Blackberry Creek

Rachel McCoy

AuthorHouse™
1663 Liberty Drive
Bloomington, IN 47403
www.authorhouse.com
Phone: 1-800-839-8640

First published by AuthorHouse 1/31/2011

ISBN: 978-1-4567-1747-6 (sc)
ISBN: 978-1-4567-1748-3 (e)
ISBN: 978-1-4567-1749-0 (hc)

Library of Congress Control Number: 2010919581

Printed in the United States of America

This book is printed on acid-free paper.

Copy written by Ashley Bergman.

Rachel McCoy Books - www.RachelMcCoyBooks.com

Laugh at yourself

Love all you can

Live every moment

This book is dedicated with love to
Jackson, Darby, and Jana.

Acknowledgements

Jackson, you are a daily reminder to me that dreams can come true, and that you really can accomplish anything you set your mind to. You have taught me so much. To my parents, who have always believed in me, guided me, and encouraged me to just be myself. I love you both very much. To B.T. who helped inspire me. Ashley Bergman—I couldn't have done it without you! D.P.—Thank you for your assistance. Lastly to all my close friends; Dick, Pete, Peter, Scott and Shelly, for your continued support and for being my biggest fans—I love you all!

In life there are those who wait for things to happen and there are those who make it happen—*I chose to make it happen.*

Introduction

"What do you mean you don't know how she died? I don't understand this and you're not making any sense. Samantha Jo, who told you she was dead? Samantha Jo? Answer me! Samantha Jo . . ."

Chapter 1

It was a beautiful sunny June morning in the Midwest. The sun was shining and the day was slow to warm up from the lingering cool-morning weather. Madison sat on her patio enjoying a cup of coffee and made a list of all the things she had to do on that Sunday morning. She was full of energy, and the day was wasting. Just as she had finished her laundry list of items to do and was about to start the grocery list, Samantha Jo called. She answered the phone expecting her cheery southern accent but instead found her cousin sobbing so hard Madison could barely understand her.

"Samantha Jo, get a hold of yourself and tell me what is wrong. Is Shelby Lynn all right? Has something happened?" Shelby Lynn was her five year old daughter, and Samantha Jo had recently gone through a nasty divorce. So immediately, Madison thought the worst.

After several minutes of Samantha Jo crying and trying to talk, which all sounded like garble in between her gasps for air, Madison finally heard what she was saying: "Hazel has been found dead." Hazel, their step-grandmother, had been married to their grandfather on their dad's side for over thirty years. Their grandfather, Jethro Walker, passed away five years ago almost to the day, a fact that sent chills down Madison's spine. Jethro's death had been what Madison liked to refer to as the "Family Reunion." Most people would say family gathering for such an occasion; however, this was a reunion for the Walkers.

Samantha Jo and Madison were cousins that first met as young toddlers and did not meet again until they were in their early thirties. Their fathers, Lane and Leroy Walker, were brothers. Madison hadn't seen or spoken to her father, Leroy, since she was two years old, though she did meet him once as an adult at Jethro's funeral. Samantha Jo's father, Lane, and her mother had also divorced when she was young; however, he'd remained living in the same town which allowed him to stay in touch with his daughter.

Hazel Walker had been a beautiful, young woman when she decided to marry Jethro Walker. He was almost twenty years her senior and extremely charming. She had never been married before and came from a wealthy family in town, who, to this day, still feel a lot of resentment and disappointment because of her marriage to Jethro. Her role as his wife prevented her from pursuing the dreams and goals she'd once had. Since his death, she'd lived alone in one of the many Walker estate properties and often appeared nervous and unsettled.

Samantha Jo was trying to explain to Madison that Hazel had been found dead when they were disconnected; Madison's phone dropped the call.

"Damn cell phones!" She tried repeatedly for the next fifteen minutes to call Samantha Jo back and could not get through. Annoyed, she decided that Samantha Jo would call back and it would be best if she tried to remain calm and keep the line open. Thirty minutes passed and she still had not called back. Madison's anxiety was building as well as her fear. Her mind was racing: "Our grandmother Hazel was found dead and that is all I know. I need details! I need to know how, when, and who found her. This is ridiculous; why isn't she calling me back?" Her heart was pounding and tears slowly began welling up in her eyes. "Answers! That's what I need."

She tried her phone again, and Samantha Jo answered on the third ring.

"Samantha Jo, what happened? I've been trying to reach you for the last thirty minutes."

"I don't know; I couldn't get to you either."

"Samantha Jo, you're starting to scare me. What the hell is going on?"

Samantha Jo explained all that she could recollect: "There was a break-in to the house. Hazel had come home early from the riding stables and must have caught the intruder off guard and her . . . her . . . her throat . . ."

"Her throat was what?" Madison screamed.

"Was cut with a knife," she sobbed.

"Oh my God, this can't be for real." Who would do such a horrible thing? Blackberry Creek, North Carolina was such a small town; everyone knew everyone and their business. "Samantha Jo, who told you this? Did the police call you or Hazel's sister?"

As she answered, her voice became nervous. "Lane did. He called me this morning and told me that she was dead, or, rather, found killed three days ago on Thursday. The *Blackberry Creek Reader's* obituary said her funeral and burial will be on Friday in town at Bethesda Baptist Church at 10:00 a.m."

"Samantha Jo, none of this is registering with me right now. I can't even find the words to speak. None of this makes any sense!"

"I know. I can hardly believe somethin' like this could happen, either, in Blackberry Creek."

"Something's not adding up here. I mean, how would Lane know she was dead before anyone else?"

"Well according to him, he was called by the Sheriff claiming to notify her nearest relatives. Y'all, I really feel like we should go to the funeral, but I'm not wantin' to go alone. Is there any way that ya can get some time off work and meet me there?"

"Look, Samantha Jo, I'm not exactly crazy about going back to Blackberry Creek again, especially for another funeral, but I will if you do?"

"Yeah, I feel like we have to. It's the right thing to do."

They agreed to fly in on Tuesday and meet at the Comfort Inn in

Blackberry Creek. Both Madison and Samantha Jo had to rearrange their schedules and would need a day to do so.

After Madison hung up the phone, her mind began to race. "How could such a horrible, violent thing happen? Who would do such thing?" Hazel had been in her early seventies and kept to herself outside of visiting her sister, Tessa, who lived in town and the horse stables where she boarded her three horses. Things were not adding up by her count, and she needed more information. Madison didn't believe for one minute this was a robbery gone bad. Her instincts told her that Hazel's death was no accident, and she intended to find out the truth, one way or another. She felt a darkness closing in around her as thoughts drifted towards Leroy and Lane. Were they responsible for Hazel's death? It wouldn't surprise her one bit, as shocking as that may seem to outsiders. They were crazy, vindictive, and dangerous men. It was possible.

She sat on the patio in a trance, staring out at nothing in particular. Samantha Jo's call had completely immobilized her and she couldn't move. She suddenly had a lot to do in a short period of time, leaving her first "To-do" list no longer relevant. She tore a fresh page from her notebook and began a new list that would prepare her for the following days.

To-Do

1) Pack
2) Travel Arrangements
3) Mason – stay with his father
4) George – call Michael
5) Work
6) Call Mom??

Madison felt uneasy and restless. She couldn't stop her mind from going over and over the call with Samantha Jo. None of it made sense at all. "Why was Lane the one to call Samantha Jo and tell her? How did he know before she or I did? Why, Why, Why? . . ." kept playing in her head like a broken record.

Abruptly, Madison's thoughts were interrupted when she remember to call her boss. Madison had been with the same advertising agency for the last fifteen years—Alexander Koplin, located in downtown St. Paul, Minnesota. She was a dedicated and loyal employee and one of the best account managers they had. She called John Alexander, her direct boss and a partner within the firm, to let him know that she would be needing time off for a family funeral. Ten days, to be exact. He assured her that she could take the time she needed to be with her family. They would talk after the Monday morning meeting before she left to ensure that her accounts would be tended to in her absence. John Alexander was a very understanding, kind man; however, he did enjoy making money, lots of money, and was very business driven, so Madison was surprised by his generosity.

"One down, four more to go," she said to herself as she scratched items off her To-Do list one by one. She went to her computer and made her travel arrangements. Next, she called her colleague and closest friend, Joe, to arrange for him to watch her dog, George. The last call she made was to her ex-husband explaining why she needed to leave town and asking if it would be all right for Mason to stay with him the next couple of weeks. He assured her it would be fine and would give him some extra time with Mason. As Mason was graduating from high school in June and leaving for college in August, both parents were aware of how little time they had left to spend with him.

Packing could wait until tomorrow evening leaving the last item on her list: Call Mom?? She decided to wait on making that call; she did not want to deal with the questions and concerns that she'd be pressed to answer. Although Madison was good at dealing with conflict, she decided to take the road of avoidance for now. She loved her mom very much, but knew that her mother would do everything she could to keep her from going to this funeral. Madison's mother, Ann, was deathly afraid of Leroy and had spent all of Madison's childhood years protecting her from him. There was no way to know for sure if Leroy would bother to show his face for Hazel's funeral or not, but, still, he was a threat to Madison and she knew it. Inside Madison wanted to pick up the phone and tell her mother everything, knowing full well it wouldn't help ease her fears but would only upset her mother. They had a very close relationship since they were all each other had for many years and, like a little girl, Madison wanted to run to her. She resisted making the call and decided to rethink it in the morning after she slept on it.

Chapter 2

It was 7:30 a.m. when Madison arrived at Alexander Koplin Associates and unlocked the door to her office. It was a spacious office with a dark cherry wood desk, two matching bookcases, and an oversized-plush brown leather chair with a matching ottoman. The chair sat in front of one of the three large picture windows that overlooked the Mississippi River. She had spent many hours in that chair gazing out at the view—watching boats maneuver up and down the river, joggers on their morning runs, mothers with strollers on afternoon walks, and various others enjoying the trails that ran parallel to the river. This was where she could take a break when stressing or agonizing over which advertisement she would present to her client. On her office door, her name was etched on the frosted glass—Madison Slone.

It was good that Madison loved her office because she spent a considerable amount of time there. She put down her purse and oversized leather work bag and booted up her computer. As the computer turned on she walked out into the hall and headed for the lunchroom where she found coffee already made. She poured a cup and retreated to her office. This was going to be a busy day, and the Monday morning meeting began in twenty minutes.

She wasn't ready for the meeting as she usually spent Sunday evenings planning for the week to come, but she was confident she could wing it. She was good at improvising when times called for it. In light of the call yesterday, Madison was very distracted and really had only come to the office to prepare for her leave of absence. She sat at her desk and stared at the client files in front of her, debating. Joe would have to take over her clients while she was gone. He was one of the greatest graphic designers in town. Joe would work the graphics angle and her assistant, Tamara, was more than able to handle all client relations.

Tamara had been Madison's assistant now for nearly ten years. They had worked side by side during that time and spent many hours deliberating over which advertisement would best suit a client's needs. Tamara knew Madison's clients just as well as she did and would be more than competent to handle any situation that should arise. Besides that, Madison would only be gone for ten days.

She sorted through the folders and made a few notes in each for Tamara. Joe would know what to do; she didn't worry about him and besides, he would call if necessary. She gathered her files and coffee and walked down the hall to the conference room where everyone was slowly gathering.

John Alexander began the meeting with a quick greeting and got right to the point. There was an important new client, Landis McNeil, considering Alexander Koplin and Associates to be their new advertising agency. It would be the kind of account where everyone collaborated and each person added value.

As John began discussing updates on the progress of the project, he couldn't help but think about how Madison's expertise was needed. She was one of the best when it came to presenting to clients with finesse. He knew that Tamara was great at keeping the ball rolling and things organized for Madison, but she was not a senior rep of the company and the client would see through that. He needed Madison.

For a moment he wondered if they should hold off on having the Landis McNeil meeting next Wednesday without Madison. Maybe they could postpone it to the week after her return. He could feel the tension gnawing at him as his thoughts raced. He pulled at his collar as if to loosen it and sat back in his chair while everyone gave their progress updates. There was still so much to do. He decided that he would consult with Madison privately after the meeting. Knowing full well she was not going to be back from the funeral until later the following week, he toyed with the idea of asking her to come back early.

The meeting ended and everyone scattered back to their offices and cubicles to get started on the long week ahead. As Madison exited the conference room, she asked Tamara to meet her in ten minutes. Madison walked briskly back to her office and set her things down. Before the phone or anyone in the office could distract her, Madison quickly made her way to the bathroom. It was going to be a busy day and bathroom breaks would seem to be a luxury—not only for the relief but because there were no distractions. Ironically, it was the quietest place to have a moment's thought.

She hurried back to her office and pulled out several notes she had to review with Tamara. She still had not told Tamara that she would be leaving town. In fact, no one really knew yet. Madison felt uncomfortable about the whole situation and the unknown circumstances that surrounded the death, so she had asked John to hold off on saying anything until she was gone.

Madison glanced down at her list of "To-Dos." Lists were good. They helped her feel in control and organized. Scratching something off the list was a joyful accomplishment and provided personal recognition. Any additions to a list were mere raises of the bar in Madison's mind.

At that moment her list consisted of the following:

1) Confirm flight/hotel/car arrangements
2) Dinner with Mason
3) Drop off George
4) Meet with Tamara
5) Meet with Joe- lunch
6) Discuss loose ends with John Alexander
7) Tell mom? Undecided.

Tamara arrived and had brought two cups of coffee for their meeting. Madison thanked her before saying, "There's been a terrible accident over the weekend, and I will be leaving town for ten days."

Tamara asked, "God, Madison, is everything okay? Is it Mason?"

"No, he's fine. It's my grandmother in North Carolina: she was found murdered in her home."

As Madison began to tell her about Hazel, Tamara intently studied her face, trying to pick up on the emotion Madison was displaying. She couldn't put her finger on it. Losing a loved one is painful enough and then finding out they've been murdered must be torturous. As Madison kept talking, Tamara noticed and thought, "She seems more upset over the murder than the actual loss." Then again, she herself had never experienced the murder of someone she knew. Maybe that was just another step in the grieving process she was obviously not familiar with.

Madison reminded her that she would only be a call away if Tamara had any problems or questions and to not hesitate in calling. They went through each file, and Tamara wrote feverishly for the next hour. As they wrapped up, Tamara looked at Madison and said, "What about the Landis McNeil project? Everyone is killing themselves on this project and we need you!"

"Tamara, you will be just fine. I've laid out for you all that needs to be done and you will do great! I wouldn't leave this in your hands if I didn't feel confident in your abilities. I'm only a call away if you need me, and I will have my computer with for any drafts needing my approval."

After they adjourned their meeting, Tamara came over to Madison and gave her a hug. "I don't know exactly what to say right now except please be careful and I really am sorry for your loss."

"Thanks Tamara. I'll be fine. Just call me if you have any questions. Really, it's all right. Besides, I'll be back before you know it."

Joe and Madison had lunch plans at their favorite Irish Pub,

Flaherty's, in forty minutes. Madison figured that would be enough to time for her to lay out her afternoon as well as confirm her travel arrangements, but before she could pick up the phone, it rang. She looked down and noticed the name on her caller ID: John Alexander.

She picked up the phone. "Hi, John."

"Hi, Madison. Would you please come to my office in five minutes? I have a few things that I need to review with you before I leave for my luncheon at the University Club."

"See you in five then." Madison hung up the phone and thought for a minute: "We just had a two hour meeting discussing every project under the sun, what could possibly be left?"

Landis McNeil.

She knew how much was at stake with this project, and she knew from day one that John wanted her as the key account manager. She thought to herself, "Shit! This is bad timing. He has got to hand this off to someone else." Madison could feel her angst building. She hated that she had to leave town in the midst of a big project, and yet a force inside her kept telling her she needed to go to North Carolina. Was this going to put her career in jeopardy? She hoped not and reasoned with herself that those thoughts were irrational. After all, she had a family funeral to attend. "Calm down, girl, and take a deep breath. Let's just wait until the meeting with John before you melt down and unravel inside."

Madison went down the hall towards John's office and opened the door to his office. She noticed him pacing back and forth with his putter in hand. John was an avid golfer and played any time the opportunity presented itself. He had a small turf putting green off to a corner in his office. Personally, Madison felt golf itself was a stressful game that only increased her blood pressure; however, John found it relaxing and enjoyed being able to work on his putting at the office.

"Hi, John, how's your game coming along?"

"Today? Miserably! Madison, we have a dilemma on our hands. The Landis McNeil presentation is next Wednesday, and I was counting on you to be our presenter."

"Shit! Shit! Shit! I knew it!" thought Madison.

"John, I really hate to leave town so suddenly. Believe me I would rather I didn't have to go but you know the circumstances. I have to."

"I know, Madison. I've gone around and around in my head trying to come up with another solution. We could always postpone the Landis McNeil presentation until after you return the following week?"

"John, I don't think you should do that. Timing is everything; you taught me that the first day you hired me. You know as well as I do that postponing the meeting will send a signal to Landis McNeil that we are struggling with their ad, which we're not."

"I agree with you, Madison, but outside of that, I would need you to come back earlier from your trip."

Madison felt her temples start to pulse. "I knew it! I knew he would finally arrive at his real motive." John was not a crafty man nor was he malicious or manipulative. He was fair, yet he was also a businessman. And, in business, getting caught with your skirt up was a sign of weakness. "John, you and I both know that is not a plausible option right now for me. God, if I didn't have to tend to this family crisis I would be right here at the helms with you. But I can't and I really need to go and take care of this. There is a whole office out there with talent, and surely one of my colleagues can manage this one time."

John rested his putter against his desk and slumped into one of his black leather chairs. He dropped his head low and cocked it to the right as he peered up at Madison. "Madison, you are one of the most talented people within this firm and one I hold a great deal of trust in. You've been here fifteen years, and I've never regretted hiring you. I guess I do forget sometimes that we have a firm full of talent at our disposal, and I realize I put a lot of weight on you to carry. You're right! The meeting should remain as scheduled. But help me out here, Madison, who do you think can handle this project and the presentation for Landis McNeil?"

"Honestly, John, I think you are the best person to decide that. All of my notes on the project are with Tamara; she can help out whomever you decide to put in my place. Joe is almost done with the first draft of the graphic layout, and I will review it this afternoon for approval."

He straightened his head, looked her straight in the eye, and said, "I always knew you would someday make a great successor after I retire, and I've never thought otherwise. You are calm and collected under pressure and act efficiently with a proactive view. I honestly don't know what we'd do without you."

"Thank you, John, but that still doesn't change the fact I'm not coming back early."

Giving her a smirk he said, "You can't blame me for trying." John thought for a moment then looked up at Madison and said, "What about Nelson Thomas? He would be a good suitor to fill in for you."

"Sure, I think that is a great choice."

"Great, I will meet with him this afternoon to let him know and send him down for a briefing from you and Tamara before the day is done."

"Perfect. I will get everything ready to hand over to him today." As she left his office, she turned and said, "John, thank you."

"No need to thank me, Madison; go be with your family and we will see you when you return."

Joe was waiting in her office. He sat in the oversized chair near the picture window looking out at the river. She studied him for a moment and thought about how long they had known each other. She confided in Joe a lot. Not only were they colleagues, they were also very close friends.

Joe was forty-four with dark brown hair and steel-blue eyes. He had a chiseled-looking face that he kept shaved and a dimple on the right side when he smiled. Joe was 6'3" with a toned body. He worked out regularly at a gym in the early morning before getting to the office. Had he been any other guy, she would have been in love with him the day they met. However, Joe was gay and had been in a committed relationship for the past 8 years with a man named Colin. Colin was a CPA at one of the few larger firms in town and was similar to Joe in appearance but without hair. They were a great couple, and Madison enjoyed spending time with them over long dinners while drinking way too much red wine. She loved Joe, as he did her, and they were each other's sounding board and confidants in the workplace. They kept each other sane.

Joe looked up after a minute and noticed Madison standing behind him staring off at the river as well.

"You ready?" he asked.

"Yes, I thought you'd never ask!" She grabbed her purse and they left.

At the restaurant, they both ordered the daily special and two Diet Cokes. As they sat and ate in silence, Joe finally looked up at Madison and asked, "When were you going to tell me about Hazel's death and your leaving town?"

Madison stopped chewing her bite of burger and stared at him from across the table as if someone had hit the pause button on a remote. After an uncomfortable amount of silence, she put down her burger, swallowed her mouthful, and took a sip of her Diet Coke. Looking at him with amazement, she asked, "How did you find out? I mean, I was going to tell you Joe, I just—well it's been so crazy today . . . You know."

"Not good enough, Madison," Joe replied.

Madison knew he was right. After all, he was one of her closest friends and knew her well enough to call her out when she was wrong. He continued with, "Tamara came to me today and asked about the drafts you needed to approve before you left town. I guess my puzzled look must have been a dead giveaway because she turned red and said, 'oh, shit!' Tamara, I guess, assumed I already knew."

"Joe, you have to understand, I meant to tell you, it's just that I feel like I am a chicken running around with my head cut off right now."

Joe stared Madison down—eye to eye as if it were a showdown from an old western movie—and said, "No, Madison, that is not the truth and you know it. You knew I would be concerned and tell you not to go! It is too dangerous down there for you to go by yourself."

It was no use trying to argue with Joe, she knew he was right about everything and he had called her out on it. But she argued anyway: "Joe, I have to go down there! Dangerous or not, this is my family. And I won't be alone; I'm meeting Samantha Jo there."

"Madison, the last time you were there was five years ago when your grandfather died. I was with you, remember? It was unnerving then, and I doubt much has changed since. Both your uncle and father creeped me out. I'm just amazed that both of you are even considering this. In fact, in light of Hazel's death, it's probably even worse now and all the more reason neither of you should be even considering going. I bet you haven't even called your mother yet to tell her, have you?"

Again, Joe was right. Shit! She hadn't decided whether or not she would call her yet. It made Madison angry that he knew her so well; he knew her to the point where she couldn't deny any of his accusations. She knew herself it was dangerous to go back to North Carolina alone, especially after her last visit. But deep down she felt that there was no choice, and it was not up for debate with Joe or anyone. Things didn't add up, and there was a truth out there somewhere that she knew would never be uncovered if she didn't go and that was something she could not live with. Right or wrong, she was going!

"Joe, we weren't working on a project like Landis McNeil five years ago, and it just so worked out that you were able to get the time off to join me. This time is different—that is not an option. In fact, John called me to his office this afternoon to ask me if I would consider cutting my trip short and returning earlier."

Joe knew John just as well and his request for Madison to return early did not surprise Joe in the least. "What did you tell him?"

"I told him that I couldn't and that there was an entire office full of talent, and that he should look to them and delegate a new lead for the project."

"And his reply was what?" Joe asked.

"He agreed after a while and is going to ask Nelson Thomas to replace me."

Joe spat the bite of burger he had just taken onto the top of his ketchup-covered fries. Madison gave him that disgusted look a mother gives when her child displays a rude behavior. Joe wiped his mouth with his napkin and apologized for his immature behavior.

"Are you kidding me? Nelson Thomas?"

"Ah c'mon, Joe, he's not that bad." Madison couldn't help but smirk and giggle as she said it. Joe was uncomfortable around Nelson and, if Nelson took over for Madison, Joe would have to work side by side with him for the next week.

Two years ago at the annual company holiday party, Joe was in the lunchroom getting more champagne to bring out to the group gathered in the conference room. As he began to uncork the champagne, Nelson, who had followed him into the lunchroom, came up so close that he was practically hugging Joe from behind. He pressed his body up against Joe's while groping his butt with his hands, caressing it ever so slightly. Softly, he whispered into Joe's ear his desire and need to be with another man.

Joe had squirmed away, moving forward, and turned around to let Nelson know he was not interested in his advances but Nelson had already started to walk out of the lunchroom. Joe confided in Madison about the incident, feeling embarrassed and ashamed. He'd decided that since it was a party where everyone had been partaking in a bit of champagne that he would not report it. It would've been his word against Nelson's and, after all, there was alcohol involved. Plus, everyone knew Nelson had been married for over eighteen years to a beautiful wife and had three kids. Nelson never brought it up and acted as if nothing had ever happened. However, Joe would forever be uncomfortable around Nelson.

Madison reached out to comfort Joe by putting her hand on his. As he pulled away, he smiled and told her she was an evil bitch.

"Joe, you are going to have to find a way to deal with this. You know as well as I do Nelson can handle this project and will be great. I know you are uncomfortable, but you've either got to confront him or find a way to live with your decision not to take action. You still have to work with him."

Joe knew she was right—my, how the tables could turn fast between the two of them. They could always be honest with each other and consoling at the same time.

They finished their lunch and began walking back to the office. Joe put his arm around Madison like a big brother as they walked back. She promised him she would call or text daily to let him know she was okay and give him updates. In return, he promised to work as best he could alongside Nelson. She gave him a big hug and a kiss on the cheek.

"Joe," she said, "Do me a favor, though, and send me the drafts as soon as you can so I can get Nelson up to speed, okay?"

Joe looked at her, smiled, and said, "Already done before we left for lunch, babe."

The rest of the afternoon flew right by and, before she knew it, it was 4:30 and she had to leave. She ran to the restroom again, and reminded herself to quickly text Mason to let him know she'd be home in forty-five minutes and would make dinner before sending him off with his dad.

She ran through the afternoon in her head again: Joe had sent over the drafts she had finalized, Tamara and Nelson were good to go, and she had emailed John to remind him to call her should there be any unanswered questions and thanked him again for his understanding. The final thing she had to do was turn on an automatic email reply that said she would be out of the office for the next ten days and, in her absence, all questions should be directed to Tamara.

Returning to her office, Madison sat for a moment and looked around. She would miss being a part of the Landis McNeil project. She loved the intensity of deadlines and collaborating with everyone to get the project right and wow the customer. They would be just fine without her, but she was envious of the colleagues she was leaving behind. She smiled to herself and whispered, "Next time, girl." She grabbed her purse, made sure her laptop was in her oversized bag, shut off the lights, and locked the door.

Mason was waiting for her when she got home. He was anxious to eat and get settled in at his dad's. They ate dinner, and Mason gave her a hug and kiss before loading his car and driving to his dad's. Madison and Mason's father had divorced when Mason was two years old. Since then, her ex had remarried while Madison remained single.

It wasn't that she didn't want to be with someone else, but her inability to trust men in any relationship made it hard. Madison struggled with that and knew from a psychological standpoint that it had everything to do with her relationship with Leroy. She'd decided that Mason was her focus and once he went off to college, she would address that issue and be more open to working on a relationship.

After Mason had left, it dawned on her that she had forgotten one of the To-do items—Confirm Travel Arrangements! Madison pulled out her itinerary and checked to make sure her flight would be on time tomorrow. She was flying out late Tuesday morning so it shouldn't be too busy at the airport; nevertheless, she wanted to confirm that flight as well as her hotel and car arrangements.

She packed George's favorite blanket, his toys, and a bag of dog food and threw them in the car. She would bring him to Joe's in the morning. Now, all she had left to do was pack and she'd be set to go.

Chapter 3

It was 8:30 p.m. when Madison finally changed into her comfy clothes. She'd managed to get her packing done fairly quickly and could finally relax out on her patio with a glass of Shiraz and George at her feet. Madison had dug out a pack of cigarettes. She wasn't a smoker, but she kept emergency cigarettes around for moments when she craved one. They helped her relax.

She sat outside and admired both the wonderful weather and the plants blooming around her. The temperature already began to drop for the evening, and, feeling a bit chilled, Madison wrapped herself into a blanket. As she curled up in the Adirondack chair, sipping her wine and lighting a cigarette, her memory opened up to her last visit in North Carolina for her grandfather's funeral. He had been sick for the last two years before his death so the news of his passing was not a complete surprise. On the other hand, meeting her father Leroy for the first time since she was two years old was.

Madison's mother had tried over the years to protect her from Leroy and, at times, was brutally honest about who he really was—a Monster. Going to Jethro's funeral had made Madison uneasy. It had been almost twenty years since her last visit to Blackberry Creek, and she knew without a doubt that Leroy, as well as his brother, would be there. She had been lucky that Joe was able to join her on that trip as her body guard, so to speak. This time she would be going alone. This time it was personal!

While visiting for the funeral, she did indeed meet the Monster who did not appear as scary as the stories made him out to be. He was older now, mid-fifties, nearly the same height as Madison, 5'8", and had apparently put on weight. Madison figured he had to be at least thirty pounds overweight. He had long hair that he pulled back into a ponytail and kept a five o'clock shadow on his face.

He had a self-inflicted limp from when he had purposely shot himself in the leg; he then tried blaming the injury on his girlfriend at the time. Luckily for her, with the help of the police, she'd made her escape from him and the relationship. Standing there in front of him, Madison could remember thinking, "You're not so scary and tough! I could outrun you in New York minute." That was the truth, physically; mentally, however, she had no idea about the Monster that still lived inside him.

After the funeral and luncheon, Leroy had approached Madison alone and asked if she would meet him alone for an hour or so before everyone met up for dinner that evening. She wanted to say no just to spite him but at the same time something inside her said yes. It was as if her lips spoke before her brain had the chance to consult with them. She figured she would never have the chance again for this moment, and she had some questions she wanted answered. It was now or never. Game on!

Joe was nervous and tried to persuade her to let him come with, but Madison knew this was between family—just her and the Monster. Samantha Jo, along with five-year-old Shelby and her mother Charlene, was going to stop by the hotel to pick up Joe at seven p.m., exactly one hour later, and then meet up with Leroy and Madison at the restaurant. Madison took the rental car and told Joe that if she was not at the restaurant when they all got there at seven p.m. to call the police immediately and put an all-points bulletin (for those in the know, an APB) out for her. She didn't want to take any chances and knew that Leroy, even as aged as he was, was still a Monster who had no conscience or remorse whatsoever. He would just as soon cut the line on your car breaks in the middle of the night and then wait to read about your crash in the daily reader. Monster!

Madison arrived promptly at six and found Leroy in a booth centered in the middle of the restaurant. She felt comfortable enough to join him as long as he wasn't in some dark corner. She sat down, ordered a beer from the waitress, then focused her attention on Leroy. He watched her like a loving father with tender and caring eyes.

At first, they just made small talk, and Leroy was careful not to give away too much about himself. When Madison asked him for his mailing address so they could have future correspondence, he smiled and said, "Anything for me you can simply send to Gram in Mississippi." Virginia, generally referred to as Gram, lived in a small town in Mississippi and was Leroy's and Lane's biological mother. Hazel had been Jethro's second wife years later. Gram and Jethro had separated back when Leroy was fourteen and Lane was twelve.

Leroy claimed that he missed Madison and wondered if they could bury the hatchet, but before Madison would say yes, she had some questions of her own that needed answers. She began her interrogation by asking, "You are trying to act as though you care about me when, in fact, I haven't heard from you or seen you in over thirty years. Why is that?"

Leroy's eyes began to change, and she could see that the caring look she saw when she first sat down left in a matter of seconds. His eyes turned cold and his voice became firm when he said, "That was your mama's doin'! She did everything she could to keep me from you and hide you away! And you're wrong! I did come to see you when you were three after she didn't return home from her trip with ya to Minnesota to see her family."

Madison looked at him with surprise and in sarcastic voice said, "We had already been gone for nearly nine months and that's when you realized we weren't coming back? Are you kidding me?"

Leroy shot back at her, "You forget cuz you were so young, but you sat on your tricycle in the sidewalk and were cryin' big crocodile tears as I drove away screaming 'Daddy, come back!' I know because I watched you out of the rearview mirror as I drove away."

So it wasn't a dream—Madison had a vague memory of such an incident but never knew for sure if it was real or one of the many dreams she'd had about a father she thought she loved. She fantasized for years that one day her real daddy would come back to her and her mother and be a good, loving man. That he would be the husband and father he should have been, like the ones she saw on TV.

Madison knew this was not going to be an easy discussion, and she knew he was proud of himself as well as his actions. He was arrogant, manipulative, and crazy! He continued by saying, "There isn't day that goes by that I don't regret not having the chance to raise you myself, and I never meant y'all any harm."

Madison narrowed her eyes and said, "Really, is that why you kept threatening to kidnap me? Do you have any idea how much that scares a ten-year-old child? Honestly, how was that taking care of me?"

"That's your mama's fault—she just kept comin' after me for child support, and I figured if she couldn't take care of you on her own than I'd do it myself. Besides, she went and remarried that David guy who adopted you. I know cuz I signed the paperwork!"

"Leroy, he never adopted me. The papers were never filed."

"Yes he did; I told you, I signed the documents!"

"Well, you may have very well signed them but they were never filed with the courts. He never adopted me!"

"Why'd you go by his last name, then, for so many years if he didn't adopt you?"

"Because my mother figured it would be hard for me to explain why I had a different name and where my daddy was."

"Makes no difference to me, you're just like your mama! In fact, you look like her with your big feet and small tits! All you care about is money, and you're not getting' a cent out of me. She shoulda done a better job raisin' you."

"Leroy, you should've paid your child support. We lived on welfare until my mother remarried. We had nothing!"

"She's the one that left; that makes it her job to take care of you.

And I was payin' fifty dollars a month to the county to send to you, that shoulda been enough! But no, she always kept tryin' to come after me for more."

"That's funny, Leroy, because we never saw a dime of it!"

It was useless to argue with Leroy and expect to hear the truth. Madison began to wonder why on earth she had even agreed to this meeting. What was she really expecting from him? How could she even think for one moment that he would tell her the truth? Ah, but he had. The Monster had shown his true colors. Madison reminded herself that Leroy had been diagnosed with schizophrenia nearly forty years ago and so he *was* telling the truth—the truth that he knew.

Leroy had been suspected of suffering from schizophrenia since he was around fifteen years old. It is usually around that age that symptoms start to appear in young boys. It didn't help Leroy much that Jethro and Virginia fought constantly and that Virginia had wanted girls. Instead she had two boys: one who could do no wrong and one she despised.

Jethro had met Virginia while on a brief pass between his assignments as an Air Force pilot in WWII. They found each other one evening as Jethro and his friend were cruising the town. Virginia was with a friend of hers and the four all hooked up. Two weeks later, their friends decided to elope. Jethro and Virginia figured, "What the hell?" and they did the same. It was, however, a marriage doomed from the beginning. They fought constantly, and it became increasingly worse when the boys arrived.

By the time Leroy was fourteen and Lane twelve, Jethro had left Virginia in Mississippi and moved to North Carolina. Over the years, the boys bounced back and forth between their parents, depending on who would put up with them. By this time, they were a handful and had already started a life evading the law. Who could blame them for their conniving and mischievous behavior; they never really had a fair chance from the start.

Crazy and dysfunction were in Leroy's and Lane's lives from the days they were born. They never had a fighting chance for normalcy. Virginia was not happy getting pregnant right away and even less happy that, nine months later, Leroy was born. Instead of the daughter she wanted, she had a son. She would purposely forget to put the child gate up at the top of the wooden staircase, and, as a result, Leroy had taken several tumbles down them before the age of two. Strangely, it would seem that Virginia was trying to allow the baby to get hurt—if she couldn't have a daughter, she'd rather not have any children at all.

Two years later, Lane was born. Again, Virginia would conveniently forget to block the staircase, and Lane would fall down and hit his head repeatedly just as Leroy had done. Once, Lane fell out of an open window after she'd put his crib next to it. Luckily he only suffered some bruising and a broken arm. His injuries could have been much worse.

As the boys grew up, she still had a yearning for girls. She must have finally decided that, although they were born boys, they could be made up to look like girls. Lane was the lucky one chosen for that craziness. She let his dark blonde hair grow long and used rollers to dress him up in ringlet curls. She bought a light-blue dress with a white crochet trim around the neck line that she made him wear. And, to prove it, she marched him down the main street to the photographer's and had his picture taken. As if that wasn't enough, she also performed her personal douching in front of the boys. Madison guessed that after a while Virginia figured maybe should could somehow change them or convince herself that she had two daughters rather than two sons.

Madison couldn't imagine the horror her father and uncle endured while Virginia raised them. While on a visit to see her grandfather and Hazel when she was fifteen, Madison could remember going to one of the houses Jethro owned; here he stored old clothing from his bridle store. Rummaging through some old items and photos, Madison came across a picture of a girl in a light-blue dress smiling at the camera. Holding the picture up, she asked Hazel if it was Samantha Jo's picture. Madison hadn't seen her cousin since she was two years old and couldn't remember what she looked like.

When Hazel replied, "No, darlin', that's a photo of your uncle Lane when he was ten," Madison thought Hazel had lost her mind.

Utterly puzzled by Hazel's reply, she held the picture up closer to her and said, "No, Hazel, this photo here of the girl in the blue dress."

Hazel replied with, "I know, dear; that is your uncle Lane."

Madison's mouth was gaping wide open, and she had an obviously perplexed look on her face when Hazel began to tell her the stories of Virginia dressing the boys up. She had not seen any with Leroy in dresses and figured they had probably existed at some time but were now destroyed.

One of the last arguments at the Walker residence happened before Leroy turned fourteen years old and included a baseball bat and a shotgun. Leroy had come home to find Virginia and Jethro in one the worst arguments they'd ever had. Jethro had such a hard grip around her arm that he broke it. She also had some bruising and a bleeding cut on her lower lip. Leroy ran to his parents' closet upstairs and came back down with his father's shotgun. He aimed it right at Jethro and shouted at him to get out of the house and never return. Jethro grabbed the baseball bat lying on the floor by the front door and chased Leroy down the street, threatening to kill him. Leroy stayed away from the house, and it wasn't long after that night that Jethro left for good and headed to North Carolina. It was hard for Madison to imagine such events ever took place and she couldn't decide who was crazier—Jethro or Virginia.

As Madison had been estranged from Virginia for most of her life, she really didn't know much about her or her family. After her divorce from Jethro, Virginia remarried several years later to a man named Grady Harrison. Leroy and Lane had been bouncing back and forth between North Carolina and Mississippi but after the marriage, Grady didn't want them around. He didn't trust them and for good reason.

As the boys grew older and became adults, they turned into manipulative parasites. They constantly looked for handouts of money from Virginia and were in trouble with the law on a regular basis. Leroy was always Virginia's favorite, and she would sneak him money, including paying thousands of dollars to keep him out of jail. Lane was a different story. He had to beg, steal, and borrow to get by without the help of Virginia.

Right after Jethro left and before she married Grady Harrison, Virginia had to move in with her mother in a small two-story house on Bunch Street in Blackberry Creek. Her mother didn't like the boys and thought they were dirty and messy. Virginia's mother felt the boys were a nuisance and she didn't want them in her house, but let them live there anyway under her strict rules.

She was aware that they were costing her both in food and utilities. So she tried to save money by conserving water. She made sure the boys had no more than two inches of water in the tub when they bathed. They also had to bath together to conserve on the water usage, and she would walk right in the bathroom with a ruler to make sure they had not used more than the two inches she allowed them. The humiliation they must have felt. No matter where the boys were, craziness and dysfunction would surely follow.

As time went on, Leroy joined the Navy looking for some structure and belonging while Lane stayed back and tried to make his own way. He was not close to Jethro and, by the age of sixteen, had given up on going back to North Carolina for good. However, he had nowhere to go but to his mother's and beg for a place to stay. Virginia was still living with her mother, and the old woman was still as mean as a rattlesnake and refused to let Lane sleep in her house again. Even though all the furniture was covered with protective plastic and there was an unoccupied spare room upstairs, she refused to let him sleep in the house. He slept in his car, parked in front of the house, for weeks.

After a while, Virginia convinced her mother to let Lane sleep on the back porch so that folks wouldn't talk. From then on, Lane's life was about survival, and he figured out quickly that he would need a woman who worked and could afford to take care of him. Thus, the ten marriages to date.

Lane was married to his first wife, Charlene, Samantha Jo's mother, when Leroy was dishonorably discharged from the Navy. The two lived next to each other in a double bungalow house in Mississippi. Samantha Jo was a little more than two years older than Madison, and their mothers bonded very quickly. They were each other's sanity during all they endured in their marriages to the Walker boys.

Once Lane divorced Charlene, he went through a string of marriages; finding women he thought could financially take care of him. He still called on Virginia now and again for money and sometimes she would give him a handout but usually not. Lane was always lying and cheating someone out of their money; he was a notorious swindler. Like his older brother, he never paid child support and had a very strained relationship with Samantha Jo.

When his daughter was in her early twenties, Lane gave her an old Mercedes convertible that was pale yellow and in mint condition as a birthday present. There was a catch though—in exchange, he needed her to rent out a storage unit for him using her name. She drove the car for several months after until the police pulled her over.

When she asked the officer why he had pulled her over, he replied, "M'am, are you aware this is a stolen car? License and registration, please!" Lane had placed his own daughter right in the middle of one of his law-evasion schemes. Samantha Jo explained that her father had given her the car and that she did not know where it had come from nor did she have the registration. She then told the officer about the storage unit she had signed for on behalf of Lane Walker.

The officer listened to her intently and, due to Lane's past run-ins with the law, had no reason not to believe Samantha Jo. He drove her to the storage unit and the owner let them inside. It was large, similar in size to a one-car garage. Once the door was fully opened, the officer called on his radio for immediate back-up. Inside were stolen goods that filled the unit from top to bottom.

Because Lane had not signed for the storage unit and his name was not tied to it, the authorities were never able to convict him on theft of stolen goods. In fact, he walked away without as much as a slap on the wrist. Samantha Jo was not prosecuted as they knew she was not responsible, but the humiliation it brought upon her and the shame of having Lane Walker as her father were prosecution enough.

Lane, however, did eventually spend time in jail years later. Not for theft but, rather, arson and attempted murder. He set fire to the house of his tenth wife while she and her children were still inside. He was in another financial bind and probably owed some bad people a large amount of money. As the sole beneficiary to her life insurance policy, he was sure that he would be able to secure the funds shortly after her death and pay off the thugs that were after him. To his surprise, his wife escaped with her children and when she found Lane outside holding a book of matches, she turned his ass into the authorities faster than the blink of an eye.

He served five years for that stunt before being released for good behavior. It amazed Madison that Samantha Jo could still stand to be in the same room with her father after all his lies and deceit.

Now Madison found herself sitting across from her own Monster that she hated and despised. She knew about Leroy's demons and treacherous ways from the stories she had heard. Leroy was not a man who could keep his hands to himself and had repeatedly cheated on her mother during their several years of marriage.

Madison found herself listening to Leroy gloat about the fact that she had an older sister in California and two younger siblings that were twins—a boy and a girl. They were less than a year younger which meant he had been running around town while her mother was pregnant with her. She couldn't decide whether he was telling the truth or trying to upset her. Either way, it made no difference to her; it wasn't as if she wanted anything to do with them and she assumed vice versa.

When Madison was a year old, the family left Mississippi and moved to North Carolina. It was there, on one occasion, that Leroy had gone off with some woman again and contracted a permanent venereal disease. Leroy didn't know he had contracted such a disease, and Madison's mother found out while at the doctor's. She confided in the doctor about Leroy's constant unfaithful behavior as well as his physical abuse. The doctor pleaded with her to leave him, take Madison, and get as far away from North Carolina as possible. It would be another year and two more attempts on her life before she would leave him.

Leroy was always full of anger and deceit. When he first met Ann, he was on a quick leave from the Navy in Minnesota. She was a senior in high school when Leroy talked her into marrying him. They waited until she graduated before he moved her to the south, far away from her family and friends. He was handsome and charming, and, as a young girl looking for a ticket out of home, Ann found herself quickly falling for him. Madison would come along three years later.

As Leroy's schizophrenia got progressively worse over the years so did his abusive temper. Just after Madison had turned a year old, Leroy was on one of his rampages. He began to hate Madison's mother so much that he tried to get her arrested by hiding marijuana in her dresser. Before he could concoct a story to tell the police so that they would search the house, her mother had found the bag by accident and when she started questioning him, a deadly fight broke out. He chased her through the house, screaming and hitting her, claiming she was the one to blame. Blame for what, though? His unhappiness? His insanity? Only Leroy knew the answer to that one.

He followed her into the bedroom and pulled out a pistol from his back pocket. He held the barrel right against her forehead, cocked and ready to shoot, and said, "What'd you do if I shot you right now?"

Her mother's only reply was, "If I could still manage to get up, I'd take Madison and leave you." He left and didn't come back for nearly a month.

The fights got worse, and Leroy would take off for long periods without as much as a call. During these times, Madison's mother found consolation in Jethro and Hazel who helped her with bills, groceries, and taking care of Madison. But this was still a time and place where people didn't hang out their dirty laundry for others to see.

After awhile, Jethro's tolerance for his own son's behavior ran out. He expressed his disdain for Leroy's habit of running around and leaving his wife and child without food or money. It was then Jethro told him he was no longer welcome at their home and if he ever stepped foot on the property again he'd shoot 'em at first sight. Leroy sensed that Madison's mother would leave him sooner or later, so he tried to coerce Ann into thinking that he'd get help and they'd be fine, but, deep down, she knew better.

They decided to take a Sunday drive into the mountains and have a family day together with a picnic lunch. On the way back, Leroy had a plan. Anyone who has driven up through the mountains knows there are many twists and turns, leaving the terrain deadly if not respected. Leroy drove around a corner where there was a straight stretch for about a quarter of a mile. As he looked ahead, he noticed a semi-trailer coming from the opposite direction. He pressed his foot down on the gas and sped the car up nearly twenty miles past the forty miles per hour speed limit. As the truck came closer, Leroy cranked the steering wheel to the left and the car began to skid sideways toward the oncoming truck.

Madison's mother was in the passenger seat and in place to take first impact upon crashing. She screamed and begged him to stop before he killed them all. He was going too fast and the impact would have killed everyone, not just the one intended. Maybe he really did love Madison in his own way and the fear of her being killed troubled him or maybe it was the screaming from Ann; whichever it was, he drove the car onto the shoulder of the road and put it in park. As the dust began to settle around them, he looked over at Madison's mother and all he said was, "You bitch!"

Shortly after that incident, her mother used her last dime to call her father, asking him to drive down to North Carolina and bring Madison and her back to the Midwest. Jethro and Hazel also begged her to get out of town before Leroy actually did harm her and the baby. Jethro could only do so much to protect her from his own son. Two weeks later, Madison and her mother were on their way to Minnesota and never returned.

Back in the present day, Madison looked up at Leroy and said, "Why'd you try to kill us all in the car when I was little?"

"Is that what your mama told ya, huh?"

"Yeah it is! Why'd you do it?"

"I wasn't tryin' to kill you. I knew your mama was gonna leave sooner or later and I figured hell, if I swing her side of the car into the truck, that you and I might just make it outta there alive and I'd just raise you myself."

Madison's eyes widened as she sat there in silence, thinking: "The son of a bitch just admitted he tried to kill my mother. This man is sick. I mean, this is the shit you see in the movies! But this isn't a movie: this is my father, this is the Monster!"

Before Madison could reply, the others arrived and were looking for Leroy and Madison to join them for dinner. In Madison's mind, this discussion was not over, not even close! Leroy sat there staring at her and thinking to himself: "She'd best be headin' back to Minnesota if she knows what's good for herself and stay the hell outta my way and my business. It was a mistake to think I coulda convinced her otherwise."

Shivers ran down Madison's spine and the hair on her neck stood on end as she brought herself back to reality. Her memories were nightmares—the kind she couldn't wake up from. It was nearly 11 p.m. when she realized she had drank nearly two-thirds of the bottle of Shiraz and smoked 5 cigarettes.

She petted George and called him into the house. Though her flight was later in the morning, she needed her rest for the day of travel and for all the emotions that awaited her in North Carolina. She lay restless in bed, tossing and turning until about 3:30 a.m. Before she knew it, the alarm went off at 6:30, and she hit snooze for the next thirty minutes. Eventually, she showered and then sat for moment while sipping her coffee. It was going to be a stressful day for her and the uneasy feeling she had since her call with Samantha Jo was increasing at a fierce rate.

Chapter 4

Madison dropped off George at Joe's and drove straight to the Minneapolis-St. Paul International Airport. She had made the decision the night before that it would just be easier for her to park her car in the airport parking ramp rather than look for rides. She hated having to ask for favors from her friends. Her flight home was scheduled for the following Thursday evening and arrived back in Minnesota at 10:35 p.m. Technically she was off for 10 days, but she felt better knowing that she would be home a day earlier to go into the office if she felt the need.

To her surprise the parking ramp was extremely packed, and she drove around for over twenty minutes until she found one of the last spots on the top level. Madison made her way fairly quickly through the check-in counter with time to spare.

Once through security, she stopped by the Starbucks near her gate and grabbed a large coffee and a blueberry muffin. She realized that she had not eaten yet this morning. Madison didn't like to each much when she flew; she felt it made her stomach more upset. Motion sickness sometimes bothered her and she hated taking drugs like Dramamine.

She made her way to her gate, B9, and found an open chair. The flight screen above the attendant's desk read: Charlotte, NC - On Time. She made herself as comfortable as she could and sipped her coffee while enjoying her muffin. The plane with the arriving flight was just taxiing into their gate; it was 11:05 a.m. Her flight was scheduled to depart at 11:55 a.m. So far everything appeared to be moving on schedule.

She fumbled through her large bag and pulled out her book, *Flamingo Heights*. At times Madison enjoyed reading a romance or suspense novel to distract her from thoughts of her everyday life. Those books helped her escape and relaxed her mind. She almost felt embarrassed dragging it out of her bag, thinking about how stereotypical she must look: a single woman on a flight with a romance novel. It practically screamed to every single man around her—I'm single and looking, please talk to me.

In reality, that was anything but the truth. Yes, she was single but she was not looking for a male companion to sweep her off her feet and consume her every waking moment. Quite the opposite was true for Madison. Over the years she had become so accustomed to her single life that the only thing of importance to her right now was that Mason finished high school and went to college. She planned to move from Minnesota once he was settled in college, and she figured then she could focus on herself and her dreams. Charleston, South Carolina, was her destination of choice.

She had visited a friend there over a long Thanksgiving weekend and fell in love with the people, culture, and history of the charming town. On her visit, she had done some sightseeing and took in the town. Though the Atlantic was not her favorite, she had also considered somewhere in Florida on the Gulf side. It was warmer and the ocean was a bright, tropical blue. Madison hated the winters in Minnesota and counted down the months until she would finally leave behind her shovel and boots.

But for now, she sat at the airport alone, holding a romance novel. She tried to read the introduction and quickly found that her attention span at the moment was not going to allow her to begin a book. She was too busy watching people exit through the terminal doors of B9 and was overwhelmed with thoughts of what she was about to find in North Carolina. They would be boarding in twenty minutes and she figured, "Why bother, I can read this later on the plane or at the hotel."

Once boarded, Madison pulled out her iPod, notebook, and novel, placing everything in the back pouch of the seat in front her. She had grabbed a blanket from the overhead on her way to her seat and made herself as comfortable as she could. After all, it was a plane and she was in coach seating.

The seat next to her was occupied by an older woman who had been in town visiting her daughter and family. She attempted to break into conversation briefly with Madison and inquired about her visit to North Carolina. Was it personal or business? What was her line of work? How long was she staying? Madison lied and said that she would be in Charlotte for work and tried to give the woman short answers, not wanting to elaborate on details any more than she wanted to engage in conversation.

Once airborne, Madison pulled the blanket up to her chest and grabbed her iPod to listen to music. The woman noticed her body language and acknowledged that Madison looked tired. She said she'd wake her when they came around with beverages and pretzels. Madison thanked her for her kindness but told her it would not be necessary, she just wanted to rest and would be fine.

Once the plane was in the air, Madison got lost in thoughts and time passed quickly. She remembered the last time on a flight to North Carolina. She'd been going to her grandfather's funeral, and she'd tried to prepare herself in her mind and heart for seeing Jethro lying in his casket, completely lifeless. She had long ago given up trying to analyze her feelings about Leroy and what would be of that reunion, but Jethro was different.

She had gone to see him when he was first placed into the home for people with Alzheimer's, three years before his death. He had been struggling with the disease for some time before Hazel could no longer manage his Alzheimer's and feared for her own life. Several nights Jethro had woke her up by screaming vile obscenities at the top of his lungs while pointing his rifle at her. He claimed there were thugs outside hiding and waiting to kill him. He'd point out the window and say, "He's right there behind the old car, you see 'em?" It was then she realized he needed to be in a more confined environment; otherwise, he'd probably kill them both.

When Madison had gone down for that visit to see her grandfather that time, she suspected it would be the last time she'd see him alive. She went to the closest Wal-Mart and bought him three pair of sweatpants with matching sweatshirts, socks, five t-shirts, and some slippers. She wanted him to be comfortable and didn't really know what else to do. When he was having a good, lucid day and had some memory recollection, he recognized Madison and asked about his grandson, Mason. He asked how he was doing and how old he was now. That would be the last time she would see Jethro alive.

During her visit, she spent some quality time with Hazel. Madison would come by at night, and they'd eat dinner together before pulling out the Jack Daniels and talking for hours. Hazel would say, "How many jiggers y'all want, honey?" By the second night, she'd no longer ask and instead just put in two jiggers, a few ice cubes, and a splash of Coke. During their conversations, Madison learned things about her family she didn't know and some things no one knew but her. She left Hazel's house feeling sad that Jethro was not the man she had thought he was—not even close. While Jethro loved his granddaughters more than anything in the world, there was a side to him that was meaner and crazier than the devil himself.

Jethro Walker was born in Pike County, Kentucky, in October of 1922. His father was killed when he was a baby and his mother had remarried in 1925. Jethro Walker was not the name he was given at birth. He was born John B. McCoy. His family was of the famous McCoys that inhibited the Kentucky side of the river, known as Tug Fork, while the Hatfields homesteaded on the other side of the river in West Virginia. The history of the two families was well known throughout the south as well as their hatred and anger towards one another. Although the feud that consumed the two families was resolved in 1891, it didn't officially end until 1901.

Shortly after Jethro's father's died, his mother, Polly, left him with his father's mother until she could return to care for the child. She'd been gone for nearly five years before she came back for him. When she finally did, she was married and expecting her first child from her latest husband, Calvin Walker. Polly and Calvin left Kentucky with Jethro to move to West Virginia where Calvin's family owned a clothing store.

Over time, that clothing store evolved into what would be considered a high-end men's clothing store with a second location in North Carolina. Once settled in West Virginia, Calvin and Polly both agreed that it would be best to change Jethro's last name from McCoy to Walker. Calvin adopted Jethro and when the adoption was final, they had also changed his first name from John to Jethro. No one really ever knew or understood why his first name was changed as it was never discussed. Nonetheless, Jethro it was and soon he had a sister, Ella. Polly and Calvin went on to have three more children (Cal Jr., Lou, and Chloe).

Jethro was closest to Ella as the others were quite a bit younger than him. Jethro missed his grandmother, Mamma Nan, more than anything, though. He had become very attached to her and saw her as more of a mother than Polly. Who could really blame him; Mamma Nan had loved and raised him as her own for nearly five years. He visited and spent time with Mamma Nan every chance he got, but, as he got older, he began working at the family store and in the other family business—moonshine—leaving him with less and less time to visit her. Mamma Nan eventually passed away and some say that Jethro was never the same after that.

By his late teens, Jethro had already started bootlegging moonshine to Tennessee and North Carolina as well as learning the family recipe. His younger brothers learned the business too and soon Cal Jr. and Lou would take over for Jethro when he enlisted in the United States Armed Forces. At the age of twenty in 1942, Jethro became a fighter pilot. He met Virginia while on a pass back in the south in between training and operations. They married, as mentioned earlier, after knowing one another only two weeks. He left right after they said their vows and went back to serving his country.

Jethro was a fighter pilot and one of the largest missions he was assigned happened on August 1, 1943 and was known as operation Tidal Wave. Of the 178 planes that left Libya that day, only 88 would return. One of the last planes to return had 365 holes in it. In that operation the pilots and planes were broken down into five different squads. Jethro's plane was shot down somewhere above Romania during Tidal Wave.

He had been able to eject from his plane and land with his parachute. Once landed, he gained consciousness and realized the five other pilots around him, who had also ejected, were not so lucky. They had either died from gun fire or complications with their landing. Jethro quickly got himself free from his parachute, folded it up, and carried it into a remote place in the woods. He knew the Germans would be looking for survivors and a parachute left behind without a body would alert them of a living survivor.

After burying his parachute, he wandered through the woods for nearly three days until he fell upon a farm house just outside of the woods. He quietly crept up to the barn and hoped to be able find some refuge and food. What he found inside was a drunk and passed out German soldier in full uniform. Jethro assessed the situation and realized very quickly that his only hope of survival and making it back to the U.S. station was the obvious. He quietly moved towards the snoring German soldier and snapped his neck. From there, he removed and put on the soldier's uniform which, luckily for him, fit.

The wife of the farm house had come out to the barn to check on the German soldier, whose role was to watch for fugitives, but instead found Jethro. She did not say much by way of words but gestured for him to rest on the bench. She went back to the house and came out with a warm meal for him. Jethro knew he could not stay in the barn for too long as he did not want to put the woman and her husband at risk any more than they already were. He stayed until dawn the next morning and walked down the dirt road that led to the nearest town.

From there, he walked down Main Street amongst other German soldiers and just nodded his head in acknowledgement when they said hello or waved to him. They didn't know or recognize that he was actually an American. Jethro found his way back to safety and was returned to base with his fellow pilots. How he managed to live through that awful experience to even tell it was a miracle.

Jethro returned home after the war ended in 1945, forever a changed man. He and Virginia fought constantly and, in 1949, Leroy was born and Lane followed two years later. Jethro had a mean streak and a temper that was like no other. Madison knew where the Monsters' demons had come from—they were in the DNA.

In 1962 Calvin Walker passed away and left Jethro the executer of his estate. His will specifically explained who was to get what and how much. But Jethro and his sister, Ella, had other plans. They had always been closer to each other than the other siblings and, with Ella working at a bank in West Virginia, they had devised a plan for the money in the estate. They agreed that Polly would be taken care of financially because to do otherwise would raise flags and the other siblings would ask questions. They kept the money at Ella's bank and began to invest it into various stocks and bonds. For years they made enough money to live comfortably off the interest alone and left the principal amount untouched.

During that time Jethro and Virginia separated and, to keep it hidden from Virginia, Jethro kept all his money at his sister's bank in West Virginia under her name. Virginia knew he was keeping money from her but she couldn't prove it. Polly eventually passed away in October of 1971 and that was when Ella and Jethro decided to disburse the original funds left to the other siblings.

By then Cal Jr. and Chloe were the remaining siblings. Lou had been involved with the wrong crowd from an early age. During his time bootlegging moonshine during the prohibition, he started moving in circles that included the mafia. Lou's activities included doing drugs, drinking and gambling. At the age of twenty-five, he was found dead in his apartment a week after he'd been killed. They never did catch the murderer but it had always been suspected his untimely death was due to his illegal activities.

So Jethro and Ella split the appropriated funds and disbursed the amounts to Cal Jr. and Chloe. Neither wanted to get on Jethro's bad side and accepted the funds given to them without dispute.

Jethro sat a very wealthy man though few knew. They wouldn't have known it from the way he lived. For many years, he owned and operated the Walker Men's Store in Blackberry Creek until he converted it into a bridle shop that carried cowboy boots, Stetson hats, high-end embroidered and gemmed shirts, chaps, and a variety of other products.

He loved horses and began breeding and showing his own. Tennessee Walking Horses were his love and passion. It was then that he met Hazel. She was twenty years younger than him and a stunning beauty with thick, long, black hair, green eyes and long, slim legs. He spent the next year courting her and showering her with his charm in order to gain her love. She was lovely and came from a very prominent and well-to-do family in town. Before meeting Jethro, her plans had been to go to college to study art as she was an extremely talented artist and to marry another man she'd had her eye on.

In the end, Jethro won her over and from that point on she would live a life full of regret. Madison was positive that Hazel had no idea who Jethro Walker really was, just as many didn't. Maybe Hazel was attracted to the "bad boy" in him that gave her a sense of thrill and excitement or maybe she thought she could change him. Either way, her family never approved of the marriage nor did they accept him. Whatever the attraction, she spent the next thirty-five years wishing she could go back in time and marry the other fella.

Jethro was a womanizer who loved beautiful women. He didn't care if they were married or single—he was a charmer, and if there was a will, there was a way. Of course, there was always moonshine too, which often left him with poor judgment. Somehow Hazel must have assumed that she would be the only one and he'd need no other, but it wasn't long after they married that she found out otherwise.

Madison remembered a story her mother had shared with her when she was old enough to hear it. According to the story, Ann and Hazel snuck out behind the shop one night and found some of the moonshine buried out back. They began drinking and soon found themselves laughin' and talkin' up a storm. A couple weeks prior, Madison's mother caught Jethro in the back room screwin' around one afternoon with a young store clerk who worked for him. She knew not to say anything—Jethro was not a man you wanted to piss off. While the two women were drinkin' and got a bit tipsy, Madison's mother told Hazel what she had seen. She loved Hazel, and she hated the fact that everyone else in town knew Jethro was runnin' around on Hazel while she appeared to be none the wiser.

Hazel, of course, immediately went to confront Jethro, and Jethro made sure to inform Leroy to keep his new, young bride under control. She needed to learn to keep her mouth shut and stay outta other's business. Madison's mother had just married Leroy and experienced her first violent argument with him. He, of course, would apologize a couple weeks later and come home with a peace offering of beautiful jewelry. He'd learned from his father how to be a "real" gentleman.

Madison felt a tap on her shoulder. Pausing her iPod, she opened her eyes. "Something to drink, m'am?" She shook her head.

"Would you like some peanuts or pretzels today?"

"No, thanks."

The woman next to Madison turned to her and said, "I told her you didn't want nothing, but she insisted you be asked."

"It's all right," Madison said as she patted the woman on the arm. "No harm."

The woman looked at her, nodded, and went back to her Sudoku puzzles.

Madison was, for the most part, an extrovert and loved meeting new people and talking with them. She always enjoyed learning about who they were, what they did, where they were from . . . but on this trip, she really just wanted and needed to be left alone. She turned back on her iPod, situated herself into a new position, and closed her eyes.

Moments later she was back to thinking about Jethro. God, she'd loved her grandfather. The few trips she had taken to North Carolina when she was younger to visit him were memories she'd never forgotten. The first trip she could remember she was thirteen years old. She'd gone to stay for a week with Hazel and Jethro. When she arrived at their farm, she couldn't believe her eyes. It was not a farm by any standards at all! She expected to find the typical big, red barn and white house with blue trim. She found otherwise.

On the farm, there were several acres of land surrounded by woods. The nearest neighbor lived nearly a mile back down the dirt road. Their car came to a stop, and Madison looked out into a field where she saw five Tennessee Walking Horses grazing. They seemed so beautiful to her as she had never been up close to a horse before in her life. She watched as Jethro got out of the old 1959 Oldsmobile and approached the fence. She remembered finding the state and age of his car odd, thinking, "Really? This is the 80's—was he that poor?" It was an old, dusty, and dirty olive-green colored car, with its share of rust. But she didn't think on it too much; at the time Madison was just happy to be in the presence of her grandfather that she loved and dearly wanted to know.

Jethro undid the latch on the makeshift fence, then got back in the car and drove through. Once through, he got out and reattached the thick wire. It must have been an inch in diameter and when he returned to the car, she inquired as to what it was. His reply was, "An electric fence, darling. Ain't you seen one of those before?'

"An electric fence?" Madison asked inquisitively. Jethro explained to her that if she touched the fence it would give her a big shock: one that would knock her right on her ass.

He claimed it was to keep the animals in their fields. It was years later that Madison understood that it was really more to keep unwanted visitors away. Without a key, the only other way in was to drive through it.

The road extended for another few hundred yards. The left side was lined with trees and to the right was another field that had a couple of bulls that ran free. She soon saw sheds on her left and standing outside of them were goats. As the road veered to the left, Jethro pulled off to the side in the woods and parked the car. The road kept winding down a hill but, after a while, Madison saw that it looked more like a path than anything else. The path looked to be steep.

As she stepped out of the car, she noticed what appeared to be a barn, though it wasn't red, and it looked to be in dire need of repair. It was not fully enclosed and appeared to have some sort of roof attached to it. In it was Rawhide. He was Jethro's pride and joy and an award-winning stud. Rawhide was twenty-five years old and missing most of his teeth.

Next to Rawhide were cages containing several rabbits. Madison was young but she knew it wouldn't take long for that number to multiply. Looking back, she'd thought it was so cute to pet the bunnies and hold them. It never once occurred to her why they actually had bunnies until years later when Hazel sent her a small handwritten book full of family recipes; it all made sense then.

To the other side of the road were more little shacks stuffed with old farm equipment and junk. Next to those sheds were homemade dog houses. Madison counted eight dogs running about and one exception who was chained to his house—Cooper. Cooper was a Basset Hound and Madison fell in love with him the minute she saw him. He was tri-colored with white, dark brown, and black. Madison used up a whole roll of film, thirty-six pictures, on Cooper alone. He loved the attention and affection he received for the week Madison stayed. It was more than he'd probably ever had.

Cooper needed to stay chained up for his own good. Basset Hounds tend to catch a scent on something and head off with their noses down.

You can call at them and try and chase them down but, once on the loose, all you can do is wait. Madison guessed Jethro was afraid he'd get loose, take off, and get killed. The bitch of that was that he could get killed by being chained up, too. North Carolina has some of the most poisonous snakes in the United States including the Rattle Snake and Cotton Mouth. So, either way, poor Cooper was potentially in danger.

While continuing to look around, Madison noticed there were also roosters and chickens running wild amongst them. Near Rawhide's quarters, she heard a commotion. As she moved in closer, she saw three geese waddling around squawking at the top of their lungs. She thought to herself, "What kind of place is this? There are animals everywhere. And where is the house?" She looked but couldn't see one near.

After the commotion settled down, Jethro walked up to an old golf cart that was parked near the car. He started it up and told Madison to grab her suitcase and hop on. The look on her face must have been one of dazed confusion. He looked at her as though time was a-wastin' and she did as she was told. Hazel sat in the front next to Jethro. They began driving down the hill where the road got narrower and basically turned into a path, and soon Madison could see a small white trailer home right in the middle of the woods. As they pulled around to the front of it, three white German Spitz dogs came running and growling.

The mother and her two offspring were mean as hell, with the mother being the worst of them all. She hated Madison instantly and began showing her teeth and snarling. One day, Madison went back down to the trailer by herself to use the bathroom, and when she got near the door, the mother began snarling and creeping in towards her. Frightened to death, Madison stood frozen in place. Madison was so scared that she peed in her pants.

Hazel yelled at the dogs to shut up, and they ran back to their dog house that sat by the wood-burning stove. Hazel used the outdoor stove quite frequently to make homemade cornbread muffins for dinner so the trailer wouldn't get so hot, but more often than not, she'd used it to boil up chicken parts and feed it to the dogs for their dinner.

Once in the trailer, another three dogs, all poodles, came yappin' to the door to greet everyone. "How many dogs could one have?" Madison was amazed and in shock at the same time. If the electric fence didn't keep intruders out, the alarm system of dogs would. Unbelievable!

The trailer was very small. To the right was a tiny kitchen and space for a table and chairs. On the wall next to the kitchen table was a hutch containing miscellaneous pieces of china and crystal. It was far too big a piece of furniture for the trailer and it took up the space that was probably intended to be a living room. To the left of the door was a hallway that had a bathroom on the immediate right and a bedroom at the far end.

Off from the kitchen was an addition that was made into the living room. It was man-made with pine walls, a door leading outside, and large windows on the roof. Hazel motioned for Madison to put her things in there as that was the only room for her to sleep in. There was no spare bedroom, so it was either that or sleep outside with the dog that wanted to tear her into shreds. She graciously accepted her new accommodations. At least there was a TV, albeit black and white.

Hazel let her get settled before showing her to the bathroom and explaining how it worked. "It's a bathroom; they all worked the same, right?" Madison wondered. The thing was that there was no running water or sewer system. So, if she went to the bathroom, she sat on a bucket instead of a toilet. If she wanted a bath, water was heated for her on the stove and mixed in with buckets of rain water from the barrels outside. Fear and panic ran through Madison as she realized she would not be able to poop for a week. How embarrassing—she could hardly go at school or a friend's house, and now she had to go in a bucket for others to see. It was going to be a long week!

Morning came early; there were mouths waiting to be fed. Madison threw on some shorts and a shirt and jumped in the golf cart to head back up towards the sheds. The goats needed milking daily, and it would take Madison four days to finally get the hang of it. It took nearly an hour to feed all the animals and when they had finished, they hopped back into the golf cart to have breakfast back in the trailer.

Madison decided she would just have cereal, and Hazel put the carafe of milk on the table for her. She took one bite of her cereal and looked up at her grandmother, stunned. "This milk tastes funny," she said. Hazel told her it was the milk she'd gotten that morning from the goats. Madison didn't care for it much at all but had no other choice. Two hours later, red bumps began forming on her neck and chest. It was official—Madison was allergic to goat's milk. "No loss there," she thought.

Later that morning they all got in the car and headed to town for more food for the animals. They pulled into a grocery store and, instead of parking in the front lot, they drove straight to the back and grabbed plastic bags from the trunk. Madison was asked to hold the bags while Hazel and Jethro sifted through the garbage for old produce that could no longer be sold. They said it was for the goats, bunnies, horses, and all the other animals.

Once done, they drove over to the feed store to get more food for Rawhide, dry dog food, seed for the chickens, and pellets for the rabbits. The last stop would be at a day-old bakery store. Again, they drove to the back of the store and went through the large garbage bins full of old bread and expired pastries that could no longer be sold. They filled the entire back seat of the car with bread, Hostess Pies, and Twinkies. Madison sat in the front between Jethro and Hazel for the ride home. The car was packed to the gills. She asked on the way home what they were going to do with the Twinkies and Hostess Pies. They were way past expiration, and Madison had no intention of eating them after taking them out of the garbage can—the reply: "It's for the animals, honey." The goats, horses, dogs, bulls, and Rawhide received the baked goods either as part of a meal or a treat. Madison had never heard of such a thing in all her life.

It was at that moment she realized she was on adventure like no other she'd experienced.

The next day they spent in town visiting other properties owned by her grandfather. Blackberry Creek was a charming, small town that sat at the bottom of the beautiful Blue Ridge Mountains and was full of lush green forests, babbling creeks, and catfish ponds. Madison remembered thinking about how beautiful things were there and how laidback the people were. Everyone said hello to one another in a deep southern drawl with smiles on their faces. The days were long and hot in the summer and folks would often rest in the early evenings on their porches sipping cool lemonade or homemade iced tea. Madison found out quickly she preferred the sweetened iced tea over the unsweetened which tasted bitter to her.

On the outskirts of town, they pulled over off the beaten path and stopped by another large forest. They walked uphill through woods and admired the natural beauty of the wild flowers growing. Jethro explained to Madison that this, too, was one of his properties. She thought it was beautiful and learned later that this particular piece of property held enormous value as prime property. They walked a bit and picked a small bouquet of wild flowers to bring home.

Returning to the car, they drove into the far end of Blackberry Creek which was filled with quaint neighborhoods and small homes. They pulled up to a dark blue house on a corner, and Jethro told Hazel to take Madison inside if she wanted while he got something from the shed.

The house was tiny and had only two bedrooms, a small living room, kitchen, and bathroom. It was dusty and smelled of mildew. Inside, Madison noticed there were boxes everywhere instead of furniture. It had become a place for storage and held a lot of items leftover from the bridle shop that Jethro once owned. They didn't stay long as Madison's allergies began to act up from all the dust and mildew inside.

Back in the car, they began driving back towards the farm only to pull off onto yet another road. By way of the crow they were only about ten minutes away from the farm. Slowly the car drove through four feet of overgrown weeds before stopping in front of yet another trailer.

Across from the trailer was the largest vegetable garden Madison had ever seen. There, Jethro and Hazel grew beans, corn, squash, lettuce, tomatoes, cucumbers, and even strawberries. They spent the remainder of the day tending to the garden. Madison and Hazel pulled weeds, and Jethro spent a lot of time in the corn applying insect repellant to ward off the beetles that could destroy a crop in no time.

While in the garden, Hazel told Madison to be on the lookout for Indian arrowheads. Hazel had found nearly a dozen and showed them to Madison later that evening. The dirt was red and oftentimes the arrowheads blended in with the soil, making it hard to see them at first glance. An hour later, as she was weeding by the cucumbers, she stumbled upon a perfect reddish-color stone. Madison had found an arrowhead. She couldn't believe it, and Hazel and Jethro admired her finding, saying, "I told ya they were here." Madison treasured her new finding and made sure to put in a safe place for her return home. She couldn't wait to show her mother.

They loaded the car with some ripe vegetables and corn on the cob for dinner. They drove back out to the main road again and turned just a few miles up onto yet another road. This time they didn't get out of the car but Jethro pointed out another house that was his. No one lived there; it just sat empty. In total, Madison figured her grandfather owned at least 5 pieces of property.

What she couldn't figure out was why he and Hazel lived in a tiny trailer in the middle of the woods with animals everywhere and no running water or a real bathroom. Surely both the houses she saw today had more amenities than where she was staying. Why would they choose to live this way like hermits? She, for the life of her, could not figure it out. It was all just part of the adventure.

That night, Hazel made homemade cornbread on the cast iron stove outside of the trailer. While the cornbread was baking, she'd boiled up miscellaneous chicken parts and gizzards to feed to the Spitz dogs and the three poodles that lived in the trailer. Madison was yet again dumbfounded that someone would intentionally cook up chicken to feed to dogs. Hazel kept the thighs, wings, and breasts out and made homemade southern fried chicken, mashed potatoes, and gravy and biscuits, along with the corn on the cob they'd brought back from the garden.

It was the best meal she'd tasted in her life. She remembered wishing her mother could cook like that but, then again, not everyone has a cast iron stove right out their back door. Hazel would include some of these recipes in the small recipe book for Madison years later.

Most days were the same: feed the animals, pet and ride the horses, and walk the land. Madison fell in love with one of the horses that had been born just before she arrived. Her grandfather saw how she loved the horse and said she could have the colt as her own and name it. She named her Strawberry. Strawberry was a beautiful white and pink Tennessee Walking Horse, and Madison thought the name suited her well. Strawberry was too young to be ridden or broken in, but she let Madison pet her and feed her apples and carrots.

Near the back end of the horse pasture housing stood more woods. Madison and her grandfather walked towards the back of the pasture together one day, talking, and she finally built up the courage to ask him, "Why do you carry a gun on your belt, Grandpa?" He'd replied that it was for protection due to the abundance of snakes everywhere. So young, she believed him. "Of course! The snakes! I'm walking next to him, closely," she thought.

As they walked through the forest, Madison heard the sound of water and soon they had walked right up to a small, babbling brook. She noticed a shed off to the side where Jethro had already opened the door. Inside, he kept old jugs and other various containers. Some were plastic while others were ceramic or glass. He grabbed a couple of the plastic milk jugs, and showed her how to hold it and fill it up with water from the brook. These were natural springs and the water they contained was of the purist.

While filling the container, she looked around and noticed a couple old, barrel-shaped oil drums. At the time she didn't give too much thought to why those were in the middle of the woods near the water. It was later in her life that Madison learned from her mother that those oil barrels had never been used for oil. At least, not since Jethro had owned them. Those were used for making moonshine; hence, the reason for keeping them hidden. The shed held quarts of moonshine for both his personal consumption and for sale.

She had loved that trip to North Carolina but remembered an uncomfortable moment. The fourth day of her trip they had decided to go visit the local flea market that sat on the edge of town in a dusty field. In the field there was an aluminum building with tables where people sold their goods.

While inside, Madison came upon a peddler selling paraphernalia of Michael Jackson. He'd become a huge hit after his Thriller album and this table had posters, t-shirts, purses, pins, and much more for sale. Madison had brought her money with and wanted to buy one of the posters to bring back home and hang in her room. Jethro forbid her from purchasing the poster. He would not have it, and it was not welcome back at the house. Madison was embarrassed as she had not even thought to ask permission to buy the poster. Back home if she would have done so, her mother would have just said, "It's your money. If that's what you want to spend it on, then it's your decision."

Without any argument, she put her money back her wallet and walked away feeling deflated. She wanted to cry she felt so humiliated. Not a word of the incident was mentioned the entire way home. Two days would go by without Jethro saying a word to Madison. She could tell he was upset and disappointed with her but she couldn't figure out why. Finally, one afternoon, while helping Hazel peel apples in the kitchen, she asked, "Hazel, why is Grandpa so mad at me? He won't look at me or talk to me."

Hazel set down the paring knife, looked up at Madison, and said, matter-of-fact, "Because you like a black man, honey." That was Madison's first lesson on the Confederacy.

Looking back, she realized that even in the small town of Blackberry

Creek in the 1980's, there were few black people in town and they did not socialize with the white people. It was voluntary segregation at its prime. That experience left Madison hurt and confused and it would take her years to work through.

Though it bothered her very deeply unfortunately it was not the only experience of its kind. Madison's trip back to Blackberry Creek after Jethro was placed into the Alzheimer's home brought back a similar memory. While driving around town she slowly noticed the flags hanging from people's garages. They were not the American flag—they were Confederate flags. For a moment she wondered if it was even legal to hang such a discriminating thing on one's house and then remembered quickly where she was. She was in the south, the Deep South. Hoisting the Confederate flag on your garage or slapping it on the bumper of your truck was perfectly acceptable. Some things would never change, but she had a hard time seeing it hang so freely.

Later that same evening, Hazel and Madison were sitting around after dinner enjoying their usual Jack and Cokes when they found themselves on the topics of confederacy, slavery, and discrimination. It was painfully apparent that they had opposing viewpoints on the matter. Hazel raised her voice, one of the first times Madison had ever heard her do so, and said, "I don't hate black people; they're just not the supreme race like the white folk. It's the way God made it. Why, I loved Miss Massy who cared for me!"

Madison looked at her sharply and exclaimed, "She was practically a slave! She may have cared for you and raised you but she also cleaned the house while her mama did all the cookin'!"

The argument ended the evening early and left both women not speaking to one another. Madison got up, threw her drink in the sink, and turned around to tell Hazel, "I think it would be best if we just called it a night and I left." Hazel agreed but kept on after Madison for having the wrong opinion of the Confederacy and raising Mason to have the same misunderstanding. Unwilling to respond to the ludicrous, Madison stood there silently and shook her head back and forth in astonishment at Hazel. When she had enough, she grabbed her things and left. She was upset and, even though they'd been drinking, knew deep down that she couldn't change Hazel's or anyone else's mind in Blackberry Creek no matter what she said or did.

Back at her hotel, she took a shower to cool down. When finished, she threw on a white tank top and cut-off denim shorts and sat outside in front of her door smoking a cigarette. She decided that tomorrow she would apologize to Hazel in hopes that it would bring peace. Madison didn't want to fight with her step-grandmother; she was all the family she had left on that side. True, Virginia was her biological grandmother back in Mississippi, but their relationship was very distant, consisting of an occasional exchange of letters.

The next day, Madison apologized to Hazel, and they agreed that it was a subject that should no longer be discussed between the two.

Later that day, Hazel and Madison drove back to the old blue house in town so Madison could pick up some of Jethro's belongings and some items from the bridle store to take back home. The house looked even more run down than it had twenty years ago. It had suffered structural damage due to negligence, and when she walked inside she saw that the floor of the living room had completely caved in. Hazel warned her to be careful and watch her step. While Hazel dug through some old boxes, Madison picked up a framed photograph and turned to ask Hazel if it was a picture of Samantha Jo. This was the day she'd found the photo of Lane in his dress with his hair curled, smiling at the camera. The picture did exist and, so, the stories were true. Madison had thought to herself, "What sick person dresses up a male child in a dress, curls his hair, and takes him to town to see the photographer? What insane family did I come from?"

That night, after dinner at Hazel's, they again began with the Jack and Cokes. This time Madison reminded herself to the keep the conversation as far away as possible from taboo subjects. Hazel talked about Madison's daddy and made reference to his craziness while in the next sentence telling Madison how much he loved her. Madison found it odd since Hazel didn't care for Leroy much and those feelings were mutually shared.

While the two women sat at the kitchen table drinkin' and tellin' stories, Madison realized that Hazel knew a lot more about her family than she realized. Madison had been told that Jethro was once a grand dragon in the KKK. She inquired about that story and Hazel lazily dismissed as untrue. She didn't deny that he may have been active with the KKK, though, and how could she? Jethro himself had made it very clear to Madison that he hated black folks.

They finished the last of their drinks around midnight, and Madison gave Hazel a farewell kiss and hug. She would be heading home for Minnesota in the morning. She told Hazel to keep her informed on Jethro's health and give him her love. That night as she drove back to the hotel, her head was wild with stories she'd been told. Yet they weren't just stories, they were the Walker truths. The next time she saw Hazel was at her grandfather's funeral, three years later.

She called Joe that night from her hotel to tell him about her trip and the stories she'd been told. Joe started laughing and Madison curtly said, "What the hell is so funny to y'all?"

It was then that he really began to roar on the other line. "Madison, honey," he said. "How long did it take you to find your southern accent?"

She burst out laughing, too, when she realized she had been talking with the southern accent that came naturally to her. "I suppose I've had it since I've been here."

They laughed some more, and Madison told him the stories Hazel had shared and the fight they'd gotten into the night before. Joe just kept saying, "I can't believe it! Seriously, Madison, you could write a book about your family! That is just messed up!"

"I know, right? I couldn't make these stories up if I tried!"

What began as an adventure at the age of thirteen soon became a wake-up call and then a nightmare. The nightmare was a terrible trip for Madison when she returned to Blackberry Creek for Jethro's funeral.

She buried her grandfather and met the Monster. That was also the first time she met her uncle Lane and the adult version of Samantha Jo.

Lane looked like the devil's son himself. He was tall and lanky with dark hair and eyes so dark they looked black. He scared Madison with his looks alone, and she made sure to keep her distance from him the remainder of her trip. Samantha Jo was just as beautiful as Madison had imagined. She had long, wavy, blonde hair and green eyes. She looked more like her mother than Lane, and her daughter, Shelby Lynn, was a smaller version of her.

After the funeral, folks went to Hazel's house for a luncheon and to give their condolences. It was a small crowd of about twenty-five people. Upon Jethro's admittance into the Alzheimer's home, Hazel had moved into the house Madison had only seen from the outside as a teenager. It brought her comfort to know that she was not living alone in squalor out at the farm.

While others chatted, Madison stepped out for a cigarette to calm her nerves. Standing out back, she peered around the corner and noticed Leroy and Lane leaning over the hood of a car with documents spread out. Madison shivered and recognized they were up to something. Watching them closely, Madison became extremely worried. Her grandfather had only been six feet in the ground for two hours and here those two were already working up some sort of scheme to get their hands on what they felt was rightfully theirs. Madison kept her thoughts to herself and waited to share them until she spent some time alone with Hazel.

Later the next day, Madison and Hazel sat at the kitchen table, pulled out the Jack Daniels, and again found themselves in deep conversation. Hazel admitted she was a little nervous about Lane and Leroy, and Madison made her promise to be on alert and take safety precautions. Hazel waved her hand in the air and claimed the two men were heathens but she didn't fear they'd do anything to harm her.

Heathens they were! Leroy had already rifled through Hazel's house the day before the funeral looking for things he claimed were the

Walker's and should stay in the family. He took a few pieces of jewelry and miscellaneous odds and ends. Hazel knew better than to try and stop him as she figured he'd probably been the one who'd broken into the trailer at the farm a few days back, looking for things of value.

Madison asked Hazel why she didn't seem to mind that Leroy was breaking in and taking things with little respect to her. Hazel looked down at her glass thoughtfully then back up at Madison with a serious look that made her a bit uneasy. "Look, darlin'," she said, "He can take all that he wants. He and Lane are trying to plan a way to fight me for your granddaddy's money. They know there's a will, and they're claimin' that it was changed and that they're entitled to the land and money."

"Hazel, I think you need to take what's goin' on a little more serious. Those two are crazy, and I worry about you. What are you going to do?"

"Right now, the will states that the two boys get nothin' until I die and then they can fight over it."

"Hazel, you really need to get an attorney."

"I have, and he's taking care of things for me."

"I don't like this at all! Those men are awful! I can't believe they would bother to attest the will and fight you on it. You were his wife and you lived in a shack for years with no running water. Who do they think they are?"

She looked at Madison and said, "Honey, there is somethin' you need to know that I've never told no one about it. I have documented proof and your daddy and uncle know nothin' about it."

"What kind of secret are we talking about?"

"You've got to promise me, Madison, that you ain't gonna say a word. This needs to stay quiet and remain at this table. You promise now."

"I promise, Hazel, I swear! Now you're scarin' me, so just spit it out!"

She finished her drink and sat the glass down. The room was quiet, and Madison almost jumped when the ice in Hazel's glass settled on the bottom of her cup. Hazel sat silent for a moment before saying, "Your daddy and Lane are not the only sons your granddaddy had."

Madison slumped back in her chair and stared at Hazel. Hazel shocked her with that one; Madison hadn't expected that to come at her. "What do you mean, they don't know? Wait, how is it you know?"

"They don't know and it needs to stay that way. It would just mess things up and possibly ruin lives."

Madison's eyebrow raised, and she said, "What do you mean when you say 'ruin lives?' Why didn't Granddaddy tell them they have a brother? This had to be before he met you, then?"

Hazel shook her head in response. "Honey, I don't mean to be talkin' disrespectful of your granddaddy so soon after his death. I know how much y'all loved him just as I do, but there are just some things about your granddaddy that ya should know."

"What kinds of things are you talkin' about, Hazel?"

"Honey, he loved you more than anything, and you were too young to know and understand many things about him. He is not the man you've made him out to be. He's done some things, bad things, and you should understand who he really was."

"Hazel, just tell me what kinda things are you talkin' about? I know he's not perfect and I know he's done some horrible mean things, but what you're sayin' is scarin' me."

"Y'all remember when you had come to stay with us when you was thirteen years old?"

"Of course I do, how could I forget meetin' you, really, for the first time since I was a baby?"

"Well then, y'all remember that grocery store we went to, the one we parked behind to get the old produce from the dumpster?"

"Yeah."

"Remember that day we stopped back to actually go in and buy some groceries to bring home?"

"Yes, I remember. What does this have to do with anything?"

"Your granddaddy stayed out in the car while you and I went to fetch the groceries. There was a woman who worked at the registers. Her checkout lane was movin' quicker than the others that day but I held you back to wait in the other."

"I vaguely remember, but, yes, go on."

"Madison, what I'm goin' to tell ya maybe hard for ya to hear, but it's the truth. Your granddaddy and I had only been married for a short time. He'd been out drinkin' with the boys after he'd closed shop and on his way home, he saw a young girl walkin' on the side of the road. Your granddaddy offered to give her a ride home, and she got into the car. Only he didn't take her straight home. He drove her out into the country where he raped her for over two hours. He was drunk on moonshine and not thinkin' straight."

"I'm sorry; did you just say my grandfather raped a young girl? I . . . I . . . Jesus Christ, Hazel! What kind of shit is this? How old was she?"

"Madison, ya gotta know he was bit by the moonshine and not thinkin' clearly!"

"Are you gonna sit there and justify what he did? How old was she?"

"She was fifteen years old."

"What the hell does the grocery store have to do with this at all?"

"That was her mama that worked the checkout lane we avoided. Your granddaddy told the girl that if she told anyone, he'd come after her and have her mama fired from the grocery store. She musta told her mama because from that day on that woman stopped sayin' hello to me and wouldn't ring my groceries up. She'd walk away from me."

"Do you blame her? I mean, my God, Hazel, my grandfather rapes her daughter and she knows you're married to the man, what did you expect from her? And what happened to the poor girl?"

"Well, nine months later she had a son that she kept and raised as her own. He don't know your granddaddy is his daddy, and that is why you need to keep this to yourself, now, ya hear?"

"Hazel, you swear this is the truth? I mean, I just can't believe this, that poor girl and her family."

"You think it's been any easier for me? I have spent most of my married years to your granddaddy in shame livin' in a shack. We didn't talk to no one, and we certainly didn't get no visitors. Your granddaddy kept us hidden from everyone and everything! I have been livin' with this and humiliated! This is one of those things, Madison, ya keep to yourself and don't talk about. It will destroy lives!"

Madison was in shock. There were no words to describe the emotions she felt and the rage running through her. She looked up at Hazel and said, "Why, then, are ya tellin' me about this? If it is so detrimental then why tell me and why now?"

"I suspected somethin' bad had happened once that woman started ignoring me and stopped speakin' to me. Your granddaddy stopped comin' in the store with me and would just say he'd wait outside and to not be long. It wasn't after I had to put your granddaddy in the Alzheimer home that I stumbled upon the papers and learned of the entire incident."

"What papers are you talkin' about?"

"After the young girl had the baby, she sent your granddaddy a letter letting him know that he was the father of her baby. She didn't want nothin' from him and wouldn't tell a soul who the father was. She promised she'd keep it to herself and didn't want no trouble or harm to come to the baby. I kept the letter and placed it in a safe spot to keep it outta reach from Lane and Leroy. They're not to find out about this."

"Hazel, I am so sorry. I can't imagine how this must have hurt you, and you've been livin' with this all to yourself. Why tell me now if I'm not to share this information with anyone?"

"There will come a day when I'm gone that you should use this information only if absolutely necessary. You are not to say a word until then. Your cousin Samantha Jo is not to know about this either. Y'all have to trust me; I've got my reasons. I trust that you will do as I've asked?"

"You have my word, I promise. But, Hazel, where is the letter? How will I know where to look for it when this supposed time comes?"

"Trust me, darlin', y'all find it. It'll be right under your nose." She gave Madison a wink and they changed the subject.

Madison felt a tap on her shoulder and when she opened her eyes, she noticed the woman next to her motioning something. She, again, paused her iPod and took one ear bud out to hear what she was saying: "Honey, we're gettin' ready to land. You should put your seat up now."

Chapter 5

It was three o'clock in the afternoon when Madison received her luggage and loaded up her rental car to begin the trip to Blackberry Creek. The drive, which was mostly highway driving, would take nearly two hours. She pulled out her map and began driving. Her emotions were all over, and it frustrated her that she couldn't get a grip on them.

She was excited to see Samantha Jo, scared as hell that she'd see the Monster, upset to be attending Hazel's funeral, and anxious knowing there was something more lying ahead of her that she couldn't even begin to comprehend. Tears ran down her cheek at the very thought of everything. She wiped them away and licked her lips, tasting the salt from her tears. Madison quickly cracked the window to let in some clean, southern air. She wanted a cigarette but decided to hold off until she could pull over and dig them out. For now, she needed to pay attention to the road until she exited off near Pigeon Ridge and followed the back roads the remainder of the way.

While driving, she found herself thinking about Hazel and the distance that had built between the two since her grandfather's death. She couldn't understand it and was hurt that Hazel wanted nothing to do with her once Jethro had died. It didn't make any sense. She'd really only had Hazel as a grandmother since her relationship with Virginia was so distant. She had always considered Hazel her grandmother even though they weren't blood-related. That hadn't mattered to Madison.

But, for some unexplained reason, since Jethro's death, Hazel had more or less disowned Madison and Samantha Jo without so much as a word.

Jethro had been dead nearly one year when Hazel stopped returning calls or even picking up the phone. In a letter, Madison begged and pleaded Hazel to please contact her and let her know that she was all right. Madison worried about her and desperately wanted to know if she was alive and well. Hazel responded with a very short and cool letter to say that she was fine and that she appreciated the letter. That was all she wrote.

Samantha Jo tried calling her the following year, and Hazel answered the call. Samantha Jo inquired why she was not returning calls or sending letters; why she was ignoring and avoiding her step-granddaughters. All Hazel said was, "I just think it's for the best, honey. Y'all take care and it'd be best if ya didn't call here in anymore." Samantha Jo had called Madison to tell her about the conversation and how cool Hazel's voice was over the phone—almost as if she had never known who they were. Both women struggled to understand the situation. Samantha Jo had spent vacations with Jethro and Hazel, too, and was also deeply hurt. It was obvious that she no longer wished to accept them as her granddaughters and wanted no further contact with them.

It ate away at Madison and bothered her something fierce: "Why would she do this? She loved us. Didn't she? Weren't we her granddaughters? She always acted like she cared and made sure we received holiday and birthday cards. She even handmade the cards most of the time." In spite of it all, she still loved Hazel and would never have wished her any wrong. Never! The only thing that made sense in Madison's mind was that this had to do with Leroy and Lane. She didn't know for sure, but it was the only reasonable answer. Maybe Hazel became paranoid the women were in cahoots with their fathers, or maybe she just wanted to protect them from the danger she feared herself. With Hazel dead now, they would never know her real reason. Madison kept asking the same questions over and over in her mind—"What happened to her? Who would want to break into her house and for what? What had she done that someone would kill her?" And then it surfaced again—that sickening feeling of knowing somehow, someway this had everything to do with Leroy and Lane.

Madison didn't like the fact that Lane was the one who called Samantha Jo to tell her the news. "Why hadn't the sheriff called instead? Or Tessa, Hazel's sister? Was Lane in town?" As far as she knew, he still lived in Mississippi. The more Madison tormented herself, trying to make sense of it all, the more unanswered questions she came up with.

Madison thought about a call she'd had with Samantha Jo several months back. She hadn't thought too much of it at the time other than that it was just more crazy bullshit. It was just talk. Virginia was experiencing some health complications, and she'd be in the hospital for a few weeks for a hip surgery. Lane and Leroy were still fighting and not speaking to one another—but that was nothing new. Virginia was eighty-six years old, and Madison worried that her body may be too tired to endure the surgery.

Samantha Jo had also mentioned in her call that Leroy, the Monster, had called her to make amends since their last conversation ended in a fight. Leroy occasionally came through town, unexpectedly, to visit Virginia. Madison knew his visits were because he needed money rather than because he actually wanted to visit his mother. He and Samantha Jo had some words a few years back, and he wanted to set things right with her. He acknowledged that he would be coming to town in three weeks to help care for Virginia and didn't feel it was right for them to continue fighting at a time with Virginia needed them both.

Madison immediately questioned his motive. There was always a devious motive driving Leroy to do anything he did. There was something in it for him, and in order to get it, he needed to be the doting favorite of Virginia's, at her side and assisting with her recovery.

Leroy hated his brother, and the two were often fighting. If money was involved, they'd appear to be working together and joining forces.

But when the plan failed or took too long, they'd begin doubting one another's real motive and begin fighting. At the time of the call, the two had been fighting since Jethro's death, nearly a year ago. Madison stiffened her body and her knuckles gripped the steering wheel so hard they were white. She repeated the words out loud while driving in the car—"Since Jethro's death." That was too coincidental for her.

First, Hazel cut off all communication with her and Samantha Jo around the same time that Leroy and Lane began sparring. The last time she saw her father and Lane was after her grandfather's funeral when the two men were bent over the hood of car discussing and pointing to the papers they had laid out. Madison flew home with Joe right after the funeral and never did learn what information those papers contained. Why was it that these two incidents happened in such quick succession?

During her call with Samantha Jo that day, her cousin also mentioned that she had to make up with Leroy because she was nervous about his reasons for coming back to town. Like Madison, she obviously didn't believe that he was concerned for his mother. Virginia didn't have much left to offer. Grady had passed away fifteen years ago from a sudden heart attack, and Leroy and Lane made sure they stood in line and took turns bleeding her dry of any money that she received.

She continued to work two jobs until the age of eighty-two, trying to support herself and her two parasitic sons. Even at the age of eighty-six, she was still paying bills totaling nearly 1100 dollars a month for each of the two men, leaving her 20 dollars a week for food. Samantha Jo checked on her often to make sure she had food and to see if she needed care. Lane was supposedly tending to her; however, Samantha Jo stopped by one day and found out that Lane had not seen Virginia in over a week.

Her mail was piling up in the mailbox and she had run out of food. When Samantha Jo asked her what happened and why her daddy had not been by, Virginia said he was mad at her because she told him she could no longer afford to pay some of his bills. He had stormed out of the house, angry, and had not returned since. Madison screamed into the phone, "That is his own fucking mother, for God's sake! What the hell is wrong with this family?" Samantha Jo could only agree with Madison. There was no sane reason for anything Lane or Leroy did.

Madison had told Samantha Jo to be careful and to keep a close eye out for herself while Leroy was in town. "Madison" she said, "There's something more."

"What do you mean? More about Virginia's health? What?"

"No," she said "It's Leroy. He just scares me sometimes."

Madison thought to herself, "Try having him as your father," but said, "What is it that's got you upset, other than the fact he called you and is coming to town? I mean, you know you can't believe a word he says!"

"Madison, if there's one thing I know about y'alls daddy, it's that he never lies."

Madison thought for a moment and came back with, "You might be right about that, but it's only his truth and it's crazy talk! What did he say?"

"He said that he would be comin' back to take care of Virginia and as soon as she takes her last breath, he's gonna hunt down Lane and shoot him dead."

"Are you serious? He really said that?"

"Ya, he did and you know what? I believe him some."

"So after his own mother dies, he's gonna go and shoot his own brother?"

"That's what he said."

Madison sat for a second and thought to herself, "Even if he did intend to do this, surely times have changed even in the south so he wouldn't be able to get away with such a thing. I mean, really, this is just ludicrous."

As it was, Virginia managed to pull through the surgery and return home. Leroy left town after she'd been home for nearly a month. Madison figured he got tired of waiting to for her to die and when it was apparent she'd be okay, he left. There was nothing else for him to do but wait some more. Wait some more for her to die, get his inheritance, and then kill his brother. Like a snake in the weeds he could be—just patiently lying in the grass, waiting for the right moment to strike.

Samantha Jo may have been right about Leroy not being a liar, but he sure was full of talk that seemed to be idle threats more than anything. Nevertheless, he was crazy and there was just no reasoning with crazy or knowing what crazy would really do.

Madison was about fifteen miles from her exit to Pigeon Ridge when it dawned on her she had not called her mother. Not that it was intentional but she'd just had so much to do in a short period of time that . . . Ah hell, who was she kiddin'; she had avoided the entire thing all together.

She knew her mother would be upset and scared that Madison was going back to Blackberry Creek. She also knew that the conversation would be long and drawn out; exhausting was more like it. She was already on an emotional landslide, trying to keep herself calm, without explaining to her mother why she needed to do this. Her cell phone beeped, and she saw that Joe had sent her a text.

It read: Be careful and don't do anything CRAZY! Call when you get to the hotel. Love Joe.

She smiled and repeated out loud—"Yeah, don't do anything crazy. Like come here in the first place, idiot!"

She found her exit to Pigeon Ridge and, while waiting at the light to turn right and head west, she dug out her cigarettes and lit one. She needed something stronger, she figured, to take the edge off, but this would suffice for now. She knew that at the hotel she and Samantha Jo would have their happy reunion and go for drinks and dinner. She was looking forward to seeing Samantha Jo and hoped to hear if she had learned anything more about Hazel.

While driving down the road at a steady fifty-five, she passed by an old Baptist church that was mainly attended by Black families. It was a small building with a steeple on top. The church could hold forty people on a good day. It was run down and the white paint was peeling all around it. By her count, the peeling had gotten worse since the last time she'd driven by it five years ago.

There were Baptist churches spread all throughout the southern countryside, but this particular one always gave Madison the chills whenever she drove by it. It was almost as if she'd hold her breath until she had passed it. Madison was not a religious person by any means and, in fact, would consider herself an atheist, but each time she drove by this particular church, she found herself saying a prayer.

Back in 1963 there was a lot of uproar and rioting because of the Civil Rights Movement. The Klan was busy taking care of business their way, and the government was working to bring equal rights to everyone, no matter their race or color. It was a dangerous time in the south for a black person. Most people remember 1963 as the year Medgar Evers was shot and killed outside his home and Martin Luther King, Jr. delivered his "I Have a Dream" speech in Washington. But that very same year there was much chaos across the south with the Klan working to keep control over the law and prevent the spread of equal rights by using methods of their own.

Madison knew the story well; her mother told her about it years ago after she first saw the Baptist church. It was a harrowing story full of hatred and loss that left a community in fear and sorrow for years to come.

The story is not much different than others that took place throughout the country but it saddened Madison every time she'd drive by and remember how her mother had explained to her that, on a hot summer day, five young black boys were walking home for supper together. They ranged in age from five to twelve years old. Two were nine-year-old identical twin brothers.

The boys had been working all day at the church, weeding and painting pews that needed some touch-up. They were all in the choir and had agreed to come in that late Saturday afternoon to help the minister and his family out. The boys started walking home around 8 p.m. It was summer, and the night was warm and muggy. They would be late for dinner but knew it would be waitin' for them after they got home and cleaned up.

Only, they never made it home that night.

The details are not clear and no one will ever know for sure what happened, with the exception of the guilty, but by 10 p.m., two of the fathers decided to go lookin' for the boys. They figured they were probably messing around and playin' by the creek, lookin' to cool down after such a hot day. But when the men got to the creek, the boys were nowhere to be found.

They followed the main road that led back to the church. It was a two lane road that had large trees on each side creating a canopy of shade. The men walked nearly a mile when one of the fathers noticed a shoe in the ditch. They'd just passed a dirt road about 200 yards back that led to an old abandoned farmhouse. The house had been empty for years and was so old and decrepit that it leaned to the left.

Turning back, the two headed for the dirt road and noticed fresh tire tracks that had pulled off the main road recently. Everyone knew that the house and land were vacant, leaving little reason for anyone to drive down to it with the exception of the occasional teenaged couple looking for a private spot to make out.

They started to follow the tracks and within a few hundred yards, they found another shoe, different from the first they'd found. They knew instantly that something was not right. They started running at this point and called out the names of the boys, desperately hoping to hear a sound from them. But the night was still and the only noise they heard were the sounds of the dark.

They reached the house and still saw no sign of the boys anywhere. They didn't figure to look in the house, as deteriorated it was, it would have just been plain foolish for the boys to have gone in there. They looked around, noticed the barn and started in that direction. One of the fathers looked to his right at the forest that worked as a border around the property. He shined his light and froze with terror at the sight that lay before him.

There, from the trees, hung all five boys.

They had been beaten so badly that their faces were unrecognizable. All five were completely stripped of clothing and hung by a rope around their neck. Their entire bodies had been so brutally beaten that pools of blood soaked into the dirt below them. Broken arms and legs hung disjointed. Each had been sodomized with some foreign object and their penises had been cut off. They smelled of urine and human feces.

Tears ran down the faces of the fathers who tried frantically to lower the bodies as they screamed out, "No Lord! Oh why? Why? No! No!" Their struggle to release the boys was without success. What seemed like seconds was really thirty minutes. Giving up, they ran as fast as they could back home to get help and ladders. When they returned and cut the ropes, each of the bodies fell to the ground and laid there lifelessly next to one another.

They had been dead for nearly an hour before the two fathers found them. It was of no use to try and revive them; their souls had left their tortured and abused bodies to be with God. The black community was devastated and enraged that something so awful as this could happen. Why? They hadn't done anything to anyone. They were on their way home from helping at the church.

Though they never did identify who had committed the horrible murder, everyone knew who was guilty and capable of such a crime. Unfortunately, this was a time when the KKK was making their stands to show they did not agree with the Civil Rights Movement. It was a senseless and hateful crime that would go unpunished and leave a community up in arms.

As Madison drove by the church, she looked up at the large sign that had been made in memory of the young boys that died that night. Each of their pictures was on it along with their names and dates of their births and deaths.

Above their photos read: **Not Forgotten**

It made sense to Madison why she'd hold her breath, give a moment of silence, and break into a prayer. The senselessness and anger of this apparent hate crime was more than she could stomach. As a mother, she could not imagine the pain and suffering those families would endure the rest of their lives wondering how they could have stopped this from happening and saved their babies.

The thought of those boys crying out for their parents and for help was more than Madison could bear to think about, and she felt great sadness. She drove in silence the remainder of the way to the hotel.

Chapter 6

It was just after 5 p.m. when Madison pulled into the parking lot for the Comfort Inn. She shut off her car and picked up her cell, found Joe's text and hit reply.

She wrote: I'm here at the Comfort Inn and just checking in. Will call you in the morning.

She took her luggage out of the trunk, threw her leather bag over her shoulder, and headed for the door to the check-in counter. While walking across the lot, she took in the fresh air of Blackberry Creek and whispered to herself, "Don't do anything crazy!"

The hotel clerk checked her in, gave her the room key, and said that the other party had already arrived and checked in. He told her that her room would be on the fifth floor, number 505, and to turn left from the elevators. She made her way to the room and slid in the key card.

Samantha Jo was waiting for her and flew off the bed to greet Madison. They hugged each other and stood back to admire one another and then hugged again. "Samantha Jo, it is so great to see you! God, I can't believe it's been five years and yet here we are again for another funeral."

"I know! I was thinkin' the same thing when I got here."

"I need a drink! Is there any liquor there by the fridge?"

"No, I checked right away when I got here."

"Fine, let me throw this bag down and lets go find a place to grab a bite to eat and drink."

"I thought y'all would never ask!"

The two women walked into the Sawdust Bar and Restaurant and grabbed a booth where they could talk with some privacy. They both ordered a Jack and Coke, in Hazel's memory, along with a cheeseburger. When the drinks came they gave a toast, "To Hazel," and took long sips. Madison set down her glass and asked Samantha Jo, "Have you been thinking since our call how strange all this is?"

"Girl, that is all I've been thinkin' about! And I'll tell ya somethin' else, those two Lane and Leroy, they scare the dickens outta me."

"I'm glad to hear you say that. Otherwise I'd have to think you're just as crazy as they are." They gave each other a crooked smile and toasted their glasses again.

"Honestly, though, Madison, I just don't know what to think about all this goin' on. I can't make heads or tails of it none. Maybe it was just a burglary that went wrong . . . Ya know?"

"I don't believe that for one second, Samantha Jo, and I know you don't either! What I don't understand is why Lane was the one to call y'all?"

"I asked him the same thing when he called and he'd just told me that the sheriff had been the one to let him know. He apparently knew granddaddy very well and found his number in her address book near the phone."

"I suppose that could make sense, but I still don't buy it."

"Madison, y'all got to remember that things here ain't like they are in the Midwest. Down here things are much simpler and laid back. I know that Lane lies through his teeth, but it don't make no sense to me why he'd lie about the call."

"I know things are different down here, that's what makes me so crazy! I just have this unsettled feelin' that somethin' is amiss here, and I intend to find out what it is."

"I don't know that I'd go pokin' around too much, y'all know that those two fathers of ours will be comin' to town."

"What on earth for? They never did get along with Hazel, and for sure not since granddaddy's death. Hell, they can't even get along with each other for that matter!"

"Honey, there's reasons why those two have been fightin' and disagreein' the last five years."

Madison's voice rose as she exclaimed, "What are you talkin' about? What don't I know now? What have those two gone and done? They're up to something, aren't they?"

"Now, calm down some. I know y'all are angry, but it ain't me you're mad at!"

"I'm sorry, you're right. I just get so damn mad. Every time I turn around there's just more shit comin' outta the woodwork. What the fuck is it with this family? Somethin' in the water I should know about?"

"No, now stop y'all and listen. Y'all remember that day after granddaddy's funeral when you saw Lane and Leroy lookin' over papers on the hood of the car?"

"Of course I do. I'm the one that told you about it. What about it?"

"Right. Well honey, they wasn't just lookin' at one will, they was lookin' at two wills!"

"Come again? How is that possible?"

"Well, now, listen and I'ma tell ya. Evidently Granddaddy had a will where Lane and Leroy were suppose to get 40k each, which they did, and supposed to each get five of the twenty-one properties."

"Twenty-one? I thought there was maybe 5 or so?"

"No, honey, Granddaddy invested a lot of his money into properties that are worth a ton of money today. The other will they were lookin' at had been revised and supposedly Hazel had forged granddaddy's name when he was admitted into that Alzheimer hospital."

"Are you kidding me? How do you forge a signature on a will and not get caught? First of all you need to have it notarized, and secondly, why would Hazel do that?"

"Well, yeah, ya do, but she coulda had someone do that for her."

"So what is the dispute, then, between Lane and Leroy?"

"They didn't get the properties. The revised will says that only when Hazel dies do they inherit them. They was fightin' because Lane wanted the properties sooner and he went and got himself a lawyer that was makin' all kinds of fuss. The judge in town decided that the revised will would stand and that was it. Nothin' Lane's attorney could do would change it none. It pissed Leroy off somethin' fierce cuz now rather than reasonin' with her, he's gotta wait it out. And on top of it, share it with his brother!"

"Good God! You know all they're gonna do is sell those properties for the money!"

"I suspect y'all right 'bout that one. But the other properties, the remainin' fifteen, stand to go to Hazel's family now."

"The hell you say! That property belongs in the Walker family and should stay there. Why not leave it to us or somethin'?"

"Well, there again, honey, since granddaddy had purchased those properties while married to Hazel and her name is on the titles and all, she can do as she pleases."

"So what you're sayin' is that nothin' is left of the Walker estate and those two fucking parasites of fathers get the remaining to sell off and that's it?"

"Now y'all are gettin' it, sister!"

"Samantha Jo you do realize that our fathers could very well be responsible for Hazel's death, don't you? I mean they have the perfect motive."

"I know. I've been thinking about that too and tryin' to convince myself otherwise. I just can't believe that they could be capable of murder. These are our fathers we're talkin' about, Madison."

"I agree it's a hard one to swallow, but there is a strong chance that I'm right, especially after what ya just told me."

Their burgers came, and they each ordered another drink. Madison felt like asking for the rest of the bottle of Jack to take back to the hotel with her. She felt the need for alcohol to dull the headache that had started. "Hey, Samantha Jo, which funeral home did y'all say Hazel was at?"

"The only one there is in town, darlin', Rutherford Funeral Home. It's not too far from the hotel. Why?"

"Well I was just thinkin' that we should go over there tomorrow and find out when the actual viewin' will be and the details for her funeral. See if there's any loose ends or something we can do help."

"Y'all, I suspect Hazel's sister has pretty much got that bull by the horns."

"God, I'd forgotten all about her. Tessa. Such a cheerful woman. Ya think she'll have a big hug for us?"

"I doubt that. That woman's been acting like someone dropped a house on her sister for years!"

The two women couldn't help but burst out laughing. They laughed so hard tears began to run down their faces.

Madison exclaimed, "I'm goin' to hell now; I'm sure of it!"

"Nonsense!" roared Samantha Jo. "Y'all, I couldn't of said it better myself."

"I never met such a mean and spiteful woman. I remember meetin' her once when I was younger; we'd gone to visit her at the family estate. She didn't seem to care for me none and didn't want me sittin' on the furniture or touchin' anything in the house."

"I'm sure she ain't changed none and has the whole service and everythin' all tended to. I'm almost afraid to see her. Now all I can imagine in my head is her wearin' striped tights and a witch's hat!"

"Wouldn't that be a sight?"

Again the two women couldn't help but snicker each time they looked across the table at one another.

"Ya know, Samantha Jo, the more I think about it, the more I think we shoulda never come here in the first place!"

"I know what y'all mean, it's not like we have a family that is forgivin' and welcoming. I gave up a long time ago thinkin' we could be a normal, lovin' family. It's just a shame bein' that we're so small and all."

"I've got you and Shelby Lynn, Samantha Jo, and I'll take that any day over havin' none."

They finished their dinner and drinks, and walked out to the parking lot to head back to the hotel. It was dark out and nearly 9:30 p.m. Madison was exhausted from her travels and from the newly learned information from Samantha Jo at dinner. It seemed every time she'd try and accept the fact that the Walker family was a mess, she'd hear something new and find the rage returning.

As they began to pull out of their parking spot, a parked car in the far corner of the lot turned on its engine and lights and sat idle. Madison didn't think much of it and laid her head back, looking out the window while Samantha Jo drove. She rolled her window down to take in the sweet, warm air of the night. As they turned onto the main road heading towards the hotel, Madison glanced into the side mirror and froze for a moment. She sat up and looked at Samantha Jo with a puzzled look, asking, "Did y'all see anyone walk out of the restaurant when we did?"

"I don't reckon so but I've had a couple drinks and can't really recall. Why?"

"Well, I've had a few drinks too, and I don't remember anyone walking out with us either. Which is why I'm wonderin' why that car in the lot started its engine when we did and is now followin' us?"

"Madison, y'all stop. I'm scared enough as it is with all this crazy talk tonight. I'm sure it's just coincidence is all."

"Coincidence my ass! That car started its engine when we got in our car and turned on its lights."

"And what?"

"You're right, I'm just a little jumpy and on edge. Forget it all, let's just get back to the hotel and get some sleep. I'm sure I'm just overtired. Besides my nerves have been on overload since Sunday."

"Honey, I agree. It's probably been all that travelin' today and talk that's got y'all uptight. A good night's rest will do ya some good."

As they pulled into the hotel parking lot, Madison noticed the car that had been behind them had dropped back in distance from them.

The two women got out of the car and started walking for the main door when Madison turned and saw the car drive by slowly. It was an old car, she figured, from the '70s, and, though she couldn't tell for sure, she thought it may have been a Chrysler. She couldn't make out who the driver was, and even with the street light near the road, she was too far away to see the plates. She was pretty sure it was a shade of green. The car stopped alongside the road just past the entrance to the hotel lot and idled there.

Madison tapped Samantha Jo on the shoulder, and she turned around. The car sat for thirty seconds then pulled back onto the road and drove off into the night. Samantha Jo grabbed Madison's hand and pulled her in through the front doors and the two went straight for the elevator. "Samantha Jo?"

"Don't say it. Let's just get to our room and lock the door." She didn't want to talk about it, but, deep down, Samantha Jo knew just as Madison did that it was creepy bein' back in North Carolina and it was no coincidence that the car had stopped alongside the road. They had been followed and there could only be two logical explanations as to who was drivin' that car. She knew that no one had followed them out of the restaurant, and, in the rearview mirror, she saw the car turn onto the main road shortly after they did. She'd figured she was just imaginin' things and gettin' herself worked up for nothin'. But she knew better and so did Madison.

Once in the room, they agreed to set the alarm for 8 a.m. and stop down in the lobby for a cup of coffee and complimentary continental breakfast before heading over to the funeral home. They spent the night talking in their beds about one another and their families before falling asleep at 10:30.

Chapter 7

Madison awoke before the alarm. She rolled over and looked at the clock; it was 6:07 a.m. The sun was already coming up, and it was going to be a warm day. She'd heard that a wave of hot weather, along with high humidity, was on its way and would remain for several days. She laid there thinking about what Samantha Jo had said at dinner last night and tried to tell herself that it was not a dream; it was, in fact, real.

If what Samantha Jo had said was true, then Madison's suspicions about Hazel's murder may well be correct. But who had done? Or rather, which one had done it? Both Lane and Leroy stood to gain from her death. As long as she was alive, they'd have to wait patiently to inherit their land. Was that worth killing over? Then she remembered the value of the properties and realized, yes, of course it was worth killing over if you thought like those two.

She remembered the car that had obviously followed her and Samantha Jo back to the hotel. It sent shivers down her spine because she knew it only could have been Leroy or Lane. But how had they known where she and Samantha Jo were eating? How did they know their daughters were in town? It wasn't as if they had already been there a few days or talked with anyone. More questions, always more questions, and never any answers.

She would have to be more alert of her surroundings, more than she had anticipated. She had hoped that neither her father nor uncle would show their faces in town. However, that may have been wishful thinking. Someone was here, and they had made their presence known. The last thing she needed was to be a sitting duck.

Samantha Jo also woke before the alarm and remained still, thinking about the evening's events as well. She felt more on edge than ever and felt she had more to lose than Madison. Madison would leave North Carolina, return to Minnesota, and never have to worry about dealing with Lane or Leroy again, if she chose. But she, on the other hand, lived in the same town as Virginia and knew that both the Walker men would come to town unannounced whenever they wanted.

She'd run the chance of havin' to see them and, possibly, talk with them. She didn't want no trouble, that was for sure, and feared not only for her safety but her daughter's safety as well.

She felt a wave of nausea in her stomach, thinking about the trouble Madison could bring to her life if she pushed too much and pissed off the wrong people. She didn't know how she could keep her cousin from bringing harm their way, but she decided to keep an eye on Madison and keep her cool. Maybe Madison would let things be and accept the fact that she couldn't change the situation or why their fathers were the way they were.

Samantha Jo didn't have the same desires to dig up matters like her cousin did. Maybe she should return home earlier than planned? She'd wait and see how things went at the funeral and then decide. She could always catch a quick flight outta there, and, after all, she missed her daughter already. Samantha Jo was realizing very quickly that coming here had quite possibly been a huge mistake.

Madison got up just before the alarm went off and went into the bathroom. She quickly showered, brushed her teeth, and threw her hair up in a ponytail. With the heat and humidity, she would stay cooler with her hair up and, besides that, the humidity would ruin whatever attempt she made to style it.

When she came out, Samantha Jo was up and said, "Good mornin'," as she walked passed Madison to the bathroom. Madison threw on some shorts and a tank top and dabbed on a bit of mascara and lip gloss. She pulled out her cell as she waited for Samantha Jo and started perusing the emails on her phone. There was a text from Joe and the rest were of no importance to her at this time. Just a few work emails that could wait for her return.

She scrolled to Joe's text: Good morning! Glad to hear you're ok. Meeting with Nelson today to review account. Just checking in to make sure you're ok. George is doing just fine and sends a slobbery kiss. Miss you!

Madison smiled and hit reply: Behave yourself and be nice to Nelson. Give George a kiss and rub his ears for me. I'll call ya later. Wish you were here with me.

When Samantha Jo finished getting ready, the two women stopped by the lobby to grab their breakfast and hot coffee. They pulled out of the hotel lot and drove towards town in somber silence. They were both short on words this morning and knew that it was due to their nerves. They were heading to the funeral home to visit their dead grandmother—there were really no words to say.

They parked the car and went inside the funeral home. They were greeted by an older woman in her sixties who wore a yellow dress and had her hair pulled up in a bun. She spoke in a quiet voice and said, "Good morning, y'all, how may I help you today?" Samantha Jo introduced the two of them and explained that they had come to see their grandmother, Hazel Walker.

"Oh, dear, yes. We are so sorry for y'alls loss. Hazel was a gracious and kind woman. I didn't know her too well, but she always took the time to say hello when I'd see her at the drug store. Why don't y'all wait here in the lobby while I find my husband, Stan, and he'll take care of y'all. By the way, my name is Judy if you need anything."

They sat down and were looking at one another when they heard voices coming from another room. The voices began to get louder. From the sound of it, they could tell there were more than two people in the other room. Madison turned to Samantha Jo and said, "What on earth is goin' on in there? I thought our family was bad. That sounds like a serious disagreement goin' on."

Suddenly, the door opened and out walked a tall gentleman. He looked to be somewhere in his forties, with salt and pepper hair and blue eyes. Madison noticed his muscularity and noted how handsome he was. She was attracted to his eyes. She could tell a lot about someone by looking into their eyes. It was true what they said, "the eyes are the window to one's soul." He spoke with a deep southern drawl and tipped his head in acknowledgement to the two women staring up at him. "Good mornin', ladies. I'm Travis Jackson, and you two must be Madison and Samantha Jo?"

Madison cleared her throat and said, "That is correct. Forgive me for sounding rude, but who are you? And why do you already know our names?"

"I was your grandmother's attorney. Have been since your granddaddy fell ill several years ago. I'm sorry that we are meetin' under circumstances like this, y'all. It is never an easy time for me when a client passes away and leaves loved ones behind."

"Well, thank you for your condolences, Mr. . . uh, Jackson, was it?"

"Yes, m'am, Travis Jackson but you can just call me Travis."

"Well then, Travis, what was that we heard in the other room? Is everythin' okay?" asked Samantha Jo.

"I do apologize to y'all for havin' to overhear us. Let's just say these can be extremely emotional and challenging moments when it comes to getting everyone to agree at times." Madison nodded her head in agreement, and thought that he didn't know the half of it.

"If y'all will excuse me, I do have to be leavin' for an appointment with another client, but here is my card should you have questions or want to talk further. I knew your grandmother for such a short time but I did enjoy her company. There will be a meetin' on Monday to discuss her will and y'all are both welcome to attend. We will be startin' at 2 p.m. sharp."

Samantha Jo broke in and asked, "Excuse me, Travis, I know this is going to sound awkward and a bit awful, but is there anything you can tell us about her will?"

"I reckon, m'am, that I can't discuss any details regarding your grandmother's will with ya at this time. That will have to be done on Monday, but certainly feel free to contact me if y'all have any other questions unrelated to her estate. My office is just around the corner in the brick building with the wrought iron gate, and my number is on my card as well. Now if you'll excuse me, y'all have someone waitin' for you in the next room. Good day."

"Damn, girl, he was cute! Did you see the body on that man?"

"He certainly looks like he keeps fit."

"Madison, a gorgeous man walks into the room and that's all you can say? 'He looks like he keeps fit?' Honestly, girl!"

"Okay, busted! Yes, he is attractive; yes, he has a nice-looking ass, and he also lives in North Fucking Carolina! He is of no use to me, Samantha Jo."

"I know, but he is good-lookin' eye candy and will be fun to watch and listen to on Monday." She gave Madison a wink as the two walked into the next room.

There, standing with her back to the door, was an older woman with a slumped-over posture. She had dark gray hair and stood about 5'5". She waited until she'd heard the two women walk in to turn around. Neither Madison nor Samantha Jo recognized her. They waited for the old woman to say something.

She walked over, shook her finger at both women, and said, "I don't want no trouble from y'all. This here is all taken care of and don't concern y'all none."

Madison looked the woman in the eye and said, "Forgive us, m'am, but do we know you?"

"I'm Tessa, Hazel's sister, and this standin' over here is my husband

Edward." Edward stood there in silence. Madison had the feeling that he was used to keepin' quiet and letting Tessa rule the roost her way.

Tessa Sawyer was Hazel's oldest sister, and she still lived in the Sawyer family's estate home. The home was left to her when their parents passed away years ago. When Tessa and Edward first married, they had lived in the house with her parents. Poor old Edward had been told what to do, where to go, when to eat, and probably what to wear his whole life while married to that old bat. The Sawyer Estate home was a mansion. It sat at the end of town and was a beautiful, gated property. The house was all brick and three-stories high with ten bedrooms.

Madison remembered it from her visit when she was younger and thought that it resembled something out of a movie. It was furnished with many family heirlooms and antiques. She wasn't allowed to see too much of the house as Tessa didn't want her pokin' around, but she did remember the large black and white marble-tiled floor from the entrance. There were two staircases covered with rich, deep red carpet leading up to the second floor.

The house had been in the family for centuries and would remain so even after Tessa and Edward passed away. They'd leave it to their nieces. After Jethro passed, Hazel commented that Tessa wanted her to move in with her and Edward. But Hazel enjoyed her independence, and, after all those years of living with Jethro, she wanted time to herself to do what she pleased. She, too, knew how overpowering Tessa was to be around, though she loved her in spite of it and had been close to her sister her whole life.

It was said that Robert E. Lee and his comrades had stopped at the Sawyer Estate for a brief stay during the Civil War. All the slaves had to be confined in a secret underground room off from the kitchen. It was also known that the estate sat over the town aquifer that ran underground. The city officials established the Sawyer Estate as one of the monumental land marks in town.

"Tessa, I'm . . ."

Before Madison could say any more, the old woman interrupted her and said, "I know darn well who y'all are and, like I said, this here has all been tended to already."

"What's been tended to?" Samantha Jo asked.

"The arrangements for Hazel. They've all been discussed and planned, and the last thing I need is for y'all to be complicatin' things."

"We're not looking to bring you any headaches, Tessa. We're just here to pay our respects to our grandmother. Any plans you've made, I'm sure, will be just fine. But if it's all right with you, we'd like to know more about the details as Samantha Jo and I have both traveled a distance to be here to attend the funeral services."

"This here is between family, Madison, and, darlin', that does not include y'all!"

Samantha Jo grabbed Madison's hand as if to hold her back; she knew Madison was not goin' to take kindly to Tessa and her nasty remarks. "I don't know what y'all are talkin' about us not bein' family an' all; she was our grandmother."

"Your family, the Walkers, honey, are not my family. There is no blood between us therefore that don't make y'all family to the Sawyers. Y'all Walkers are the same, nothin' but trouble and shame. Now I want my sister to rest in peace with dignity. Ya hear?"

"Tessa, this here is not up for debate. As far as Samantha Jo and I are concerned, she was our grandmother, and we intend to bury her and pay our respects. Now, if you all are done, we will be excusing ourselves to go and say our goodbyes to our grandmother."

"Now, you listen here, missy, y'all stay outta my way and my business. There ain't nothing here concerning y'all."

"Well, Tessa, I'm gonna have to disagree with you there. Blood or not, we came here today to see our grandmother and pay our respects. Now, if you'll excuse us, that's what we're going to go do."

"I'm warnin' y'all, don't go messin' round with business that don't concern ya none."

"I could say the same to you! Goodbye, Tessa; we'll see you on Friday at the ceremony."

The two women turned and left the room. As they walked out, Samantha Jo turned to Madison and said, "Damn, that woman chaps my hide! Did y'all see the meanness and spite in her eyes?"

"She hasn't changed a bit, cuz."

As they walked back out into the lobby, they saw that the woman in the yellow dress, Judy, had returned and the man standing next to her must be Stan.

He walked forward and extended his hand out to greet them. "Good morning, ladies. If y'all follow me, I'll take you back where you can be alone with your grandmother. Her body was embalmed yesterday, and I need to warn y'all that this may be difficult for ya to see. The circumstances of her death were quite grotesque leaving us much work yet to complete. We've gotten the body preserved but still have yet to address her make-up, hair, and the like."

Madison and Samantha looked at one another and took deep breaths. Stan stopped in front of a door that read: **Private Viewing**. He opened the door for the women as they entered into a room with two sterile, metal tables in the center.

To the left was a wall that held what looked like large filing drawers. Each was marked with a number—there were ten in total. There were two chairs off to the right. A white curtain hung from ceiling to separate the two tables.

Stan asked the women if they were ready, and they nodded in agreement. He reached for drawer number 5, turned the metal handle downwards, and opened the door. It made the sound of something decompressing, and he reached in and pulled the drawer out toward him. He gently pulled the white sheet that lay over Hazel's head downward and folded it just above her chest.

"I will be right outside the door if y'all need anything. Please, take y'alls time." He walked out the door and the two waited until the door closed before they made a move.

They grabbed each other's hand and walked towards the body. They both gasped when they saw the body in closer view. "Oh, dear God," cried Samantha Jo. "I've never seen anything so awful as this. Why did this have to happen?"

Madison leaned forward to study the body, squinting from the tears that filled her eyes. Hazel's neck had been cut from one ear to the other. The stitches reminded her of a Raggedy Ann doll. This was not at all how she remembered Hazel looking nor did she want it to be her last memory of her grandmother.

She reached out to touch the cold body; it felt more like a wax dummy than an actual person. It always amazed her why people did this. Why did they have viewings of a dead loved one when nothing about them was real? The loved one was really nothing more than a wax dummy slathered in make-up, combed hair, and put in a nice suit. It seemed ridiculous when she thought about it.

Samantha Jo interrupted Madison's thoughts and said, "I suppose Tessa's got this under control, too, with what she'll be wearin' and all?"

"Yeah, I'm sure you're right about that one. She's got everything under control, according to her, and we should just mind our own P's and Q's."

"Well, I hope she puts her in something nice cuz this is just awful lookin'."

"I'm sure Stan will have her lookin' real nice for the funeral with her hair done and all."

"Samantha Jo, did you look at her neck closely?"

"It's hard not to. Would y'all just look at all those stitches?"

"Yeah, but I'm looking more specifically at the cut itself. I mean, think about it for a second—why would a burglar go through the trouble of such precision from ear to ear? Why not just the main area of the throat?" Madison used her index finger as if she were slitting her own neck to show Samantha Jo what she'd meant.

"What's the difference? She's dead, ain't she? We're sittin' here tryin' to understand why someone would even kill her and y'all are worried about how they did it?"

"It was just a question. It just doesn't make sense to me why the trouble of it all. Certainly there are other ways of killing someone."

"Madison, I've been thinkin', and I don't think we should go pokin' around here none. Let's just get through the funeral and attend the meetin' on Monday with Mr. Jackson and go home! I just feel like we're askin' for trouble here, and I don't want no part of it, ya hear? I gotta family to worry about."

"You're not the only with family to worry about, Samantha Jo!"

"True, but I live in the south, y'all don't. Lane and Leroy come around when they feel like it to visit Gram, and I just don't need to be lookin' over my shoulder every day because you're diggin up things that ain't of no concern to us."

"No concern? So what you're sayin' is the truth is of no concern to you? And, by the way, you should be lookin' over your shoulder everyday anyway; those two are crazy!"

"Of course the truth is, but at what price, Madison? Y'all gonna risk your life and possibly others? It ain't gonna bring her back, honey! And it certainly ain't gonna change the crazy and dysfunction of this family none."

"Look, Samantha Jo, I've spent my entire life lookin' over my shoulder and afraid to trust. I don't like what's going on here and all I'm saying is that it wouldn't hurt to understand what's really happened. In fact, I'd like to go and see Hazel's house and the crime scene."

"Oh, Madison, y'all have lost it! What on earth would you want to see that for? What good can possibly come from that?"

"I want answers and I want the truth! You can either join me or step aside, Samantha Jo, but don't stand in my way. I respect you're scared and want to stay out of harm's way, but this needs to be done. I've made up mind, and there's no changin' it!"

"Well, I've said my piece and how I feel about it, and I've made up my mind, too. I'm headin' back home the first flight out Monday evening to go back to Mississippi. There ain't nothin' to keep me here after the funeral and readin' of the will."

"Look, Samantha Jo, I'm sorry; the last thing I want right now is to fight with you. Nor do I want to put you in harm's way any more than you already feel. I am going to look into this further, and I will do it on my own time without involving you. I really would like for us to have some time together and . . ." Madison paused for a moment as a wonderful thought came to her.

"What y'all thinkin' about?"

Madison looked over at Samantha Jo with a mischievous smile and said, "What do ya say we leave town early Saturday morning after the funeral and drive to the beach for a few days? We can get back in time for the meeting on Monday. It'll do us good to get out of this town and away from all this mess. Come on, what do ya say?"

"I think that's a great idea. If you promise we'll be back Monday for the meeting then I'm in! Now, can we leave this place? I'm beginnin' to get creeped out in this room with the dead, frozen bodies." Madison smiled, leaned down to kiss the side of Hazel's cheek, and whispered, "I'll find it."

The two walked out into the hallway and found Stan waiting there patiently for them. He led them back to the entrance where Judy was waiting for them at the front desk. She spoke again with her soft voice and said, "The service is scheduled for 10 a.m. on Friday morning at Bethesda Baptist Church: it's just at the end of town off Main Street. From there, the funeral procession will head out to the Blackberry Creek cemetery for the burial. I heard Miss Tessa talkin' of havin' a luncheon afterwards."

"Thank you, m'am," Madison said. "We appreciate all your help and letting us see our grandmother."

"Think nothin' of it, honey. Now, here is our card; if you have any questions or concerns you just call us. Remember we are here to help y'all through this tough time." She gave each of them her card as they left and patted them on their shoulders.

Walking towards the car, Samantha Jo turned to Madison to comment on how sweet Stan and Judy were when she noticed Madison kneeling down to the ground. She acted is if she was tying her shoes, which would have been plausible if she weren't wearing sandals that day. "Madison, what y'all doin'?"

"Don't look to your left, Samantha Jo, just keep lookin' ahead."

"What's wrong?"

"I think the green car from last night is a block down the street."

"Are you sure? It's not like we got a good look at it. There could be a hundred cars that look similar to one last night."

"Maybe. But just hold up a second." Madison stood up, walked over to Samantha Jo and said, "Just keep walking." They reached the end of the sidewalk, and Madison turned around again to see the car but it was gone.

They decided to walk through town and find a café where they could have an early lunch. It was a beautiful day out, and the town looked so lovely and charming. Madison enjoyed the clean air. She was used to big city busses roaring by, leaving the smell of exhaust in their trail. Downtown Blackberry Creek was adorable with its tree-lined boulevards and old buildings. A few of the store fronts had flower boxes with bright and vibrant colors growing out of them.

They approached the town square park and admired the creek running through it. They walked over the bridge towards the town band shell. This was where the city hosted its main outdoor events. Surrounding the entire park were tall oak trees and Weeping Willows. They walked through the park talking, laughing, and comparing stories about how fast Mason and Shelby Lynn were growing up. Both were divorced and commented on how hard it was at times being a single mother.

Walking back through town, they found a small café. As Samantha Jo opened the door to go in, Madison looked down both sides of the street to see if the green car had returned. There was no sign of it. During lunch the two discussed their short trip to the ocean and decided when they got back to the hotel they'd call and make arrangements. Madison pulled out her blackberry cell and found a resort called Ocean Isle

Beach Hotel. It was less than a four hour drive away and was situated right on the ocean. The accommodations also mentioned that there were spa services available. It would be perfect.

Madison finished her tuna sandwich and said, "If you don't mind, I'd like to go back over to Travis Jackson's office when we're done here to talk to him further."

Samantha Jo looked up and said, "Y'all gonna ask him out?"

"Don't be silly."

"Why not? You saw how handsome that man was."

"Yes, I did see that. No, I want to talk to him more about Hazel and see if he has been contacted by any other family members."

"Like who?"

"Our fathers, for starters."

"Now why on God's green earth would you go askin' him that?"

"You said it yourself, Samantha Jo, there were two wills, and, if you're right, Lane and Leroy stand to gain out of this mess. Surely one of them has been in touch with Mr. Jackson?"

"He already said he couldn't discuss none of the details with us all."

"I'm not lookin' for any details, I'm just curious if either have contacted him. Besides, what was that whole mess about back at the funeral home with Tessa?"

"You're right; he didn't say much 'bout that did he? Well, I suppose it's none of our business or he would have."

"Would have or couldn't have?"

"What do y'all mean?"

"Well Tessa was in the next room, how could he have said anything to us?"

"Madison, I'm gonna say it again, don't go kickin' dust up around us. Let it all go!"

"I promise I'll be quick; I just want to talk a bit further with him and see if he can tell us anything more."

"All right then, y'all, I'm gonna visit some of those cute boutique shops we all passed earlier. Don't be long and call me on my cell when y'all are done with Mr. Handsome."

"I will." They paid their bill and left the café. Samantha Jo found a shop just a few doors down and ducked in, waving goodbye to Madison.

On her way to Mr. Jackson's office, Madison continued admiring the quaintness of the town, and wondered, "How could such a beautiful town be filled with such anger and violence?" She came to a light, and turned left to wait to cross the street. She looked behind her, and there, again, was the green car. She thought to herself, "Maybe Samantha Jo was right. There could be a hundred green cars like that. But then, why was this one always in sight when I turn around?" She admitted to herself that it was no coincidence and that the two were being followed.

It was a good idea for Samantha Jo and her to leave town for a few days. Even though they'd just got there the night before, things were already strangely disconcerting. The light turned and she crossed the street. When she reached the other side, she looked back again and saw the car still parked on the street. She couldn't be sure, but the engine didn't appear to be running.

She found her way to the address on Mr. Jackson's card and saw that the front of his office was just as he described. There were two six-foot stone archways in the front and a plaque that read: T. Jackson Esq. A wrought iron gate sat between the archways and continued out beyond the stone, wrapping around to the sides of the building.

She opened the gate and noticed the landscaping surrounding the sidewalk that led to the front door. It was a small space, but someone had taken the time decorate it and had done a beautiful job. Inside the space, she noticed a small, white, iron loveseat bench beside a matching table. Surrounding it were lovely bushes and flowers leaving a sweet fragrance in the air. A trail made of large flagstones led the way to the bench and table.

To the right was a large cement fountain with a cherub in the center.

Both hands were situated on each thigh while his penis streamed water into the basin. She laughed and thought, "Typical but tasteful."

Opening the door, Madison found a woman sitting at a desk. "Good afternoon, m'am. How can I help y'all?"

"Hello, I'm Madison Slone. I was looking for Mr. Travis Jackson? We met briefly this morning at the funeral home."

"Well, he's on the phone right now but if you have a seat over there in the chairs, I'll let him know y'all are waitin'."

Madison sat down and looked about the room. It was filled with rich colors from the Persian rugs on the floor to the hunting-themed artwork on the walls. The furniture was dark-brown leather with ornate gold tacking. Madison looked up when she heard, "Can I get y'all something while you're waitin' for Mr. Jackson?"

"Thank you, m'am. I'm fine."

Madison began to feel the cold air from the air conditioning hit her skin, sending chills throughout her body. The heat and humidity was so intense that she'd broken a sweat on her way over. Her clothes felt ice cold next to her body, sending goose bumps down her arms and legs. She looked down at her chest and noticed her nipples had hardened and were pointing outwards through her shirt. Embarrassed, she quickly folded her arms around her chest remembering she'd worn her unpadded bra due to the heat. "Real nice, Madison," she thought to herself. "Way to make that first impression."

Suddenly the woman picked up her phone and said, "There is a Madison Slone waitin' in front to see y'all." She hung up the phone and looked at Madison. "He said it'll just be a moment."

"Thank you." Madison sat patiently, looking about the room until the double doors to her right opened and out walked Mr. Jackson.

He walked up to Madison and shook her hand. "Pleasure to see you again, Miss Slone. Won't y'all please come in and have a seat? Can I get y'all some coffee or water?"

"Thank you but I can't stay too long, and I know you're real busy."

"All right then, come on in. Doris, please hold my calls for me."

Madison walked into his office. It took up the entire corner of the building. To her right were huge paned windows that looked out at the front of the street. His desk sat straight ahead and had two leather chairs in front of it for guests. They, too, were brown leather with gold tacking. There was a large painting hanging on the wall behind his chair—it depicted a hunting scene with coon hounds, horses, and men holding rifles.

The far wall to the left was his library. It went from floor to ceiling and was filled with law and reference books. Madison liked his office and wondered what Travis's story was. Was he gay, too? He didn't wear a ring, and, from her quick assessment of his office, she couldn't see any pictures alluding to a family or wife. He also had great taste in clothing and décor. He was like the male version of Martha Stewart.

She sat down in one of the chairs in front of his desk. "You have a very nice office, Mr. Jackson," she said while looking about the room. "Thank you for seeing me so out of the blue like this. I promise I won't take much of your time."

"Actually, Miss Slone . . ."

"I'm sorry to interrupt, but you can just call me Madison."

"All right, Madison. I half-expected you to stop by after our meeting this morning."

"You did? Why?"

"Well, I know that you and Samantha Jo had heard the ruckus in the waitin' room while I was talkin' with Tessa and figured y'all would have more questions after you spoke with her."

"Well, she certainly was no peach to talk to, I'll say that much, Mr. Jackson. I mean, Travis. She didn't have one nice thing to say to either Samantha Jo or myself and made it very clear that we should keep out of her way."

He chuckled, "Well now, yes, Tessa can be a bit curt in her words."

"That's putting it mildly!"

"Well don't mind her none, she is just uptight about making sure things go according to her plan for your grandmother's funeral on Friday."

"Well, why would she think we'd want to make trouble for her? We were hoping we could help her any way we can. She's not the only one grieving; we lost someone we love very much, too."

"Madison, let's not pretend that your family, the Walkers, are the most loving and forgiving. She's afraid that with the two of you in town, Lane and Leroy won't be far behind."

"That's ridiculous! Samantha Jo and I want nothing to do with those two assholes who claim to be our fathers." She felt her body temperature rising as well as her frustration level at the very mention of Leroy. "Forgive me, Travis, for my angry outburst; it's just that hearing their names makes my blood boil."

"I'm sorry for touchin' on such a sore subject, Madison, but it does raise questions to some folks in this town."

"You've got questions? I have questions to the day is long!"

"Well then, let's see if we can find some answers for y'all and see about workin' through this mess together. I don't have any other appointments today and would be happy to assist in any way I can."

Madison quickly glanced down at her chest before unfolding her arms and sitting back in her chair to relax. She had been sitting straight as a board since she sat down in his office. She thought to herself, "He's just as charming when he talks too." She found it hard to stay focused on the business she'd come to discuss with him that afternoon.

"Why don't you start first," he said and leaned back in his chair. He had a pen and pad in front of him and was ready to take notes.

"I'm not sure where to even begin with this all. These last few days all seem to blend together into some sort of bad nightmare."

"Oh, how so?"

"The Walkers, as you say, are a messed up bunch, and I suppose that is no secret to many folks here in town. But since Samantha Jo called me on Sunday to tell me of Hazel's death, I just have this unsettled feeling that this was no accident."

"I'm afraid y'all are right. It was no accident. Hazel returned home early from the riding stables that day and caught the intruder off guard."

"See that's just it, I don't really believe that. I'm finding it hard to accept it as the truth."

"What do you think is the truth then?"

Ah, there was that word again—truth. Madison knew she was treading on thin ice looking for the truth when it came to the Walkers, and, at this time, she couldn't decide how much she could trust Mr. Jackson.

"Listen, all I know is that I got a call saying that my grandmother had been killed with her throat slit. The next thing I knew, a car followed Samantha Jo and me home last night from the Sawdust Bar and Restaurant, and today the wicked witch of the west is telling me to stay out of her way because I'm not a blood relative. Now, you tell me why I shouldn't suspect something else here is going on?"

Travis arched a brow, leaned forward to write on his notepad, and asked, "What did the car look like that followed you?"

"I don't know—old and green. I could have sworn I saw it again this morning when Samantha Jo and I left the funeral home."

"And y'all are sure that a car followed ya last night?"

"Look, I know this sounds paranoid and crazy, but we two are a bit on edge being down here for the funeral. The last time I was here was for my granddaddy's funeral, and I met Leroy and Lane for the first time. They both work like the devil and scare the livin' shit out of me. I'm positive we were followed back to our hotel!" Madison explained in detail as best as she could about the drive home the night before.

"Travis, I have so many questions and no answers, and all I'm looking for is to know what really happened when Hazel came home. Have you seen the police report? Was anything taken? Do they have any leads on who the murderer could have been?"

"I have not seen the police report, didn't think there was a need to look at it. But if what you're sayin is true about someone followin' y'all, then I can see why you'd have the suspicions y'all do."

Madison was beginning to feel as though finally someone believed her and was on her side. Though she found comfort in Travis's company, she still didn't know him or trust him enough to tell him about the secret Hazel had shared with her five years back. Granted, he was an attorney and there had to be something about client /attorney privilege to make him keep what she said in confidence, but he was not her attorney therefore it really was none of his business.

"Tell y'all what, let me give Bud a call and see about getting you a copy of the police report to look at."

"I'm sorry, but who is Bud, did you say?"

"Ole Bud? He's the sheriff in town and a family friend. His name is Francis Sheldon but everyone just calls him Bud. I don't reckon I've ever heard anyone call him Francis."

"Travis, I appreciate your help with that, but I'm more interested in visiting Hazel's house to see where this happened. I need to see it for myself."

"Well that will be up to Bud, but I suspect he's done with the crime scene itself and I don't see why it would hurt none to let you in and take a look around. After all, ya are family."

He gave Madison a wink, picked up the phone, and spoke: "Doris, can y'all get me Bud Sheldon on the line? Send the call in when ya track him down. Thank you."

He put the phone down. "This may be hard for y'all to go and see. As ya know, it was a violent murder leaving the room a bloody mess where they found her . . ."

"Did you see her after she was killed? Her body, I mean."

"No, I can't say I did. I called Tessa after Bud had called me, and she went to identify the body. Why do you ask?"

"Well it's just that her throat was slit from ear to ear—I just find that a strange death for just a burglary that's gone bad. To me, it seems like more of an effort than to just make a quick slit. It appears more personal, if you know what I mean?"

"I think I do. Tell y'all what, let's wait to hear back from Bud and if it's all right with you Madison, I'd like to go along with you to Hazel's home."

Madison couldn't see any harm in that and felt comfort in having someone go with her. She hadn't yet figured out how or where to look for the information Hazel had left behind for her with regards to her grandfather's third son. She needed time to assess the situation first then come up with a plan. All she remembered was Hazel saying, she'd know where to look and that it'd be right under her nose. Then it struck her: maybe Mr. Jackson was of more use than she'd originally thought. After all, he was Hazel's attorney, and surely she would have confided in him with instructions upon her death.

Madison looked at Travis and said, "You mentioned that Tessa was nervous about Lane and Leroy coming to town; have you contacted them or heard from either of them?"

"Well, as a matter of fact, I met with Lane this morning after I left y'all at the funeral home."

"You what? When were you planning to tell me that? If he's in town, he's probably the crazy fucker that's been following us!"

"Look, Madison, Hazel left pretty strict instructions as to her last wishes in her will . . ."

She cut him off mid-sentence: "You met with Lane Walker this morning? Is that what I just heard you say?"

"Yes, but as I was saying, I told him the same thing I've told you and everyone else, I can't discuss any of the details with you until Monday. Which is exactly what I told Lane Walker this morning! I'm not trying to deceive y'all or hide anything from ya. Look, my meetin' with Lane this morning was of his wishes and accord, certainly not mine. Now with that said, y'all should know he will be here on Monday for the meeting."

Madison cocked her head to one side with both eyebrows raised.

She sat with her mouth open, speechless. She thought to herself, "Did I just hear this man correctly? He invited Lane to the meeting on Monday?"

Why not just lay out the red carpet for the blood-sucking parasite. Travis had gone and quite possibly invited Hazel's murderer to the meeting. She needed to let Samantha Jo know that her daddy was in town and planning to come on Monday. Samantha Jo was not going to be happy when she heard this news. She was already upset and hearing this would only make things worse. It pained Madison to know that she would have to be the one tell her.

Madison diverted her attention back to Travis and noticed he was still talking. "That was the news I had shared with Tessa earlier today, letting her know that she should be expecting company. At the time I wasn't yet sure but I figured since he called and wanted to meet that she should know that he was in town. "

"That would explain her hostility towards Samantha Jo and me this morning. Not that she isn't usually mean but she seemed pretty uptight, more so than usual. I'm sure Tessa assumed that because Samantha Jo and I are here that our fathers wouldn't be far behind—just like at our granddaddy's funeral. And in a way, she was right."

"I reckon that was it. She really is a nice woman; she's just gotten a bit set in her ways as she's aged."

"I don't know that we're talkin' about the same woman then. She was just as mean and full of spite when I was younger. She's never cared much for me."

"Right, maybe what I meant to say is that she has always been a woman of stature and properness."

"Keep diggin'!"

Just then the phone rang. Travis picked it up and said, "Good afternoon Bud . . . Yeah, it sure does look to be another hot and sticky one . . . I sure did hear about it, and I'll see y'all on Saturday to take your money again in a friendly game of poker." He laughed and gave Madison a wink.

She thought to herself, "What is his deal—he's attractive with his distinguished looks and yet there appears to be no one in his life. Why isn't he married?"

"Say, Bud, the reason I needed to speak with y'all is I've got Madison Slone with me in my office . . . Madison, one of Hazel Walker's granddaughters . . . Yes, Jethro . . . Hold on, sir. He wants to know if y'all the Yankee from the Midwest?" Madison smiled and nodded her head. "Yes, sir, that is the one . . . Well, sir, we'd like to take a drive out to Hazel's and have a look around. Miss Madison here would like to see if anything's been taken and missin' because of the burglary. I understand and have already let her know that, sir. All right then, we'll meet y'all there in an hour."

He hit the receiver on the phone and called Doris. "Doris, I'm gonna be leavin' here shortly to take Miss Slone out to the Walker residence. I'll check in with you later. Call me on my cell if you need me."

"I really appreciate all your help, Travis. Thank you."

"Think nothin' of it. Hazel would have wanted it."

"May I ask you a question?"

"Go right ahead."

"How well did y'all know my grandmother?"

"Well now, let me see. It was shortly after Jethro had been admitted into the Alzheimer's home when she came into the office lookin' for help with the estate and will that he'd previously drawn up . . . She didn't have much by way of knowledge on what to do and needed help. She claimed she didn't care much for your granddaddy's lawyer and she asked me if I would help her."

"I see."

"Is everything okay, Madison?"

"Yeah, it's just that for the last couple years Hazel has not spoken to either Samantha Jo or me. She wouldn't even so much as send a letter or pick up the phone. It didn't make sense. She was the only grandmother I knew and then, all of a sudden, one day she stops loving us and taking our calls. And now you say she would've wanted you to help me. It doesn't make sense."

"Well, I can't speak as to her reasonin' for that an' all, but I do know that she was very uneasy and nervous about Jethro's boys. It sounds to me as if you know the uneasy feelin' I'm referrin' to."

"I do. All too well, I'm afraid."

As they were walking toward the double doors to leave his office, Madison noticed he had put his hand on the small of her back as if he was guiding her to the door. She felt the blood race to her face. "My God," she thought, "I am blushing like a damn school girl." She figured that Mr. Jackson was very much a southern gentlemen and wondered again, why was he single?

As they walked out the front door to the sidewalk, Madison remembered Samantha Jo. Oh shit! "Travis, I have to make a quick call. I left Samantha Jo in town shopping while I came to visit you. I must of lost track of time during our conversation. Let me give her a quick call and let her know I'll catch up with her later."

"Fine, I'll go and pull the car around front to pick y'all up. Let her know I'll have you back to the hotel before dinner."

"Right, a ride would be great since she and I rode together. If you're sure it's no trouble—I feel as though I have taken up too much of your time and hospitality as it is."

"It's no trouble at all. In fact, it's my pleasure." He opened the gate and disappeared around the corner of the building.

Smiling, Madison repeated to herself, "It's my pleasure." She gave a little giggle then frantically dug out her cell phone to call Samantha Jo. It rang five times before she answered, "Y'all done with Mr. Charming already?"

"Don't be foolish, Samantha Jo. What took you so long to answer your phone?"

"Honey, I found the most adorable summer dress that I was tryin' on. I think I'm gonna have to get this one, it's just too darn cute and on sale. Why y'all callin' me anyway, you ready to head back to the hotel?"

"Well, no, not exactly."

"Well then, what?"

"Samantha Jo, would you be okay headin' back by yourself to the hotel?"

"What are you doin', Madison? Are y'all runnin' off with Travis? Did he ask you out?"

"No, it's nothing like that, he's taking me to . . ."

Silence fell upon them. "What?"

"We're driving out to Hazel's house."

"Why would you want to go an' do that?"

"Because, Samantha Jo, I want to see for myself where she was murdered and see if anything was taken from the house. Now I know y'all want nothing to do with this so I won't ask you to join us."

"You can say that again! Y'all are crazy."

"Anyway, Travis is driving me out there to meet with the sheriff so that I can see the house."

"Y'all went and got the town sheriff involved, too? Jesus, Madison, the whole damn town is gonna be talkin' about us."

"Look, I just need to know if you're all right drivin' back by yourself to hotel. I'll be back before dinner."

"I suppose, but don't be too long. I don't feel right bein' alone when it's dark here."

"I promise I will be back before dinner! Hey, why don't you give a call to that Beach Resort and make our reservations for us?"

"I suppose I could. But y'all promise to be back by dinner, right?"

"Promise, cuz!"

"Madison?"

"Yeah?"

"Y'all be careful, ya hear?"

"I'm more worried about you bein' alone. I'll be with Travis."

"Don't be, this just gives me a bit more time to shop. I'll see you later."

Just as she said goodbye, Travis pulled up in an old, light-blue late-seventies model Mercedes Benz convertible with a soft, white top.

He leaned over and pushed open the door for Madison. Always the gentlemen, she thought.

Chapter 8

They drove through town and made small talk on the drive out to Hazel's. Madison commented on the beauty that surrounded all of Blackberry Creek, and Travis explained all the changes that had occurred over the years. They pulled into Hazel's driveway. It was about 250 feet in length from the street to the garage door. Madison felt tears welling up in her eyes at the sight of the house. Regardless of how strained their relationship was the last few years, she loved Hazel dearly and missed her. She smiled thinking back to her last memory of sitting at the table with Hazel talkin' and laughin' with a Jack and Coke in hand.

There were trees that lined the front of the property and made it difficult to see the front of the house from the street. To the right of the driveway was a wooded area. The only neighbor was across the street, and according to Travis, they had left town for four weeks to visit family out of state. They were an elderly couple that Hazel would often visit, bringing along gifts of fresh vegetables, apple pies, and jam.

As they pulled into the driveway, Travis said, "We musta beat Bud out here. Y'all wanna get out and walk around?"

"Sure, that would be fine." Travis came around to meet Madison as she stepped out of the car. They walked up the steps to the right of the garage that wound upwards and around to the back of the house. Hazel never did use the front door. Anyone who knew her, knew to walk up and around to the back door.

Her flowers looked to be struggling some since no one was taking care of them. Half of them were drooping to the ground, dying of thirst. It was a shame; Hazel had some beautiful roses that she'd planted and nurtured since she'd moved into the house. She had started doing things like that for herself after Jethro went into the Alzheimer's hospital.

As they came up around the back, Madison sighed in disappointment. Hazel had a large garden in the backyard where she grew all her vegetables, and they, too, were looking pretty beat up from the hot sun without any water.

"Y'all right, Madison?" Travis said as he came up next to her.

"It's just a shame," she said, pointing to the garden. "All that hard work and nurturing just gone wayside with no one to care for them."

"I agree. I sure am going to miss Hazel's visits and her homemade chicken."

"She made you her chicken?"

"She sure did, and I have to say, it was the best southern fried chicken I'd ever tasted in my life. And I live in the south!"

"Yeah, she sure could cook and bake. Did you know her apple pies won a blue ribbon in the county fair?"

Travis shook his head and said, "I didn't, but that doesn't surprise me none. I am gonna miss your grandmother."

Madison walked through the garden and admired all that Hazel had planted that spring. She, too, loved gardening and though, between her job and raising Mason, she'd found fewer and fewer hours to do so, she always appreciated the love and care one gave to their gardens.

She noticed a sun catcher at the far end of the garden. It was unusual and unique and unlike anything Madison had seen at any garden store. She leaned in for a closer look. The base was just like any other ordinary wrought iron base that went into the ground. What caught Madison's eye was the catcher itself. It was round and made of glass and looked to have an arrowhead pressed between two pieces of glass. The arrowhead was just like the one she'd found when she was visiting as a teenager. It was reddish brown and had similar markings and shape.

She called over to Travis, "Do y'all sell these in town? I've never seen anything like it before."

"I can't say that I have either. It's possible that she got that on one of her trips to Tennessee when she was looking to buy another horse."

The horses! Madison looked up at Travis and said in an alarmed voice. "Oh my God! Has anyone been to take care of the horses?"

"Calm down, Madison, I've already called the stables and they are taking care of things right now until we sort this whole mess out."

"Right. Of course you did. Thank you."

Travis nodded his head, accepting her thanks and appreciation.

Just then they heard a throat clearing, and they both turned to find Sheriff Sheldon walking around the corner.

"Hello, Bud. Good to see y'all," Travis said as he walked over to shake Bud's hand.

Madison walked up next to Travis and said, "Hello, I'm Madison Slone."

"Pleasure's all mine, Ms. Slone."

"Please, you can just call me Madison."

"Travis here tells me y'all want to go in and take a look around?"

"That's right, sir, and I really do appreciate you taking the time to meet us out here for me do so."

"Well now, like I told Travis, ain't nothin' been done inside the house since we took the body outta here a week ago. I don't reckon the air conditioning has been turned on since so brace yourselves, it's gonna be hot and not-so-pleasant smellin' in there."

Bud was usually straight to the point without much finesse in his delivery. He was a very matter-of-fact man with no fluff.

"Sheriff, before we go in, can you tell me was there anything that you found to be missing?"

"Well, no, I can't say we did."

"But when there's a burglary, it's usually been my experience that valuables and belongings are stolen?"

"Right, but we didn't see nothing of value was missing. Her TV,

VCR, and stereo are right where she kept them. I suppose if it was something of a personal nature then we wouldn't really know, would we?"

"No, I suppose not."

"Well then let's go on in so y'all can look around. I gotta be back at the station by 4 p.m. to meet Clyde from the filling station to go catfishin' this evening." He gave a wink to both Madison and Travis and walked up the four wooden stairs to the door.

Travis gave Madison a smile and let her walk in behind the Sheriff who unlocked the door. She remembered where Hazel kept the spare key and wondered if it was still there and who else knew where she kept it. They stepped into the kitchen and gasped for air.

The house was an oven, sitting and baking in the sun. There was a strong, week-old stench coming from the garbage can. Flies had taken residency in the home and covered the kitchen window. They were flying in and out of the garbage can and around the house. Madison put her hand up to her nose and mouth, trying to hold back the urge to vomit. The smell was unbearable, but she was determined to stay and look through the house.

Bud looked back over his shoulder to see if Madison was still with them or if she'd run out of the house already.

Madison glanced at the counter where Hazel kept the phone and her address book. She noticed that it was opened to the W's. Looking down, she saw the name Lane Walker and a number. She picked up the book and said, "Do you mind if I have this? I really don't see how it can be of any further use to your investigation, and I'd like to make sure that all of Hazel's friends and family know of her death."

"I don't think that should be a problem, but what investigation are you referring to?"

"The investigation of her murder? You are still investigating it, right?"

"Look, m'am, we did a surveillance of the home and found nothin' missin'. We checked to see if there was any evidence that would lead us in the direction of finding out who did this without much luck."

"So you have nothing to go on, is what you're telling me?"

"I wish we could say otherwise but at this time that's correct."

"Sheriff, was the door to the house unlocked or locked when you got to the scene and found her dead?"

"I believe it was locked when we all got here."

"Was there any sign whatsoever of a forced entry? Broken windows? Anything?"

"No, we didn't see nothin' like that."

"Well, did you take any fingerprints or something?"

"Your grandma's house is full of prints from visitors she's had over the years. Now, that'd make it difficult for us to tell if it was a friend or family wouldn't it?"

"True, but if the windows weren't broken or opened and the door was locked, wouldn't that make her attacker someone she knew?"

"I suppose it could, but, like I said, we didn't find much evidence to lead us to anyone in particular." Madison raised both her eyebrows in astonishment at the sheriff's reply. He knew damn well who Lane and Leroy were and the trouble that usually followed them.

Right then Travis came up from behind her, again touching the small of her back, and broke up the conversation by saying, "Bud it sure is hot and stinks something awful in here, why don't y'all take Madison to the bedroom where Hazel's body was found so we can wrap this up."

"Right this way, Madison."

They walked down the hallway to the master bedroom. Bud stood to the side of the door with his arm extended out towards the room. Madison walked past him and stood just a few feet into the room.

Her eyes began to well up immediately. It was the most God-awful and gruesome scene she'd ever witnessed. There was blood spattered across the far wall, reminding her of one of those paintings where the artist took a brush soaked with paint and shook it at the canvas for a splash effect. Only this was no painting. It was Hazel's blood that had run down the wall and soaked into the paint.

The floor next to the bed had also been soaked with blood that had now dried up. She looked to the bed where the comforter and pillow lay completely saturated with blood. Madison quickly acknowledged that most of the bleeding appeared to have happened on the bed. There was so much blood. Did the killer slash her throat and then lay her back onto the bed? Looking at it all, it didn't make much sense.

She turned around to leave the room, and stopped short of the door. She looked at Bud and asked, "When you found her, was she lying on the bed or the floor?"

"When we got here she was layin' on the bed."

"Didn't that strike you as odd, Sheriff?"

"Not really. We figured after the burglar cut her throat he laid her down so that she'd be out of the way."

"Out of the way for what? She was dead!"

"M'am, I've got the coroner's and police report back at the station if y'all would like to see it?"

"As a matter of fact, I would. Thank you for offering." Madison walked past him and back to the kitchen where Travis stood patiently waiting. Still the gentleman, he held out his arms as if to hug her, thinking that she needed consolation, but she held up her hand as if it was a stop sign signaling for him to leave her along.

Standing in the living room, she saw that everything was in its proper place just as the sheriff had said. The TV and VCR sat on the TV stand and the stereo was still on its shelf next to them. She turned in a slow circle, taking in the room and its contents surrounding her. She turned back towards the TV where Hazel had a small chest that held pictures of her, Mason, Samantha Jo, Shelby Lynn, and a few photos of her grandfather from when he was a pilot. Below, she kept a few pieces of china and silverware.

She paused for a moment and stared at the wall behind the chest. Hazel had mounted an enclosed case containing the American flag given to her at Jethro's ceremony along with the Medal of Honor he'd received. They were both gone. She walked closer and noticed the dust clinging to the wall as if it once sat on something, creating a slight outline of what once was there. They had obviously missed that when they inspected the house.

But how would they know anything was missing? According to Bud, nothing of value was missing as far as they could tell. But they had missed this and it was of value. It was a significant memory of her grandfather and a family keepsake. Madison suddenly realized she was in more danger than she'd known.

Those fucking monsters had been here and one of them or maybe even both of them had killed Hazel. Madison wondered how long it would be before they decided to come after her. She figured it was no use telling Sheriff Sheldon about the flag or the medal. He'd obviously made up his mind about what happened here, and, besides, he needed to get back to town to go catfishing!

She turned around and said, "I've seen all that I need to gentlemen," and walked out the back. She stood near the garden, getting a breath of fresh air, and waited for the gentlemen to close up the house and come outside. Standing with her back to the house, she stared out at the garden with tears falling down her face.

She heard footsteps behind her and recognized the cologne; Travis walked up next to hear and asked, "Do y'all wanna talk about it?"

Wiping her tears, she turned around to face him and replied, "Talk about what?"

"What you found inside that you're not tellin' me about?"

"I'm not sure what you're referring to, Travis. The only thing I found in there is the address book that Bud let me have."

"Right. Well, when you're ready to talk I'm here if you need me."

"I just need to be alone for a minute, Travis, if that's all right?"

"I'll wait down by the car for you, Madison; please take your time. I'm in no hurry."

"Thank you."

She heard their footsteps and voices fade away as they walked down the stairs and around the house. She paced back and forth in front of the garden. Her mind was racing and she did need someone to talk to before she exploded. She wanted to run back to the hotel and share what she'd found with Samantha Jo, but that was not option. Samantha Jo had made it clear that she didn't want anything more to do with Madison's little investigation that could end up getting them both killed.

She dug back through her purse, found her pack of cigarettes, and pulled one out. She lit the cigarette and took in a deep, long drag, letting the smoke burn in her lungs until she exhaled. Maybe she could trust Travis; he seemed to be genuine and honest and he certainly was picking up on Madison's intuitions. She was still undecided about Travis's intentions and, besides, why would he want to get himself pulled into this mess? He was Hazel's attorney not her bodyguard.

Still, she needed someone to talk to, someone who wasn't back in Minnesota, who would understood what she was dealing with down here. She dropped her cigarette to the ground, stepped on it to make sure it was out, and dug back into her purse for the address book. Travis had said he'd called the stables where the horses were but Madison wanted to make double sure things had been taking care of.

She paged through until she found Sunnyside Stables and took out her cell to call. A woman answered on the other end, "Good afternoon, Sunnyside Stables."

"Hello, m'am, my name is Madison Slone. I'm a relative of Hazel Walker's."

"Yes dear, we are all just so sick about what's happened to y'all. How can I help ya?"

"Well, I'm calling because I wanted to make sure that everything has been taken care of with regards to the horses."

"Why, yes, they have. Mr. Travis Jackson called to tell us of the sad news and make arrangements for the horses. Everything is fine here, dear."

"Well, all right then, I just wanted to call and make sure."

"Listen darlin', if ya got some time to come out here to the stables there is some of her personal things that she kept here, if y'all wanna come by and get 'em."

Madison paused for a moment then replied, "Yes. I could do that. Would tomorrow be fine?"

"Sure is. No need to call ahead, we're always here."

"Thank you so much, Ms. . .?"

"The name's Loretta. Y'all just ask for me when ya get here. We'll see ya then. Bye now."

Madison hung up the phone and thought for a moment. Certainly there was no harm in going out to the stables. Besides, she wanted to see the horses Hazel boarded.

She wondered if Travis had plans for the horses and if Hazel had even put them in the will? Surely she must have. They were all she had left, and she tended to them practically daily. Maybe Samantha Jo would be fine goin' out there with her. She'd ask her tonight.

She put her cell away in her purse and turned around to head towards the cement stairs when she heard the sound of a twig breaking behind her. She froze dead in her tracks and slowly turned her head back towards the wooded area that lay behind the garden.

Madison stared out into the woods but it was impossible to see anything. There were so many ferns and so much brush covering the floor like a natural carpet that she couldn't see much. Shc thought she saw something move out of the corner of her eye and she squinted to get a closer look, but all she saw was a fern with a little movement. She figured it could've been many things: a squirrel, snake, or even a small fox. Whatever it was, she was not alone.

She felt eyes staring upon her but couldn't see anything past three feet into the woods. At that moment she reminded herself that standing there alone was not the time to start imagining things like Monsters in the woods. "Madison, you've got to get a grip," she told herself and turned back around to meet Travis waiting in the car.

When she returned to the car, Travis was on his phone. "All right,

Doris . . . Yes, thank you. Y'all have a good evening as well . . . Ah huh, see ya in the morning. Bye."

Madison got in the car and asked if everything was all right. "Yes. Doris is like a mother sometimes. She wanted to check in and make sure we were fine and to see if Bud had made it. Evidently he'd called her to say he'd be runnin' a few minutes late, but we'd already left."

"Well, it sounds like you're lucky to have her. She seems like a very nice lady."

"I am lucky. She's really all I've got left." Madison nodded her head as if she understood what he was saying.

"We should be gettin' y'all back to your cousin. And, Madison, I meant what I said: I'm here if ya need to talk to someone. I promise that anythin' y'all say will be kept confidential." He gave her a sincere smile and pulled the car out of the driveway.

He stood silently behind the large, moss-covered tree another five minutes to make sure no one was coming back up. His cold eyes locked on the house with his shotgun resting at his side. He thought to himself for a moment, "That fucking bitch! She's gonna go pokin' round and causin' trouble."

He'd purposely followed her the night before to scare her and Samantha Jo some so they'd stay outta his way. He knew Samantha Jo was not the type to go causin' trouble. She knew better. But Madison was always the type to go askin' questions and gettin' herself into business that didn't concern her none. He was gonna have to keep a better eye on her.

He knew that what he was lookin' for had to be somewhere in the house and maybe now that Madison had been there she'd have no need for returnin'. The sheriff had no more reason for returnin', either, so he'd have the house to himself without interruptions. He'd expected that Madison would want to come out to the house and figured she was playing right into his plan. She was nothin' but plain trouble as far as he was concerned and trouble had to be dealt with. She needed to be dealt with.

He crept away slowly from behind the tree and started back to his car. He'd parked off the road into the woods past the street so that no one would see. He'd followed them outta town and waited until they were in the house before he crept in closer to the forest where he stood and watched. He'd find her later. After all, he knew where she and Samantha Jo were staying.

Samantha Jo had returned to the hotel around 3 p.m. from her shopping extravaganza. She couldn't believe the prices and sales and was tickled pink over her newly purchased treasures. Altogether she'd bought four new outfits, a pair of sandals, and a scarf. She threw down the bags and pulled out her cell to see if Madison had called. No calls missed.

She shrugged her shoulders and flipped open her phone to call her mamma and check on Shelby Lynn. The phone rang twice before a sweet little voice answered the phone, "Hi, Mama!"

"Hi, Shelby darling, how are ya all doin?"

"Fine, Mama. Grandma took me to the zoo today."

"She did?"

"Uh huh. And ya know what we all saw?"

"What'd y'all see? Tell me."

"We saw lions and seals and giraffes. And, oh, Mama?"

"Yeah, what is it, baby?"

"We also saw a hippopotamus!"

"You did not."

"Yeah we did! He was funny lookin'."

"Ah, that's great, darlin'. Is Grandma there with you now?"

"Yup she sure is. Ya wanna talk to her?"

"I do."

"Okay. Mama?"

"Yeah, baby?"

"How many more days till y'all come home? I miss ya."

"Oh, I miss ya too, honey. I'll be home in about four days. I love ya, and ya be good for Grandma now, ya hear?"

"I will, Mama, love ya too."

"GRANDMA—MAMA WANTS TO TALK TO YA," Samantha Jo could hear her daughter's sweet voice yellin' across the room.

Charlene took the phone from Shelby and said, "How ya holdin' up, darlin'?"

"Fine, Mama. We're just fine."

"Everthin' okay there in Blackberry Creek?"

"As good as it can be I suppose. We went to see Hazel's body this morning. It was awful lookin', Mama."

"I can only imagine it was. How's Madison takin' everything?"

"She's Madison. She thinks that somethin' more has happened and is startin' to ask questions."

"Well, y'all tell her to be careful. Blackberry Creek ain't no place to be stirrin' up trouble!"

"I did, Mama, but y'all know how she can be. She gets somethin' stuck in her head and just chews on it like a dog with a bone."

"Samantha Jo, I don't like it, y'all down there alone. I wished y'all woulda listened to me and not gone there in the first place. There's nothin' but trouble and ain't no good gonna come of it."

"I know, Mama. I've decided to come back earlier than planned. I'm catchin' the 8:30 p.m. flight out on Monday evening. I miss Shelby something fierce, and I don't much like it here."

"Samantha Jo, I wished y'all would come home sooner."

"Mamma, I can't. Now, the funeral is on Friday and the readin' of the will is on Monday afternoon."

"What are y'all gonna do in the meantime, then?"

"Well, we've decided to get outta here for the weekend and go stay at some fancy ocean resort. I think it was called Isle something; it's in North Carolina 'bout 4 hours away."

"I see. Well, it's gotta be safer there than where y'all are now. Ya be careful now, and let me know y'all are doin' all right."

"I will, Mama. I promise."

"Good then, say hi to Madison and try and keep yourselves outta trouble!"

"I will, Mama. Give Shelby a kiss and hug for me. I'll be home before y'all know it. Bye."

She hung up the phone and remembered she was supposed to call and make the reservations for the weekend. She pulled out the piece of paper in her purse with the name and number to the resort. She called, and they were in luck! There had been a last-minute cancelation for an Oceanside suite. Perfect! Without hesitation she said, "We'll take all three nights!" Samantha Jo gave her credit card information and wrote down the confirmation number. She was in a hurry to get the hell out of town and figured after the funeral, since the meeting wasn't until Monday, there was really nothin' for her and Madison to do but wait. Samantha Jo hung up the phone and took a sigh of relief.

Getting the hell outta this crazy town was a good idea. Madison was gonna get the two of them killed if Samantha Jo didn't find away to keep her occupied. Two full days of sun and spa treatments at the ocean was what they needed, and maybe it would relax Madison and take her mind off all the troubles here. She'd come back with a different view point too; Samantha Jo was sure of it.

She decided to cool down with take a bath before dinner and filled the tub with water. Madison would be back soon, and she was starting to get hungry. Shopping could wear a woman out, she thought.

On the drive back, Madison looked over at Travis and said, "Do you mind if I ask you a personal question?"

"Not at all. Ask away."

"You commented back in the driveway that Doris was all you had left?"

"That's right, she is."

"What happened to your parents? Did they move or something?"

"My parents are both deceased."

"I'm so sorry. I shouldn't have asked such a personal question like that."

"Madison, it's okay. My mother passed away about fifteen years ago, and Doris sort of took me in, if you will, and has been like a mother to me since."

"What about your father?"

"I never knew him. He died before I was born."

"How awful! Did your mother say how?"

"He was in a car accident up in Virginia while passing through. He was hit by a drunk driver they think."

"They think?"

"Yeah, well, the police were called to the scene after a car drove by and saw my dad's car all banged up. When they arrived all they found was just my dad's car. They figure the person responsible was able to drive away and they never did find 'em."

"I don't know what to say. That must have been hard growing up without your daddy."

"Well, I imagine that's something we have in common then, don't we?" He looked over at Madison and raised a brow.

She figured he'd known some of the family drama, being Hazel's attorney and all. Of course he did, Hazel had gone to him and confessed she was nervous about Lane and Leroy. Travis knew they were dangerous. Madison wondered what else he knew. It made her somewhat uneasy not knowing how much Travis really knew about her and her family. At the same time, she felt extremely comfortable in his presence and was beginning to enjoy his company.

"What did your mom do, if I might ask?"

"She worked at a store in town for many years until she was forced to quit."

"Why'd she have to quit?"

"Well, I was just finishing up law school at Harvard and studying for the bar exam when she called to tell me that she had been told by the doctor she had breast cancer."

"Oh, Travis, that must have been hard for you to hear and not be home to care for her?"

"They thought they'd caught it soon enough, but back then they didn't have the resources like we do now. She fought it as long as she could. I wanted to come home, but she begged me to stay and finish. She'd worked so hard her whole life to be able to put me through college that I felt an obligation to not let her down."

"That must have been one of the hardest decisions for you to make?"

"It was. But I made it through and passed the bar exam and returned to town before she passed. An elder gentleman, by the name of Andrew Perkins, owned the firm before me and hired me right out of college. He passed away nearly ten years ago, and I took over the firm. Doris was there before I started and has been with me since."

"She would be proud of you today, your mom. You've obviously done well for yourself and, from what I can tell, she did a great job raising you to be a perfect gentlemen."

"Thank you. I miss her every day."

They drove in silence for the next several minutes until Travis leaned over and asked, "How would you and your cousin like to join me for dinner tonight? Now, I'm warning you, I really can't accept no as an answer. Besides, it's not much fun eating alone."

"Well, I don't know if Samantha Jo will be up for it . . ."

"Great! Then it's set. I'll pick y'all up at 6:30 p.m. sharp, and we'll head over to the Blackberry Creek Country Club."

Madison looked over at him and exclaimed, "Country club? When did you all get a country club?"

"Oh, about five years ago the city bought some old property that had been for sale for some time. They completely overhauled the property and put in a regulation 18-hole golf course and a fancy country club.

There's a private ballroom on the lower level that occasionally gets rented out for weddings and such."

"Do y'all golf?" Madison was flabbergasted by the fact that Blackberry Creek had built a country club. Some things appeared to have changed since her last visit.

"No, I'm afraid I don't. Never really did understand the game."

"Yeah, well it is a love/hate type of game for sure."

"I'm not very good myself, but I try to get out a few times a year with the boys."

Madison was laughing, and Travis looked over with a puzzled look and asked, "What's gone and got you going?"

"Nothin', it's just that a lawyer who only plays golf a few times a year? Who's ever heard of such?" Back in Minnesota if you were a banker, a CPA, or an attorney, you golfed. Weekly, that is.

Travis had a perplexed look on his face and apparently didn't understand Madison's joke. He just gave her half a smile and shrugged his shoulders. They pulled into the parking lot of the hotel and, after Madison got out, Travis yelled through the window, "6:30 sharp. I'll see y'all then."

Chapter 9

Madison had to hold her hands over her ears when Samantha Jo squealed in delight. "Oh, that is wonderful! I am going to wear that new sundress and scarf I bought today shopping. What're y'all gonna wear?" she asked.

Madison hadn't thought too much about it yet. She felt sticky and dirty from being in Hazel's house; she felt like she was covered in fly shit. "I suppose I'll wear this summer red dress that I brought with. You think that will be appropriate?" She held up a slim-fitting, deep-red dress that came to her knees and had three inch slits on the outer sides. The sleeves stopped just after the shoulder bone with a V-neck line that came down just enough to show the inner curves of her breast. With the help of her Victoria's Secret bra, there would be ample cleavage.

"You're gonna look splendid! He won't be able to resist you in that dress, cousin!"

"Samantha Jo, it's not like that. I wish you'd stop tryin' to push me towards Travis. He is a very nice man and, yes, he's extremely attractive, but I just don't feel it's a good idea to be hitting on our dead grandmother's lawyer!"

"Well, ya don't gotta get all uptight about it. I thought you were kinda sweet on him? At least, that was vibe I was pickin' up?"

"Well, your vibe radar must be broken because that is not the vibe I was puttin' down!"

Samantha Jo gave her hug and said, "Well, maybe you weren't puttin' it down, but he sure was. Y'all didn't see the way he was lookin' at ya back at the funeral home."

"Samantha Jo . . ."

"I know, I know, I'll drop it. Now y'all git in the shower and get ready. We're goin' to the country club!"

Samantha Jo took a deep breath when she heard the shower turn on. She plopped down on the bed and wished for the life of her that Madison would focus her attention on something other than Hazel's murder, something like Travis. He was handsome, appeared to be single, and seemed to have done well for himself. He was a good catch as far as she was concerned. He'd be a good distraction, and she needed to find a way to keep Madison in his company. If she was runnin' around with him, she'd have less time to worry about Monsters and maybe the green car would leave them alone, too.

Just two more days and then Samantha Jo could relax a little more. She felt her nerves on end and the only thing that seemed to help keep her mind distracted was shopping.

Later, Madison was ready and walking towards the door when Samantha Jo said, "Before we go down to meet Travis, can we promise not to talk about Hazel's death, Lane, Leroy . . . Can we just go and have some fun tonight?"

"Sure. You're right; we deserve to enjoy the evening."

Travis found that after he'd showered he was having a hard time deciding what to wear. That was funny, he thought. He never had that problem before. He'd been out with women many times and, besides, this wasn't a date. He was just escorting two lovely women to dinner. He decided on the black dress pants and periwinkle button oxford. He rolled the sleeves up to his elbows and splashed on a touch of cologne.

In the background, he had the music of Otis Redding playing and every once in a while, he'd add a little skip in his step. He had a glass of Malbec to calm his nerves. He was excited and figured it was because of the new acquaintances he was lucky enough to share the evenin' with. Not too much changes in Blackberry Creek, and the thought of having someone new to talk to was exhilarating.

He arrived at the hotel at 6:30 p.m. sharp, and the two women walked out and got into the car.

He returned to the farm where he knew he'd be alone and not bothered. Besides, it was a good hide out, away from any traffic, where he didn't have to worry about someone noticing his presence.

His cell phone rang. He flipped it open and said nothing. A voice on the other end said, "They've left again for dinner, but they're not alone."

"Who are they with?" he replied.

"That attorney fella."

He flipped the phone shut and ended the call.

It was hot and sticky out still even with the rise of the moon. He turned on the only fan he could find, but it wasn't much help. He took a bucket of rain water out of the fridge and used the rag that he'd soaked in the bucket to sponge off his face and neck.

Earlier in the day, he covered himself in bug spray to help combat all the bugs he knew he'd encounter in the woods. Slapping at mosquitoes and scratching himself would have left him an open target while hiding in the trees.

He grabbed a cold beer and sat in the only chair in the little trailer. The furniture left behind was sparse but he didn't need much. He sat drinking the beer, thinking about where it was hiding. He'd gone over and over the little trailer looking for it, and now he sat contemplating the next place he'd search. She didn't believe in safety deposit boxes. No, she would have kept it where no one else would think to look. He was sure it was in plain sight; he just didn't know where.

There was no use in going out and keeping an eye on the women, they had company and he didn't want to bring outside attention to his presence. Tomorrow he'd go back to the house and continue searching.

The country club was busy with many local folks dressed up and enjoying their night out. A cover band that played rock songs called the Rifters would be starting at nine. The three were escorted to a table that Travis had reserved earlier.

Sitting down, the women began to survey their surroundings.

"This is beautiful, Travis," Samantha Jo commented.

"We think so, too."

Madison gazed upon the room herself and wondered who paid for all this in such a small town. Indeed, it was gorgeous, but it must have cost a ton of money. Travis reached his hand over and rested it on top of Madison's. "How are ya holdin' up?" he asked.

"Fine. I'm fine. I think I'm just a bit tired from the heat and everything."

Travis nodded, "Yeah, that heat can take a lot out of you if y'all not used to it."

The waitress came over and took their drink orders. Both Madison and Samantha Jo decided to have a margarita, and Travis ordered a gin and tonic.

"Madison mentioned you went shopping this afternoon. Did y'all find anything ya liked?"

"Why, yes, I did. I bought this dress and scarf today and few other things as well."

"Great choice! Y'all look absolutely stunning in that dress."

Samantha Jo blushed a bit, giggled, and said, "Y'all so sweet."

They made small talk and ordered another drink before eating dinner. Afterwards, they decided to order one more drink before heading back to the hotel.

"Well, ladies, what is on y'alls agenda for tomorrow?" Madison looked back and forth from Travis to Samantha Jo who shrugged her shoulders.

"Well, I was hoping to take a drive out to Sunnyside Stables where Hazel kept her horses. Samantha Jo, I was thinking maybe we could drive out there together and then come back to town for lunch?"

"The stables? Honey, why would we need to go out there?"

"I just thought it would give us something to do besides sitting in our hotel room until Friday is all."

Samantha Jo thought about it for a minute and figured, "Hell, maybe she's right. There couldn't possibly be any harm in going to the stables. Maybe it would be kinda nice."

"Sure. Sounds fun."

"Look, Samantha Jo, if you'd rather go shopping and spend the day in town, I'd be more than happy to drive Madison out to the stables tomorrow. I don't have any pressin' appointments that I can't reschedule."

Samantha Jo was about to say yes and then she remembered the green car. She didn't wanna be alone all day without Madison, and besides, she needed to keep an eye on her to make sure she wasn't diggin' where she shouldn't be diggin'. "That's awfully generous of you, Travis, and y'all been so kind to us, but the more I think about it, I think that I'd really like goin' out to the stables tomorrow.

Madison knew what Samantha Jo was really thinking and why she wanted to stay close to her cousin. She looked straight ahead, took a sip of her drink, and said, "Did you see the green car again today at all?"

Samantha Jo kicked her under the table and gave her a curt look. "I thought we weren't gonna talk about none of that tonight?"

"Look, Samantha Jo, whether you want to believe it or not, someone is following us and they're driving a green-fucking-car!"

Travis sensed the tension between the two women and said softly, "Samantha Jo, she's right. Madison had mentioned something 'bout your situation last night and I'm here to help y'all. I believe Madison's right and that y'all need to be taking this more seriously."

Madison sat there silently, remembering the incident that had occurred earlier that day while at the house. It had been bothering her all evening, and she needed tell someone. "Travis, I need to tell you about something that happened at the house earlier today. We weren't alone there."

"Y'all mean other than Bud?"

"Correct."

"Madison, we were alone; there wasn't anyone else around for miles."

"Yes there was. After you left me by the garden to collect myself, I made a call to the stables. When I finished the call and turned to go towards the steps, I heard a twig break in the woods behind the garden. I tried to look but it was so dark in there, and I didn't dare go lookin' any further than right where I was standing."

"Madison, why didn't y'all say something when you got to the car? Jesus, woman, are you trying to get yourself killed?"

Samantha Jo thought to herself, "Finally, someone who's as sane as I am!"

"I didn't say anything because I just wanted to get out of there!" Madison said.

"Madison, I'm not comfortable with the two of you staying at the hotel by yourselves. This is becoming too dangerous. A good friend of mine called me the other day to tell me he was comin' through town soon, and I think I better give him a call back to see about comin' sooner."

"Who is this friend of y'alls you're talkin' about?" asked Samantha Jo.

"He's a good friend of mine from college. He now works for the FBI."

"The FBI? Madison, this is gettin' too dangerous for me, for both of us. I don't want no part of it. Y'all are just askin' for trouble. Now, this has gotta stop right here and right now! Please, I'm beggin' ya!"

Madison broke in and said, "Samantha Jo, I think Travis has a good point here. We are like sitting ducks in this town, and with Lane in town, too, I just think . . ."

Samantha Jo spit the drink in her mouth across the table the minute she heard his name. "Did y'all just say Lane was in town?"

"Yes, Travis told me this afternoon . . ."

"When the hell were ya gonna tell my daddy was in town?"

"Well, I don't know if he still is, Samantha Jo, but he did come to meet with me this mornin' and y'all should know he'll be at the meeting on Monday," Travis said.

Samantha Jo starting swaying from side to side, "I don't feel so well, y'all."

Madison moved closer to her cousin and whispered, "Drink some water, honey, and take a deep breath. It's gonna be all right. I promise."

Samantha Jo took several deep breaths and centered herself. She looked over at Madison and said, "I don't want nothin' to do with that man! Why does he have to be at the meetin' on Monday?"

Travis spoke before Madison could say anything. "Samantha Jo, I can't discuss the details of your grandmother's will with you anymore than I can with anyone else. But I can tell you that you're gonna be fine in that meeting; there will be several others there, including Miss Tessa."

"Well, that's more comforting," she said sarcastically. "I'm glad we're getting out of this crazy town on Friday because I don't know how much more I can take!"

"Friday?" Madison asked. "I thought we were leaving on Saturday?"

"Yes, but I forgot to tell y'all that when I called earlier, the only openin' they had was for a cancellation for a suite Friday through Monday. We gotta leave here Friday after the funeral."

"Hold up, ladies, where are y'all goin'?"

"We decided earlier today that maybe it would be best if we left for the weekend after the funeral and stay away until Monday for the reading of the will. We're headin' to the ocean."

"I think that is a wise plan. It would seem that someone is following y'all and tryin' to scare the dickens out of ya."

"Well, it certainly is working on me!" cried Samantha Jo.

"I am still going to call my friend over at the FBI; I think Bud could use a little push to get to the bottom of this situation."

"What do you mean, bottom of it? He seemed perfectly content earlier today with where his investigation had ended at."

"Who's Bud, y'all?"

"Oh sorry, he's the sheriff that met Travis and me out at Hazel's house this afternoon. He didn't impress me in the least!"

"Madison, that's not entirely true. Things do move down here at a slower pace maybe than what y'all are used to, but I asked Bud to look deeper into this entire situation before y'all came to town. I can't say much more than that other than as it may have a significant impact on the conditions set forth in the will. I know that doesn't help y'all much now, but you're makin' the right decision to leave after the funeral until Monday."

Madison asked, "Do you really think it's that serious enough that we need to call your friend over at the FBI?"

"Honestly, I do. At the very least, it can't hurt none."

Samantha Jo had grown increasingly uncomfortable with direction of the night's conversation and asked, "Will y'all be at the funeral on Friday, too, Travis?"

"Yes, m'am," he said with a nod.

The band began setting up their equipment on the stage and making strange warm-up noises. With that, Madison gave a big yawn. She'd tried to hold it back but she was tired. Tired from the heat, tired from not sleeping so well the night before, and tired of feeling like she was being followed everywhere she went. "It's getting late and I can't seem to keep my eyes open. Would you all mind if we skip the band tonight and head back to the hotel?"

Samantha Jo was feeling tired and sick to her stomach, too. She couldn't stop thinking about how Lane would be attending the reading on Monday. Why, though? It's not like Hazel was gonna leave him nothin' more than the properties she'd listed. Was she? She wondered what was so important that Lane wanted to be there and why Travis was so hush-hush about it all. Whoever this Bud person was, why was he taking so long to wrap up the paperwork regardin' Hazel's death? And, above all, where was Leroy? Was he coming too? She caught herself in mid-thought and said to herself, "Jesus, I'm turning into Madison!"

Samantha Jo repeated the word "STOP" over and over in head. Her body began rocking back and forth with just the slightest movement. Travis looked at the two of them and said, "I agree. It is gettin' late and y'all look like ya could use some rest. I'll meet ya out front with the car," he said, excusing himself from the table.

Madison looked over at Samantha Jo and put her arm around her to console her. "It's gonna be okay Samantha Jo. Just one more day and then we'll leave this crazy-ass place for a few days. I promise you'll feel better tomorrow after a good night's rest. You'll see."

Samantha Jo spoke no words; she just kept staring forward and nodded her head in agreement. They left the table and found Travis waiting in the Mercedes out front.

After Travis dropped off the two women, he parked the car in the back of the lot to wait and see if anyone had followed them home. He drove around the lot once and didn't notice any cars that fit Madison's description of an old 1970's greenish-lookin' car.

He sat for a few minutes longer and waited just to be sure. Taking out his cell, he scrolled through the address book until he found Wyatt's number. He pressed send and stared off into the night while it rang.

"Hey, buddy, how are ya?"

"Fine, Wyatt, and y'all?"

"Oh, just busy tryin' to get things packed up around here for the movers next week. It's funny y'all don't realize how much shit ya have until ya gotta pack it all up and move."

"Yeah, ya really do find out what's worth keepin' and what needs throwin', that's for sure. Say, Wyatt, the reason I called y'all tonight is more of a business matter."

"Oh? Ya got some hot case of poachers or something down there in Blackberry Creek?" Wyatt gave a little laugh.

"No more like an unsolved murder."

"I'm sorry, Travis; I thought y'all just said murder?"

"I did."

"God, what happened? It must be a serious deal if y'all callin' me for my opinion?"

"Wyatt, I was actually hopin' y'all might be able to come in town sooner."

"This can't wait a couple weeks?"

"No, I'm afraid it can't. On top of the murder, I have two women here from out of town who believe they are being stalked. It's frightening the dickens out of them, and I gotta say from what I already know I'm a little nervous myself."

"What can y'all tell me about the case?"

"It's too much for me to go into now, but I'll fill y'all in with the details when ya get here."

"I see. Is Monday afternoon too late? I've gotta get a few more things done yet here and close up the house before I leave for Charleston. I'll leave Monday morning and be there by late afternoon. Can y'all wait until then?"

"That'll be just fine. Come straight to the house, y'all know where the key is, and I'll meet ya there after work. And, Wyatt?"

"Yeah, buddy?"

"I owe ya one!"

"Actually y'all owe me more like five or six, but who's countin'? I'll see ya Monday!"

Travis ended the call and took one more look around the parking lot; everything appeared normal. He drove home and went straight to bed.

Chapter 10

Samantha Jo didn't sleep much at all that night. She laid there wide awake with all sorts of questions running through her head. She didn't like this at all. With Travis calling in his FBI friend, this is more serious than she imagined. She was beginning to fear for her own life as well as her daughter's safety.

Her eyes were tired, and there were black circles under her lower lids from the lack of sleep. She didn't feel well and her stomach was still very much upset. Her nerves had gotten the best of her. She wondered how Madison did it, not letting anything stop her from pushing further into this nightmare. She wished she could be more like her cousin. At least she got some sleep last night.

She could tell her Monday flight was not going to come fast enough, and she longed to just get on the next plane and leave for good. Just one more day, she reminded herself, and then we can relax at the beach and get away from this. She, too, knew the reason someone was following them and trying to frighten them had to do with Hazel's death. If they left town, they would be outta the danger they were sitting right in the middle of now.

Samantha Jo got up to use the bathroom and grabbed a cool glass of water. She found a couple Tylenol she'd stashed in her cosmetic bag and slammed them down with the water. She went back to bed, pulled the covers up to her head, and decided that she wasn't going to leave her bed today.

Madison dozed off around 2 a.m. She had been so worn out from the day, both physically and emotionally, but when she'd laid down her brain decided to go into overload. She couldn't stop thinking about everything that had taken place in the last forty-eight hours. She, too, missed her son and couldn't wait to get back home to her life with him and her work.

When she heard Samantha Jo come out of the bathroom, she rolled over and glanced at the clock; it was 8 a.m. She looked over at her cousin and saw that she had the covers pulled up almost over head. Madison lay there a few more minutes then decided to take a shower.

When she came out of the bathroom, she looked at Samantha Jo who was still in the same position. She sat next to her on the bed, leaned over, and quietly said her name, "Samantha Jo . . . Are you all right? It's time to get up?"

"I don't think I can today, Madison. I'm not feelin' so well and don't feel like movin'. Y'all go on ahead today without me."

Madison frowned. She felt bad; she knew that this was more than Samantha Jo had bargained for and that she wasn't helping. The more investigating she did, the more trouble came their way. "All right, if you're sure. Can I bring you anything before I head out? You want me to go down and bring you up some coffee or something?"

"Nah, I don't have much of an appetite for anythin' right now. Y'all go on ahead."

"Okay, I'll put your cell phone by the bed. Call me if you want me to stop and get you anything. All right?"

"Uh huh."

Madison found Samantha Jo's phone charging on the desk and set it on the night stand by her bed before leaving.

Downstairs, she walked over to the front desk and asked if they had maps.

"Where y'all lookin' to get to, m'am?"

She explained that she was going to the Sunnyside Stables, and the gentleman grabbed a piece of paper and wrote down the directions. It seemed pretty easy, and she was only about thirty minutes away.

She walked over to where the hotel had laid out breakfast and coffee and grabbed a bagel, cream cheese, and a black coffee. There was a little patio out back with an outdoor pool. It was quiet out there this early, and she found a shady spot with a table and umbrella. She sat, overlooking the pool and listening to the sounds of the morning birds nearby, and thought that maybe when she got back, she and Samantha Jo could come down and lay by the pool for awhile. They were safer when they were together in a public place.

She dug out her cigarettes and sat back, enjoying both the moment and her coffee.

He woke at the break of dawn and again sponged himself down with a cool rag. It was hot and stuffy in that small trailer, and it felt like it was already ninety degrees out with the humidity.

On his way into town, he'd managed to pick up enough food to last him several days. He opened a can of Spam and went out to start the cast-iron stove. There was no use in heating up the inside of the trailer any more than it was. He boiled a small pot with water and made some instant coffee for himself.

After eating, he grabbed his hand gun and hunting knife and walked up the path to his car. He drove back to Hazel's house to resume his search. There was no traffic on the road yet. He pulled off the road and parked in the same spot as the day before then walked carefully through the woods to the back of the house.

Hanging outside the back door was a small, wooden birdhouse with a magnetically-attached metal top. Pulling the top off, he reached in and found the spare key. He'd watched her for months and knew exactly where she left the key, what time she left every day, and when she'd return. He knew her schedule better than she did.

He unlocked the door, stepped inside, and muttered, "Fuck!" It was hotter than the trailer he'd been sleeping in, and the stench that had built up inside took his breath away. The flies seemed to multiply overnight and were everywhere. He waved his hands back and forth as if to shoo them away. He decided that it was too much, even for him, and that he'd have to turn on the central air to get things cooled off and the air moving around.

Today he would start in the back bedroom first and make his way to the front of the house. There wasn't much time before company became a possibility so he got right to work.

Travis awoke at 7 a.m., an hour later than usual. He remembered that he'd had three gin and tonics the night before and, though he hadn't been drunk by any means, his body still had processed the alcohol during the night and he felt tired and thirsty. He started the coffee maker and grabbed a bottled water out of the refrigerator, slamming it in sixty seconds on his way to the shower.

Once showered and dressed, he headed back downstairs for his toast and coffee. He called Doris to let her know that he'd be in shortly and that he'd been working from home this morning. "Just a little white lie," he thought. The day before had been exhilarating from the moment he met Madison, and today, since she was going to be with her cousin, would be just an ordinary day for him.

Not much happened in Blackberry Creek, and he'd enjoyed the excitement he felt yesterday. For one of the first times in his life, he realized he didn't feel like going to the office. He wanted to be close to Madison, to see what she was doing, and to make sure of her safety. He sighed, picked up his briefcase, and headed into the office.

Madison found the directions from the front desk to be just as he said. She arrived in thirty minutes. It was just before 9:30 a.m., and she figured the folks there would be done with the morning feedings and easy to find. She pulled in and parked the car.

It was a beautiful farm containing nearly twenty acres. The barn was the typical large red barn with white trim. Two large doors were perched open, and Madison figured she would start there before knocking on the front door to the house. She immediately began sniffling and sneezing when she got out of the car. Though it was hot and humid, there was pollen in the air and hay bales stacked forty feet high next to the barn. As she neared the barn, her sneezing increased. "Hay!" she thought. She reached in her purse for a Kleenex and blew her nose before continuing.

She looked up when she heard a voice say, "Good mornin'. I thought I heard somebody out here."

Madison sniffled, wiped away the tears that'd formed during her sneezing attack, and replied, "Hello. I'm looking for Loretta?"

"I'm Loretta. How can I help ya all?"

"Loretta, pleasure to meet you. I am Madison Slone; I called and spoke with you yesterday?"

"Oh yes, dear. Glad y'all could make it. Well, come on in. Would ya like to see the horses?"

"Yes, I would. Thank you."

She followed Loretta into the barn and counted over twenty boarded horses. They were magnificent looking creatures with the most beautiful eyes and stature. As Madison followed her, admiring the different breeds and markings, Loretta turned and asked, "Did y'all say you were Hazel's niece? I can't remember."

"Uh, no, m'am, I'm her granddaughter."

"Oh, ya poor thing. We really are gonna miss your grandmother. She came out here every day ya know, to take care of these horses. Ya couldn't keep her away if ya tried."

"Yes, she and my grandfather both shared a love for horses."

Loretta stopped in front of a stall and said, "Well honey, here we are. This here is Rocket; he's a fourteen-month-old stud that Hazel brought in last year. I reckon, once he's old enough, she had intended to use him as a stud. He comes from a great line of champion show horses.

And over here is Josephine; she's a two-year-old mare your grandmother had been workin' with real hard to get broken in. Lastly, this here is Starlight. She's Josephine's mamma. Your grandmother rode her just about every day. I'll leave y'all here a minute while I go get the personal things that she'd left behind."

"Thank you."

Madison reached out to pet the top of Starlight's head. She made snorting sounds and bounced her head up and down. Madison remembered her grandfather teaching her the right way to approach a horse so ya don't frighten them. If you face them head on they have a hard time seeing you. Because their eyes are situated so far to the side of their head, they actually see two different views. What's on the right is seen with the right eye and vice versa.

Standing off to the right, Madison waited for Starlight to walk closer to her so she could pet her. She was so soft and beautiful. Her coloring was mostly a liver brown with white markings on her head. Loretta returned and said, "Here ya are, honey. It's not much; just a few items she had in her cubby here."

"Thank you so much, Loretta. It means a lot."

"Speak nothin' of it, honey. I'm just so sorry for your loss."

Madison shook her hand and turned around to walk out when Loretta called out to her, "Madison! I've got one more thing I almost forgot to give y'all."

"What is it?"

"Follow me over here to the fittin' area."

Madison followed her back and watched Loretta dig around for a bit until she found the one she wanted. "Here honey, this here is for good luck," and she handed Madison a horse shoe.

"Oh, Loretta, I can't."

"Nah, I insist. Y'all take it."

Madison nodded in agreement and walked back to her car with a small leather saddle bag and the horse shoe from Loretta.

She wanted to wait until she was alone to open the saddle bag and view its contents. As she reached the car, she began sneezing again. "I've got to get out of this place. That hay is gonna kill me!" Pulling out onto the main road, Madison heard her cell ring and she reached for it.

She picked it up and noticed the caller ID name—MOM. "Shit!" She'd not called her mother to tell her about her journey back to North Carolina. She put the phone to her ear and answered, "Hi, Mama."

"Madison?"

"Yes?"

"Why is there a sudden southern twang in your voice?"

"I . . ."

"Where are you?"

Madison cleared her throat as if that would change the drawl she'd acquired over the last two days. "I'm fine, Mom. How are you?"

"That is not what I asked you. Where are you?"

"I'm on a business trip, Mom. I'm down in . . . South Carolina."

"Why did you hesitate?"

"Sorry, it's just that I've been so busy down here with our new client, and I guess I forgot for a moment where I was."

She hated lying to her mother, but telling her truth would not do either of them any good. Her mother would not understand what was going on down here, and there wasn't time to go into details. She'd tell her the truth later, she promised herself. They spoke for just a few more minutes before Madison cut the conversation short, "Mom, I'm really busy down here and have to get to a meeting. I'll call you next week when I get back, all right?"

"All right, dear, you be safe. I love you."

"Love you too. Bye." She hung up the phone with a sigh of relief and drove back towards town. She didn't really know where she was going just that she wasn't ready to head back to the hotel just yet. While driving, she found herself thinking about Travis. She couldn't figure him out which bothered her because she was usually a pretty good, quick judge of character. He was kind, charming, attractive, single (as far as she could tell), seemingly trustworthy, and he picked up on her every intuition.

She thought back to the evening before and wondered why he decided to call his friend from the FBI? He'd acknowledged that Hazel was nervous and uneasy about Lane's and Leroy's presence and yet Bud didn't seem to be taking this seriously at all. Why did Sheriff Sheldon need a push with his investigation? As far as she could tell, there wasn't one.

What was Travis not telling her? What did he know that she didn't? He always kept referring to the reading on Monday and how he couldn't discuss any of the details until then. So why was Lane at his office yesterday morning? Lane—she had no desire to see that man again either. She remembered his cold dark eyes like those of the devil. Poor Samantha Jo. If he did come on Monday, it would only mean more trouble for her down the road. Would he dare come to the funeral tomorrow?

Madison realized she'd nearly reached town when she saw a small area where she could pull off near the creek. There she found a picnic table under a shady tree. She parked the car and sat on top of the table with her feet on the bench seat. She dug through her bag and took out a cigarette. Her nerves needed calming and her mind needed relaxing before opening the leather saddle bag. She took a long, final drag in preparation for viewing the bag's contents.

Picking up the bag, she noticed for the first time how light it felt. There could only be a few items, if anything at all, in it. She unbuckled the leather straps and opened it up.

She pulled out a 3 x 5 frame and turned it over to see the picture. In it stood her grandfather, Jethro, standing next to a fighter plane with one hand on his hip and a big smile. She opened the back of the frame and took the photo out to see if it had a date or more information. On the back read: Jethro Walker, Pilot, 1943, Flying Fortress. She flipped the photo over again and stared at him for a moment. Though he was just under six feet tall, he was a handsome man with sandy-blond hair and green eyes. She could see how women were easily attracted to him. She put the photo back into the frame and set in on the table.

Reaching in again, she pulled out a set of worn, leather riding gloves. Hazel had worn them every day at the stables. Madison held them to her face and smelled the gloves. Near the wrists she could smell a faint hint of Hazel's perfume. Madison couldn't remember what the name of it was but it had a distinct scent of lilacs to it. Her eyes began tear up, and she had to look up at the sky for a second and push back the tears that had formed. Taking a deep breath, she reached back into the bag.

The last item she found was a hairbrush. Hazel obviously kept it there to comb her hair after she was done riding or feeding the horses. She shook the bag to see if there was anything more when she heard the sound of keys clanging together. She peered back into the bag but didn't see anything. Puzzled, she shook the bag again and still heard keys of some sort. Looking even closer into the bag she noticed a small zipper vertically off to the far side. She slid the zipper down, reached into a tiny pocket, and pulled out a key chain containing four keys.

He worked feverishly for over four hours, searching every nook and cranny he could find. Each room in the house was full of furniture, knick knacks, and photographs. There was a lot to go through, and to make sure he didn't miss it, he looked through everything, including between the mattresses and under the dressers.

The scene of the crime didn't bother him none. He stepped right in the dried pools of blood and ignored the fact that the room looked like something out of a horror movie He was on a mission. "Where did she hide those fucking bonds!" he muttered. He knew that his father had hidden several of the bonds that he'd purchased years ago for extra security. And he also knew from reading both wills that the bond amounts were skewed. The amount was off by nearly $250,000, which meant that the hidden bonds were still out there.

Jethro had only lived on the farm while married to Hazel, and he knew that his father would've kept them close but out of her sight. He'd gone over the farm a dozen times and the only explanation now was that she'd found them. The properties he and his brother stood to inherit would only amount to $175,000 each. He wanted those bonds. He wanted the money. She should've never have been left all the money and properties from his father.

The air conditioning cooled the house down, but he'd still worked up a sweat looking and digging. Even with the air running, the stench in the house remained. The flies took refuge in the windows for warmth from the sun shining on them. It was after 10 a.m., and he figured he would have to quit for the day and return in the morning.

He decided to go and see what that little bitch was up to and where she was pokin' her nose now. He shut off the lights in the back bedrooms and took an apple from his shirt and ate it on his way to the door. After the door was locked, he placed the key back in the bird house for the next day.

Travis sat in his office staring out the window while tapping his pencil on his desk. Doris knocked on his door and poked her head in to tell him she was leaving and she'd be back in an hour or so. "Would you like for me to get you some lunch while I'm out? I noticed you didn't bring one with you today and had no lunch appointment."

"I'm fine, Doris. Thank you. I'm just not feelin' all that hungry today."

"It's probably the heat, honey."

"Yeah, you're probably right.

"I'll be back shortly. Ya let me know if I can get y'all somethin' while I'm out."

Travis waited until he heard the front door shut before he began staring off again, tapping his pencil as if in a trance.

He liked Madison. She had a warm presence when she was in the room but a cool vibe that kept others at a distance. He, too, wondered if she was single. Hazel really didn't talk much about either of the two women, and when he tried to push her with a question, she'd just shrug her shoulders and say, "It don't matter none."

Madison was smart and quick to the punch, too. He liked that spunk in her and didn't know if she'd gotten it from her mother or from the hard knocks of life. He felt bad for Madison, wondering what was it like having an estranged father who hated her and was so troubled in the head.

Travis had always longed to know about his father and who he was. When he was little he would ask his mother questions about him, and she'd begin to tear up and say that it was just too painful for her discuss. By the age of ten, he stopped asking and just accepted the fact that his father was dead and he would never know who he was.

Madison was definitely picking up that things were not as they should be, and he had to try to find a way to keep her safe until Wyatt got to town. With the two cousins leaving, it would be a lot easier to keep Madison safe and out of danger. He wanted to tell her all that he knew, but that would break the oath he once took as an attorney and jeopardize the series of events that'd taken place. As much as he wanted her to go for her own safety, he selfishly wanted her stay, too. He wanted more time with her to get to know her. He couldn't understand his attraction to her and it was beginning to drive him crazy.

After all, she'd be leaving in a week to return to Minnesota. Her life was there and his was here.

Madison held the keychain in the palm of her hand and studied it closely. Three of the keys looked like normal-sized keys and were marked. She placed the three close together and read: **House, B.H.,** and **Farm.**

The fourth key was different in both size and shape, leaving her puzzled. It was much smaller and slimmer than the other three, almost resembling a skeleton key. "What do you belong to?" she said, holding it up.

Then the charm on the keychain caught her attention. It was an arrowhead. This one was different in color and shape than the one she'd found years ago. It was more of a quartz-type stone with a tiny hole drilled through it so that it could fit on the key ring. "You're interesting, too," she thought.

This was odd; why did Hazel keep these keys zipped up in a bag at the stables? The only rational answer she could think of was that Hazel had spares in case she forgot her keys. But wouldn't she have her keys with her if she drove to the stables? It didn't make sense, and it bothered her that she couldn't figure out what the fourth key belonged to.

She had some time yet before she had to head back to the hotel, and she was sweating profusely from sitting outside so long. She decided to stop and visit Travis before heading back. She didn't know why, but she had a longing to see him again. She put the contents back into the leather saddlebag with the exception of the keys; those she put in her purse.

She found her way into town and parked down the street from Travis's office. Madison had started for the front gate when she looked down the side street and saw that it was there again. She had to squint to see it, but she was pretty sure it was the old, green car. Standing there, she hesitated for a minute, wondering what to do. It could have been anyone's car, and maybe the heat was getting to her and making her paranoid. "Fuck it," she said and waited for the light to turn green and then crossed the street.

At first she was walking at a face clip when suddenly she started sprinting towards the car, not knowing what she'd do when she reached it. She didn't care. She was hot, pissed off, and tired of looking over her shoulder. She came within a hundred yards of the car before its engine revved up and, with its tires screeching, pulled out and sped away. Again, she was too far away to see the license plate.

She stood there for a moment, out of breath and panting, before she realized she was being watched. She turned and looked towards the flower shop she'd stopped in front of where two older ladies stood staring at her, talking to one another, and pointing. Madison couldn't read their lips, but she assumed they were saying, "What in tarnation is that woman doin' runnin' in this heat! Fool!" Madison walked back towards Travis's office and stopped to rest a minute with her back against the wall and her hands on her knees. She looked up and noticed the sky was starting to change and fill with clouds. Even with the sun hiding, it still was hot and muggy.

She walked through the gate and opened the front door to his office. She didn't see Doris sitting at her desk, so she yelled, "Hello?" She took a few steps, and Travis appeared at his door.

"Madison. Where is Samantha Jo? I thought the two of you were heading over to the stables today?" Then he noticed that she had sweat running down her face, her head was soaking wet, and her clothes were sticking to her. Jokingly, he said, "Did I miss the marathon today? Y'all look awful! Come sit, I'll get ya some water."

Madison didn't say a word. She walked into his office and sat in the same chair she'd sat in before. Travis handed her a cool glass of water and sat back down in his chair, waiting for her to speak. She finished the water and sat the glass down. Looking up, she said, "I saw it again."

"Saw what?"

"The car! The green-fucking-car!"

"At the stables?"

"No, here, in town. Just now. I got out of my car and started for your office when I noticed it parked down that block." She pointed out the window that looked out towards the street.

"What happened?"

"I started to run down the sidewalk to get a closer, and it took off before I could get close enough to see the driver or the plates."

"Madison, are you sure?"

"Of course I'm sure! As soon as I got too close, it peeled out and sped down the street like a bat outta hell!"

Travis couldn't help but crack a small smile. Madison looked up at him and said, "Y'all think this is fucking funny? Some crazy bastard is stalking me, and all ya can do is sit there and smile?"

Travis choked for a second, trying to clear his throat, and said, "No, not at all. That's not why I was smiling. This is a very serious matter, and I believe you."

"Then why were ya smilin' at me when I told you what happened?"

"Madison, please don't take this the wrong way, but your southern twang is adorable."

She couldn't help but crack a smile herself. "Yeah, yeah, yeah. I know. Every time I'm down here or talk with Samantha Jo at great lengths it starts to come out."

"Maybe y'all more of a southern belle than ya think ya are?"

"Maybe so."

That sat and talked for a short while when Travis inquired as to the whereabouts of Samantha Jo. "I thought the two of you were going together today?"

She explained to him how her cousin wasn't feeling so well this morning and decided to remain in bed. "I think the stress of everything goin' on here is beginning to wear on her. It's as if she's shut down inside."

Madison explained to him she was fine going by herself and how nice Loretta was. "Travis, what's gonna happen with the horses now that Hazel's dead?"

"Madison, you know I can't discuss at this time any of the details of your grandmother's will. I wish I could say more than that, but these things are gonna have to wait until Monday."

"Seriously, Travis, when did talking about horses become national security? I mean if we can't even talk about them, what can we talk about? Because I'm starting to get the feeling there are things you're not tellin' me!"

"There's plenty we can talk about. For starters, why don't y'all tell me how your visit was to the stables today? Did Loretta show y'all the horses?"

"She did, and they were beautiful, of course. She also gave me a leather saddlebag with a few of my grandmother's belongings that she'd left there."

"Oh, like what?"

"Nothin' really. A picture of my grandfather when he was in the war, her working gloves, and a hairbrush." She decided not to tell Travis about the keys. Not yet, anyway. Not because she didn't trust him, but she wanted more time to sit with them before anyone else knew she had them. For all she knew, Travis would tell Bud, and he'd make her hand them over. No, for now nobody else needed to know she had them.

"Well, that was nice of her to give y'all those things. I'm sure they mean a lot to both you and Samantha Jo." He was right. They did. In life it was the little things that meant more. These were things that her grandmother had touched and used on a daily basis. They meant more to her than the china, glassware, and jewelry combined. She felt the same about the framed flag and medal that were missing from Hazel's house.

Whoever took those items took them for a sentimental reason and killed Hazel. The act of sheer violence that took Hazel's life and the way in which it was done meant only one thing—it was personal. She was sure of it.

Travis interrupted her thoughts by clearing his throat and said, "Would you like to join me for dinner tonight, Madison? I could throw something on the grill and open a bottle of wine."

"Travis, I'd really love to and appreciate the offer, but Samantha Jo didn't look so well this morning and I think we'll just be stayin' in tonight. With the funeral tomorrow, it's goin' to be an emotional day for us both and then we're leavin' town."

"I completely understand. Just thought I'd put the offer out there. If y'all change your mind, ya know how to reach me."

"Thanks, Travis. Really, for everything. You've been so kind to us both."

"It's been my pleasure, too, Madison Slone."

"Travis?"

"Yeah?"

"Do you mind if I ask you why you're not married? I don't mean to put it so bluntly. It's just that, well, if you don't mind me saying, you're an attractive and charming man, stable, intelligent with a great career. Besides all of that, you seem like you would have a lot to offer in a relationship."

"Are you inquiring out of interest or curiosity?"

Madison didn't quite know how to answer him; she sat there for a moment not saying a word. Travis didn't wait for her to respond, though he found her discomfort somewhat amusing. Not in a malicious way but more out of curiosity as to Madison's real reason for asking him.

He simply smiled and said, "It's not that I haven't been looking or open to sharing my life with another. Certainly, I've had relationships over the years. I guess they weren't with the right person. And what about you, Madison? I could just as well ask you the same."

Madison knew he'd caught her. He said just enough without saying too much and turned it around on her. Typical lawyer, she thought. She loved a good debate but when it came to her personally, she avoided the subject at all costs. "I guess, just like you, I, too, have not found that person to share my life with either. After Mason's father and I divorced, I dated some but found that most of my time is consumed with Mason and my work. I guess that after a while, that part of my life was put on hold. Besides that, so much time has now passed that I think I'm too stubborn and set in my ways."

"Well, it sounds to me like we are both in the same boat and looking for our compass to find our way back home."

Smiling, she replied, "I like your choice of words."

Just then, a gust of wind picked up the branches on the tree nearest his office window and began to sway about. Travis looked over at his computer and quickly moved his mouse about. "Madison, y'all better get goin' back to the hotel. We've got a large storm coming in with wind gusts up to fifty miles per hour."

"How serious of a storm?"

"Serious enough that you shouldn't be drivin' in torrential rain."

She grabbed her purse and headed for the door. "Thanks again, Travis. We'll see you tomorrow at the funeral."

"Yes, I'll see ya both tomorrow. Now go before y'all get caught in the rain."

Madison quickly ran to her car and got in before rain drops starting pounding against her windshield. She made it back to the hotel before it began coming down in sheets.

Once back, she noticed that Samantha Jo was still curled in a ball under her covers. She set her things down and went into the bathroom. She came out and threw on some sweatpants and a t-shirt. Her stomach began to growl and make noises, and she realized she hadn't eaten since earlier in the day. She picked up the hotel room service menu and ordered a cheeseburger with fries and a large Diet Coke.

While waiting for her food, she realized she hadn't checked her emails or voicemails all day. In fact, she hadn't looked at her phone since the call with her mother.

Joe had called twice followed by a text: Where the hell r u? I've been trying to call to c how ur doing? Call me. ☺

"Oh, Joe, I was supposed to call you, wasn't I? I'm not up for any conversation right now with anyone," she thought.

She hit reply and typed: I'm a bad friend! Sorry. We've been busy today with funeral preparations. Gonna head to the beach after funeral. I promise will call then. ☺

She kept scrolling through the messages on her phone and found herself completely uninterested in any of its contents. Nothing from Mason or Tamara. "All is well, then," she thought.

Her food arrived and she turned the TV on, adjusting the volume low so she wouldn't disturb Samantha Jo. She ate in silence, trying to keep her mind occupied by the TV, but it was of no use. Her head just spun in circles with questions, and suddenly she felt a headache. After dinner, she found a few Excedrin and shut off the TV and lights. She could hear the rain beating against the windows of their room.

She saw flashes of lightening followed by loud thunder that shook the building.

Although it was only early afternoon, Madison was exhausted and decided to curl up next to Samantha Jo and comfort her. She grabbed a blanket and pillow from her own bed and snuggled up to her cousin. She whispered, "Are you all right? Can I get you anything?"

Samantha Jo mumbled back, "No. Just wake me in the morning when we can leave here." Madison put her arm around Samantha Jo and hugged her tight. She fell asleep almost immediately.

He made it back to the farm just as the rain began to come down hard. He made sure the windows were cracked just a bit to let in some air. He sat down in the chair and turned the fan so that it blew directly on him. In the fridge he found a beer and sat back down, retracing the steps he'd already taken.

Today was a close call. He had put his head down for a second to check his phone and missed her drive into town. When he looked up, he saw Madison gunning for the car on foot. His foot had slipped so that it was touching both the break and gas at the same time and, in his panic, he'd brought attention to his presence by revving the car so hard.

Damn, she was a nosy bitch! Why couldn't she just mind her own business and go back to where she came from? Then he had an idea: if she was that nosy and butterin' up to the lawyer and sheriff, she might just as well be lookin' for somethin' herself, too. Did she know about the bonds? He doubted it, but she seemed to be looking for answers and those answers would lead right back to him.

He knew they didn't have any suspects for the murder, and even if they did, they were carryin' on as though they didn't. No, Madison was looking to find the murderer and possibly something else. It'd be his luck she'd stumble on the bonds accidentally, leaving him completely screwed. He needed to find those bonds before her or anyone else.

It was harder than he thought it would be to get Madison alone, she was always with someone else. This was making it difficult for him to make her death look like an accident. He'd be patient and wait for the opportune moment. Until then, he needed to keep searching.

If the rain let up some tonight, he might be able to sneak back over to the house but it was doubtful. He reached over, turned on the radio, and stared out the window at the rain while drinking his beer.

Chapter 11

Madison rolled over and felt for Samantha Jo, but she was not in the bed. She glanced at the clock; it was 7:30 a.m. She'd slept right through the early evening and into the night. She felt exhausted still and wished that the last three days had just been a bad nightmare and that she was back home in her own bed.

Samantha Jo came out of the bathroom and, with a chipper voice, smiled and said, "Good mornin'! I didn't want to wake y'all yet, you were sleeping so sound. How are ya feelin'?"

"I'm fine. How are you feelin'? I was worried about you yesterday. Did you get up at all?"

"I'm sorry, honey. I was just so upset and overwhelmed with everything that's happened that I didn't want to leave the bed. Did y'all make it out to the stables yesterday?"

"Yeah, I went out there and met with Loretta. She was very nice and gave me a few of Hazel's things that she'd left behind."

"What'd she give ya?"

"Throw me that leather saddlebag sittin' over there on the chair." Samantha Jo handed her the bag, and Madison opened it and took out everything but the keys she'd put in her purse.

"Oh my God, would y'all look at how handsome granddaddy was?"

"I know. It's a great picture of him. Why don't you take it?"

"Are ya sure y'all don't want it?"

"No, really, Samantha Jo, you should take it."

"All right then, I won't argue with you none."

"In fact, the only thing I'd like to keep, if it's okay with you, is the bag itself."

"Really, that's all ya want?"

"I'm sure."

"Well then, it's yours. Now y'all best get in the shower and get ready so we can have some time to eat before we head over to the church. Git, y'all can't go lookin' like that!" She swatted her hand towards Madison to get her moving. Samantha Jo got up, put her new treasures in her suitcase, and busied herself with getting dressed. Still sleepy, Madison stumbled her way to the bathroom.

At the Bethesda Church, Stan and Judy stood near the door, greeting people and guiding them towards the ceremony. Madison and Samantha Jo walked in and saw the casket near the front. Madison noticed right away that it was a partially open casket, showing from the chest up.

She poked Samantha Jo in the ribs and pointed towards the casket, whispering, "Can you believe they're doin' an open casket. There couldn't possibly be enough make-up in this town that could cover up what we saw two days ago!"

Samantha Jo looked at her and just shrugged her shoulders.

The two waited in a line of folks for their turn to visit the casket and give their prayers. When it was their turn, they walked up together holding hands. Hazel looked beautiful. Well, that is, as beautiful as one can look dead. She looked at peace. Stan had done wonders with her hair and make-up.

She wore a violet jacket and skirt with a cream silk scarf nicely wrapped around her neck. Madison couldn't believe it was the same body she'd view just two days earlier. Samantha Jo leaned into her and whispered, "God, she looks so peaceful and beautiful layin' there. I can't believe it."

"Me either." They both stood there in silence for a few more minutes then turned to find a seat.

Madison occasionally looked around the room to see if Lane or Leroy had crept in and hid in the back. But they hadn't. She actually half-expected to see Lane since he had been to see Travis the other day. She was happy that he didn't show. It would have just upset Samantha Jo and put an even bigger damper on the day.

She looked to her right and saw Tessa sitting next to her husband. Tessa looked over her shoulder at Madison and gave her a nasty look, shaking her head. Madison diverted her attention from the service, wondering, "Why does that woman hate us so much! Honestly! This should be a time when family comes together and forgives each other. Let bygones be bygones. Right?" Clearly, things didn't work that way for either of these families.

The service was nice and short. Hazel didn't have many close friends. After living like a hermit for so many years on the farm with her grandfather, there wouldn't have been too many people that would've known her well enough to give a eulogy.

When it was over, the procession followed the hearse out to the cemetery, and she was buried right next to Jethro. Again, things seemed to move along rather quickly. By noon, all was said and done. They'd buried their grandmother and said their farewells just as they had intended. There was talk of Tessa having everyone over for a luncheon, and both Madison and Samantha Jo looked at one another and in unison said, "I don't think so." It was clear that Tessa wanted nothing to do with them, leaving them to feel extremely unwelcome.

Travis approached both women at the cemetery after the casket was lowered and said, "How are y'all holdin' up?"

"We're fine, I guess," said Samantha Jo. "Thank you so much for comin'. I'm sure it would've meant a lot to our grandmother."

"She was more than just a client. She was a very loving and caring woman. Will the two of you be joining everyone over at Tessa's for the luncheon?"

Madison shook her head and said, "I don't think that's such a good idea. Tessa is not very fond of either one of us, and we're not lookin' to upset her anymore than she already is."

"Oh, right. I'd forgotten about that."

"We talked about it earlier, and I think we're just going to head back to the hotel and change before we hit the road and drive to the beach for a few days."

"I understand completely. The beach will be a good little get away for both of ya. Y'all be back in time on Monday, correct?"

"We'll be there."

"Good, then at least let me escort you two lovely ladies back to your car."

"You two go on ahead. I'll catch up to you in a minute," Madison said.

Samantha Jo put her arm under Travis's and they began walking back.

Madison knelt down near her grandfather's gravestone and closed her eyes. "Grandpa, why'd it all have to be this way? Why? Our whole family is crazy and always fightin' and now I think someone is out to get Samantha Jo and me. They've already killed Hazel, and I'm really frightened!" She felt tears roll down her cheeks and watched as they hit the ground.

She didn't know why she felt the urge and sudden need to talk to her grandfather. After all, wasn't he partly responsible for all the craziness from the beginning? Kissing her index finger, Madison rested it over his name and whispered, "It stops here, today!"

She found Samantha Jo and Travis by the car chatting while they waited for her. He gave them both a hug, wished them a safe trip, and told them to call him on his cell if they needed anything.

Back at the hotel, they decided to only take what they needed and downsized their suitcases. They shut off the lights, threw on their sunglasses, and headed east towards the ocean.

He'd fallen asleep after spending more time searching through the house. He awoke to his phone ringing late Friday afternoon. He flipped it open and sat there without saying a word. He heard a voice say, "They've left, and I don't think they'll be back for a couple days."

"Why's that?"

"They had their suitcases with them. One of them has the room until next Thursday."

"And the cameras?"

"Knocked out by the storm last night. Won't be gettin' fixed 'til Monday."

"When?"

"Tonight, 3 a.m. It's quiet then."

He hung up the phone and stared at the ceiling.

Travis stopped by the office for a short while, after leaving the luncheon, to check messages and emails. There wasn't anything pressing that needed his attention. It all could wait. Besides that, he wasn't much in the mood to address any of it. He went home, made himself a gin and tonic, and sat on his deck.

He put on some jazz music in hopes of being able to lose his thoughts. He felt relieved that Madison and Samantha Jo had left town for the weekend. At least he knew they'd be safer there than in Blackberry Creek. He swirled the ice around in his glass, stared out into the yard while thinking about nothing in particular.

He pulled out his cell to see if he'd missed any calls, more specifically, any calls from Madison. He felt confused by his interest in her. He liked her a lot, beyond a shadow of a doubt, but there was something else that he had a hard time putting his finger on. She was many things to him, and still he found that something held him back from wanting to pursue anything more than friendship with her. Thinking about it only drove him crazy and he decided to just let it be for the time being.

He remembered that Monday would come quickly, and he needed to prepare for the big meeting and make sure that he'd covered all his bases. In the morning, he would call Bud and let him know that help was coming to town. Bud's capabilities were rather limited though not by any fault of his own. Blackberry Creek, unlike the FBI, was a small town with few resources available to track down a murderer.

Travis found himself thinking about his friend Wyatt. Wyatt had decided to leave the bureau after spending his entire post-college career there. Since the passing of his father, he needed a change and found himself wanting to do something different. He had sold his place in Virginia and was moving down to Charleston to start his own private investigation business. The location was based on his love for the water and the city. He had spent some time there on an assignment and felt completely drawn to Charleston in some unexplained way.

Wyatt and Travis had become close friends in college and stayed in touch over the years even as their careers took them down different roads. Travis was happy his friend was coming to visit and wished that it could've been under different circumstances.

He reminded himself to make up the spare bedroom and set out fresh linens for Wyatt's arrival on Monday.

Chapter 12

Wyatt left his home for the last time and threw his duffle bag in the back seat of his black Renegade Jeep. He sat for a moment in the driveway, staring at his home for the last time, before throwing the clutch into reverse. He was anxious to get to Blackberry Creek and see his old college buddy, Travis. Something was going on down there, and it must be serious if Travis couldn't even give him details over the phone. He thought, "What in the hell has he got himself mixed into this time?" He was joking, of course. Nothing ever happened in Blackberry Creek, at least, not anything serious. Wyatt's job with the FBI had been full of dangerous coverts and undercover work tracking down cold-blooded scumbags. Travis's law practice was nothing compared to what he had seen over the years.

He had decided, after his father passed away several months ago from a stroke, that it was time to take a chance and start his own practice. His mother had passed away a few years prior to his father, and, being an only child, there was nothing really keeping him in Virginia. He wasn't in a serious relationship so now seemed to be as good of time as any.

Over the years, he'd dated women but the demands of the bureau made it hard to maintain the relationships, and usually the women would call it quits within a couple months. He wished for some normalcy in his life and wanted to settle down with someone. Starting a family of his own at his age was probably out of the question; however, he wasn't opposed to being with someone who already had children. In fact, he felt that he would be a good father someday if he ever had the opportunity.

He hoped that starting over in Charleston would allow him more time to do more for himself and maybe, just maybe, find that special someone to share his life with. Turning up the radio, he settled in for the drive ahead.

Samantha Jo and Madison remained at the beach until the last possible minute. Neither really wanted to go back, and yet they were both anxious to attend the meeting. They walked the beach that morning and laughed about the good times they'd shared and the fun they had the night before dancing to disco music in the hotel bar. Later, they packed their suitcases, loaded the car, and made their way back to Blackberry Creek.

Arriving with three minutes to spare, Madison and Samantha Jo sprinted towards the front gate to Travis's office. Madison glanced over her shoulder at where she'd last seen the green car. She exhaled a sigh of relief to see that it wasn't there. They walked through the front door and greeted Doris who was sitting at her desk. "Good afternoon, ladies. Y'all can just go right on in to his office," as she nodded her head in its direction.

In the office, Madison noticed immediately that Travis had moved some of the furniture around to accommodate his guests. There were seven chairs situated in a crescent shape facing his desk. Samantha Jo looked at Madison and whispered, "Who all is coming to this? The town mayor?"

Madison turned and said, "I don't know, but I'm sure whoever it is, we're not going to like it."

Madison noticed Tessa standing next to her husband, talking to Sheriff Sheldon. She looked at Samantha Jo and said, "Well, there's three of the chairs." She pointed out Bud and quietly explained who he was.

Travis was sitting behind his desk before he stood up and said, "Ladies and gentlemen, we will get started here in just a minute. There's coffee and water in the back of the room for you, and if you could please take a seat, we'll get started."

Madison sat nearest to the right side of Travis's desk with Samantha Jo on her left. Across from them, Tessa took the seat nearest the left of his desk, with Edward and Bud to her right. Just as Travis was about to speak, a voice came from the entrance of his office: "Sorry I'm late, y'all."

Everyone turned at once, and there he stood—the Devil himself. Samantha Jo looked down at the ground, and Madison could tell she was shaken. She grabbed Samantha Jo's hand and gripped it hard.

"Good afternoon, Lane. We're glad y'all could make it. If y'all take a seat, we will proceed."

Lane took the chair next to Samantha Jo's. Madison heard him whisper, "Hi, darlin'" followed by Samantha Jo's, "Hi, Daddy."

His arrival sent shivers down Madison's spine as she now knew for sure who the empty chair belonged to—the Monster, Leroy. She didn't figure he would come; he hadn't made any attempt to contact anyone about Hazel's funeral or today's meeting. Besides, the way he and Lane were fighting, it would have been unlikely to see both in the same room.

Samantha Jo sat frozen in her chair and was unable to concentrate on what Travis was explaining. She hated her father, and his presence in the room was more than she could stand. "Why did he have to come here today?" She was glad that she was leaving town after the meeting. She didn't want any trouble from him and figured if she left, he would see that. He would forget about her quickly and focus his attention on whatever he stood to gain from Hazel's death.

She began tapping her foot subconsciously and didn't notice until Madison gently put her hand on her leg. She turned her head toward Travis and tried to focus. His lips were moving, but the words sounded like Japanese to her. She took a deep breath, folded her hands in her lap, and found the strength to coherently rejoin the others.

"As y'all all are aware, Hazel Walker was killed in her home upon returning and interrupting an intruder in her home. At this time, I will disclose to you the reading from both of the wills that are in question.

Tessa, Hazel left you the remaining pieces to the Sawyer family china that she'd received upon your parent's death. She also left you a few pieces of jewelry." He patted a box sitting on his desk before continuing. "And lastly, a letter written for you."

Tessa just made a huffing noise and looked the other way.

"Samantha Jo and Madison, there is a small life insurance policy of 10,000 dollars to be split equally between the two of you. I will need your signatures before you leave today and will take care of the details with the insurance company to have your checks sent to you."

Neither Samantha Jo nor Madison cared about the money. And, as far as they were both concerned, the treasures they'd been given by Loretta were enough.

Madison looked at Travis and asked, "What about the horses? What will happen to them?"

"Hazel's last wishes were for Loretta to keep them. She may do as she pleases. By that meaning she can keep them or sell them; it's up to her."

Madison nodded her head in understanding. She was glad Loretta was getting the horses. She obviously loved horses, or she wouldn't run a boarding house for them. No, they were in good hands, and Madison felt relief in knowing so.

"Now Lane, as for you and your brother Leroy, you will be given five of the twenty-one properties owned solely by your father. The two of you will decide on your own how y'all split them up amongst yourselves. However, before the titles are handed over to y'all, there is one more thing we need to address and resolve."

"What sort of thing are y'all talkin' about, Mr. Jackson?" asked Lane.

"In the first will, it was not disclosed as to whom the properties should go to. However, in the second will signed by Jethro . . ."

"You mean, the forged one?" asked Lane. "Because if that's the one y'alls referrin' to, it's wrong!"

"I'm not sure what y'all mean by wrong, Mr. Walker?"

"It's forged, Goddammit!"

"Well sir, that's where you're wrong. It is not forged. It is a real signature by your father. He was the one who decided in the end which of the properties he'd give to y'all."

"I'm not talkin' about the properties Mr. Jackson; I'm referring to the first one that said me and my brother was to receive a lump sum of money!"

Madison began to get antsy and uncomfortable in her chair. Fucking bloodsuckers! It was ALWAYS about money with them. "My God," she thought to herself. "How could I possibly have come from the same DNA? It just isn't possible."

"Lane, as I mentioned, the will had been changed at your father's request, witnessed by both his attorney and a notary. I'm afraid it's as official as can be and stands as is."

Lane shook his head in complete disagreement, and Madison noticed his face turning red. It was a good thing Bud was in the room. Travis was smart to have him present.

"Now if I may continue, we are not done. Hazel's will has a clause or an addendum, if ya will. And it states that if her death is by any other cause other than by nature or age itself, all disbursements of the properties shall remain untouched until said death is resolved. If her death is determined to be anything other than of natural causes, then all properties, along with the sixteen others, will be automatically given to the city of Blackberry Creek to do as they see fit."

Hazel knew there was a looming threat of her life being in danger and the clause was her way of having the last word.

"This is real funny! Y'all gonna sit there and tell me that because that old bag was murdered, I gotta wait to see if I get my properties or not? What the hell kinda shit is this?"

"If Hazel is found to be murdered, then all properties are given to the city. What I'm saying is that her death appears to be a murder until an investigation proves otherwise."

Madison's ears perked up. "Did I hear him correctly? An investigation?" Her head became a ping pong ball, looking back and forth from Lane to Travis then back across the room to Bud.

"So what y'all tellin' me is that because she was murdered, I get nothin'?"

"If that's how y'all choose to look at, then yes. Now, the only way that clause can be overturned is by actually catching the murderer to prove everyone's innocence. Sheriff Sheldon here is still conducting his investigation, and we are close to having this resolved very shortly."

Travis knew he was lying when he said it, and so did Bud. They were stalling in hopes that Wyatt might be able to assist with things where they had gotten stuck. Even though he'd left the bureau, he still had access to information and gadgets that both Bud and Travis hoped would find the killer. In addition, they'd hoped that if both Lane and Leroy had decided to attend the meeting, one might flip on the other and draw out the person responsible.

Lane stood up from his chair and said, "I'm not listenin' to anymore of this bullshit! My daddy worked hard his whole life and those properties belong to me, not the city or anyone else, for that matter. What about the money she'd been left by my daddy? Where's that goin', to the city as well?"

"I'm sorry, Lane, but I can't discuss that with y'all?"

"Oh, really! And why's that? You've been talkin' 'bout what everyone else in this room is gettin' in front of us all. Where's the money goin' to, Mr. Jackson?"

"Lane, I can understand y'alls frustration and bein' upset. These things are never easy for loved ones to hear. But the money portion of Hazel Walker's estate has specific instructions to only be discussed confidentially with the party involved. I'm afraid that's all I can or will say at this time."

Lane pushed his chair out of the way, hollering, "Y'all are gonna regret this!" as he left the room.

Tessa stood up and Edward followed. She looked at Travis and said, "I think I've heard enough for one day. Good day, Mr. Jackson." Travis handed her the box and letter as they left.

Once Tessa and Edward left, all that remained in the room were Madison, Samantha Jo, Travis, and Bud.

Bud pulled up a chair closer to the two women and said, "Ladies, I'm sorry y'all had to come down here under these circumstances." He looked at Madison and said, "M'am, forgive me for my behavior the other day out at your grandma's. Travis here and I have been workin' to find out what really happened and who might have been involved."

"I'm sorry, Sheriff, but isn't it obvious?"

"True as that may seem, Madison, we need more proof than what we've got at this time. I know that you and your cousin have experienced some unpleasant events since y'all arrived in town, and we've been doin' all that we can to keep an eye out for ya."

Samantha Jo hadn't said a word yet. She sat in her chair motionless since Lane had left the room. She wanted to bolt and get the hell outta that town as fast as she could. She realized right then that Madison had been right all along. Their very presence in town was dangerous. Hazel had been killed, and her father's absurd and grotesque behavior was proof that he was dangerous and only after one thing.

She looked down at her watch and noticed the time. "Madison, I need to get going back to the hotel so I can make my flight."

"Oh my God, I almost forgot."

The two ladies stood up, and Madison turned to face Travis and Bud. "Just one more thing: do you really think this Wyatt friend of yours will be able to help in some way?"

"It can't hurt, Madison"

"I suppose not."

"Look, here are directions to my house," Travis said as he handed her a piece of paper. "I'd like for you to come over tonight for dinner so I can introduce y'all to Wyatt, and together we can fill him in on what we do know so far. It will save more time that way, and he can get right to work. The sooner the better."

"I hope you're right. I'll be over after Samantha Jo leaves for the airport. Oh, and Bud?"

"Yes, m'am?"

"I'm sorry if I was hasty towards you the other day. I want you to know I appreciate your help in finding our grandmother's killer."

"It's quite all right. Let me walk you two ladies out to y'alls car."

They arrived back at the hotel by four. Samantha Jo walked in first with Madison behind her. She set her suitcase on her bed and hurriedly began running about to pack the things she'd left behind. Her flight left at 8 p.m., and she was gonna have to hurry if she was going to make it to the airport in time. She still had about a two hour drive ahead of her.

Samantha Jo was done and ready to leave in only a few minutes. She walked up to Madison, put her hands on her arms, and said, "I don't like leavin' ya here like this. It's not safe here, Madison, and I wish y'all would reconsider leavin'."

"I'll be fine. Besides, I won't be alone—I have Travis and Bud to look out for me."

"Madison, this is no time to joke around. Y'all know things is bad here. Lane is in town, and I think he's the one that's been followin' us, tryin' to scare the daylights out of us. Please, please be careful, cuz!"

"Samantha Jo, I am gonna be fine. I can't leave just yet. I need to know the truth about what happened to Hazel. I can't explain it other than that I feel an obligation to do it."

"Honey, is that obligation worth riskin' y'alls life for? Really?"

"If I don't, we'll both spend the rest of our lives lookin' over our shoulders wonderin'. Look, I'm gonna be fine. I want you to text me when you get to the airport. Promise?"

"Yeah, I will."

They hugged one another before Samantha Jo picked up her things and left.

Samantha Jo checked out down below in the lobby and loaded her car. They had used her car for the trip to the ocean, and she realized she would need gas before making it too far. She pulled out and headed towards Pigeon Creek, looking up in her rearview mirror every so often to make sure she was not bein' followed by that green car.

She found a gas station just outside of town and pulled in to fill up. She was thinking, while fillin' the car, "So far, so good; no green car. Just make it to the airport, Samantha Jo, and don't look back. Drive, girl!" She went inside to pay and grab a Diet Coke and a snack before returning to her car.

"Damn," she thought. "I shudda used the bathroom back at the hotel. I ain't never gonna make to the airport." She set the things in her car, grabbed her purse and keys, and locked the car doors. She went back inside and asked where their restrooms were. The gentlemen behind the counter handed her a key and told her they were around the side of the building, pointing in their direction.

Samantha Jo walked around the building towards the bathroom. There was still no sign of the green car. There were many cars off to the other side of the gas station that looked like they were having repair work done. What she didn't notice was the car parked on the side of the road just before the entrance to the gas station.

Leaving the bathroom to return the key was the last thing she remembered.

Lane had been waiting for her and hit her over the head with his crowbar as she exited the bathroom. His intentions were not to kill her, not yet anyway. He wanted information, and he wanted to know what she and Madison knew.

They'd been up to something, he was sure of it, and he wanted answers! "Great, now I'll have to wait till she wakes up," he mumbled. As usual his plan had not been thought through thoroughly. He got

Samantha Jo back to his tiny, seedy motel outside of town and carried her into his room.

His room was on the back side of the motel and had his own entrance to his room. He laid her on the bed and tied her hands and feet like a hog, leaving her completely immobilized. After he spent an hour watchin' TV and waitin', she started moaning and waking up.

Samantha Jo opened her eyes and saw Lane sitting on the bed next to her. She didn't say a word. He looked over and said, "Hi, honey."

"Don't y'all 'hi honey' me. What the hell are y'all doin'? Daddy? Let me go or I'll scream!"

He looked at her and said, "Y'all do that, and I'll have to hit ya again! Now hush so I can think."

"I swear y'all better let me go right now. The police will be lookin' for me soon and they're gonna find y'all. Crazy fucker!"

"I suppose your mama's expectin' ya home this evening, huh?"

Samantha Jo's eyes started to tear up. What the hell was he up to? "I swear, if he lays a hand on my mama or Shelby Lynn, I'll kill the son of a bitch myself!" she thought.

"Ain't she!" he screamed.

She nodded her head yes.

"Well then, we'll just have to take care of that, won't we?" He reached into her purse and pulled out her cell phone. He scrolled through her contacts, found her mother, and texted: Decided to stay with Madison a while longer. Be home in a few days. XOXO

"She'll never believe anything y'all type!"

"Oh, we'll see about that!"

Samantha Jo fought back the tears and laid there in terror. She wasn't gonna give him the pleasure of seeing her cry. No way. Deep down, her gut knew, "I'm gonna die here!"

Madison went into the bathroom to clean up and get ready to head over to Travis's for dinner. She was anxious to meet Wyatt, hoping he would be able to help solve her grandmother's murder and possibly put to rest the insanity of her family. She sat on the edge of her bed, wrapped in a towel, and glanced over to where she'd left her work bag and laptop. Next to it, she'd left Hazel's saddlebag. It wasn't there.

Slowly she got up and began looking frantically around the room. Maybe the cleaning lady had moved it around when she cleaned. But it was nowhere to be found. She went through her work bag and everything seemed to be in its place. Nothing was missing except for her saddlebag. She sat down and retraced her steps after the funeral on Friday.

Maybe she had put it back in the car at some point before or after the funeral. It had to be there. Yet she knew from the nauseous wave that overcame her that she hadn't taken the bag down to the car. She hadn't taken it anywhere. She knew exactly where she'd left it and now it wasn't there. She sat on the bed, staring at where she'd left the bag, and began to shake. Someone had been in their room!

She quickly threw the towel to the floor and grabbed the nearest clothes. Her hair was still wet as she grabbed her purse and a baseball cap and ran out of the room. Waiting for the elevator, she frantically hit the down arrow. "Come on, come on." Finally it stopped on the fifth floor, and she entered the elevator and hit the lobby button.

Running to her car, she dug her keys out of her purse. She stopped when she reached the car and thought, "You've got to be kidding me." There, on the driver's side, someone had spray painted "BITCH" in big black letters. She got in the car and locked the doors before starting the engine. She dug out Travis's directions. Her hands were shaking so badly she could hardly read them.

Once on the road, she dug out a cigarette and lit it. While driving it hit her suddenly—Samantha Jo. "Oh my God, Samantha Jo!" She quickly pulled off to the side of the road and dug out her phone. It was almost 6:30 p.m., and she should have made it to the airport by now. She fumbled with the phone, dropping it to the floor her hands shook so much.

She found Samantha Jo's number and called. It rang until the voicemail picked it up. She took a deep breath to make it sound as if nothing was wrong and said, "Hey, it's me. Just callin' to make sure you made it on time for your flight. Call me." She hung up the phone and waited for thirty seconds, thinkin' maybe she was in line or something and couldn't answer her call. With no reply, she pulled out back onto the road and drove to Travis's house.

As she pulled into Travis's driveway she noticed a text message had come in. She saw that it was from Samantha Jo. She gave a big sigh of relief—thank God. She read the text: "sorry I missed y'alls call. At airport will call later. XO"

"She made it," she whispered.

She ran past the black jeep with Virginia license plates and assumed it was Wyatt's vehicle. She knocked on the door and then, without hesitation, turned the knob to enter. Travis was just coming to answer the door when he looked up and saw Madison out of breath, hair still wet, and wearing her red dress from their dinner at the country club, without a bra, along with flip flops and a Nike baseball cap.

"Ah, Madison, this here is Wyatt, my friend I had mentioned to you." His face changed to a perplexed look and he said, "Is everything all right?" Pausing for a moment, she looked down at herself and realized why both men were staring at her. She touched her head and felt her wet hair. Suddenly her body began to sway, and Travis ran up to catch her before she completely passed out.

She was only out five minutes when she looked up and saw both Travis and Wyatt sitting on the coffee table next to couch where she was lying, waiting for her to come around. Wyatt had gotten a cool washcloth that he rested on her forehead while Travis had grabbed the smelling salts.

Madison sat up slowly and said, "What happened?"

Travis looked at her and said, "Y'all passed out."

Wyatt half-jokingly said, "Sometimes I have that effect on people," trying to lighten the moment.

"Madison, what's happened? You're dressed like, I don't know what, and came barreling in through the front door."

"I'm not all that sure exactly. Samantha Jo left for the airport and after I came out of the shower, I noticed that the saddlebag I got from Loretta was missing. I was positive I left it on the chair in our room next to my work bag. When I looked over it wasn't there, and I searched the entire room thinking maybe the cleaning lady moved it. It's missing! Someone was in our room while we were gone this weekend!"

Travis looked to Wyatt and said, "This is why y'all are here, my friend."

She looked at both of the men. "I guess I got so scared that I threw on what was in front of me and ran out of the room. When I got to my car, I saw that someone had spray painted 'bitch' on it in capital letters."

"Hold on a second." Travis ran to the front of the house and looked out the window. Sure enough, there on the driver's side door was the word just as she said.

"Madison, we need to call Sheriff Sheldon to come out and file a report. If someone other than the cleaning crew was in your room then you can't stay there. It's much too dangerous."

He walked into the kitchen and grabbed his cell phone to call the sheriff. It was after hours for the sheriff but this was an emergency, and he, too, wanted this case solved before anyone else got hurt.

Wyatt held out his hand and said, "I think we should start over again. I'm Wyatt Parker, pleasure to meet you." Wyatt could feel the warmth rising in his cheeks and hoped that he wasn't blushing. He was taken aback by Madison's beauty, even in her current disheveled state. For a second, he had forgotten why he was meeting her in the first place.

"Hello. Madison Slone." she said reaching out her hand to shake his.

"Madison, are you sure that someone was in your room? I'm not saying that it's not possible, but is there any doubt in your mind?"

"No, there isn't. Not after all the things that have been happening since I arrived to town."

"I hope you don't mind, but Travis filled me in some before you got here, and I understand there has been a car following both you and your cousin, is that correct?"

"Yes, but I haven't been able to get close enough to see who is driving or the plates."

Travis returned from the kitchen and said, "Bud will be here shortly. I've asked him to bring you the investigation file, Wyatt, to review and catch you up to speed on the investigation of Madison's grandmother."

Travis looked at Madison and said, "You look like you really should eat something."

"I'm not hungry, really." She glanced at the coffee table and noticed that Wyatt was drinking a beer. She pointed to it and said, "I'll have one of those if you don't mind."

Wyatt smiled and said, "I'll get ya one."

"Madison, once we are finished here, we'll follow Bud back over to the hotel to get your things. Y'all are gonna be stayin' here until you leave on Thursday, and I don't wanna hear a word otherwise."

She nodded her head in agreement. She didn't want to stay at the hotel by herself, and she felt much safer here with Travis and Wyatt.

"Bud has dispatched someone to go and talk with the folks at the hotel; we'll meet up with them there and see if they've found any leads."

Wyatt came back from the kitchen with a turkey sandwich and a beer for Madison. "Here, you really should try and at least eat something before we go since we won't be having dinner tonight."

"Thank you." Madison took a long swig of her beer then picked up half of the sandwich and took a bite. She didn't feel hungry in the least even though the last time she'd eaten was earlier that morning before she had left the beach, but it tasted good and she found herself devouring the entire sandwich. She finished her beer while they waited for Bud to arrive.

There really wasn't much for him to do other then get a picture and Madison's brief statement. It didn't take long before they were all heading back over to the hotel in Wyatt's Jeep. Bud mentioned he had a stop to make and would meet them there shortly.

Wyatt had been to Blackberry Creek many times to visit Travis and was pretty familiar with the town. Madison sat in front with Wyatt, and Travis climbed into the back. "Which hotel were you stayin' at?" he asked as he backed out the driveway.

"The Comfort Inn."

Travis leaned forward and asked, "Have you spoken with Samantha Jo since she left the hotel?"

"I stopped to call her on my way to your house, and she texted me back that she was at the airport."

"That's good news. She's better off not staying in town just as I think y'all should go home too."

"Travis, I . . ."

"I know, Madison, I get it. You don't need to explain it to me. Did Samantha Jo know about the hotel room, though?"

"No. I didn't notice it 'til after she'd left and I wouldn't want to freak her out anymore than she is. She was pretty quick to get out of here after seeing Lane at the meeting today."

"Right. I figured that may have some impact on her."

Wyatt looked over at Madison and said, "How long are you stayin' in town for?"

"I leave on Thursday afternoon to head back."

"Where are y'all from?"

"Minnesota."

"Ah, I thought I detected a bit of a Midwestern in your voice."

Madison just smiled. She hated the Midwest. By comparison with those who'd been born, raised, and spent their entire life in the Midwest, she didn't feel she came close to sounding like them.

At the hotel, Bud's deputy, Tate Malby, was already there and questioning the staff at the front desk. Travis quickly introduced Tate to Wyatt, and the men shook hands.

Wyatt asked, "Have ya got anything yet to go on?"

"Nah. We're still tryin' to figure out who was on staff on all weekend, includin' the cleanin' crew and front desk staff."

"What about video surveillance? I noticed a couple cameras when we walked in?"

"Ah, the damn things have been out since the storm we had last Thursday evenin'. There's nothin' there to look at from 6:04 p.m. Thursday until now. They got 'em fixed today."

Bud arrived and joined the conversation.

Madison stood off to the side, listening to all the conversations around her, and saw how quickly Wyatt dove right in and began doing his job. She hadn't taken too much notice of him when she reached Travis's house. She was so distraught by the time she'd gotten there that she'd barely acknowledged his presence before passing out.

Now, looking at him, she noticed how handsome he really was. She thought back to his comment about having that effect on people and smiled. He had a dry and witty sense of humor much like hers. She, too, sometimes entered humor into stressful situations to ease the tension. She liked that a lot and felt a good sense of humor was important if you were going to survive in life. Not many people understood her humor.

Wyatt was wearing a white, button-down oxford shirt with the top two buttons left undone and the sleeves rolled up to his elbows. His jeans were a pair of faded, old Levi's with holes at each knee, and he had a pair of men's thong sandals on. She caught herself giving him the up-and-down look and stopped to admire his butt with her head slightly cocked to the side.

Feeling eyes upon her, Madison glanced over to see Travis watch her checking out his friend. He said nothing and turned his head back to the conversation with Bud, Tate, and Wyatt. She thought, "What am I doing? I just got caught checking out Wyatt's ass!" She knew it wasn't the time or the place, but she found herself helplessly stealing another moment to check him out.

Wyatt stood about 6'3" and was proportion in weight to his build.

Not too skinny and not too husky. His upper body was somewhat built, and she figured he lifted weights or had some sort of workout routine. He had dark hair that was shaved like that of a Marine and wore a day-old shadow on his face.

She noticed his eyes were a deep blue like the ocean, and she found herself wanting to fall deeply into them. Her thoughts were interrupted when Wyatt turned to her and said, "Let's go up to your room so I can dust for some prints near the area you last remember leaving the bag and have a quick look around."

Once in the room, Wyatt set down a black, hard-covered case and took out what looked like a huge make-up brush and a spray bottle filled with some substance. Bud and Travis had come up too, leaving Tate downstairs to continue talking with the hotel manager.

"Where was it you last saw the bag," Wyatt asked.

Madison pointed: "Over here on the chair. I'd left it sitting right next to other bag there."

"What's in this other bag?"

"It's my work bag; I have a couple work files and my laptop in there."

"And nothing was taken from there?"

"Not that I noticed, but I didn't spend too much time checking to be honest. I was pretty freaked out. When I realized the other bag was gone, I bolted out here and went straight to Travis's."

With that, Wyatt began dusting for prints, taking samples from the arms on the chair, the handles on Madison's work bag, and the file folders inside. He thought that if it was Lane or Leroy, they would have checked through everything of Madison's; what they were looking for, he didn't know yet. He dusted all the door handles.

When they were done, he put strips taken from the dusting into a protective, sealed envelope and said, "I'm gonna courier these tomorrow up to a buddy of mine at the Washington Field Office and see if we can identify any prints other than yours and Samantha Jo's. Bud, do y'all have the original report for the murder investigation that I can review tonight? I'll get it back to ya in the morning?"

"I've got it down in the squad car, be happy to let ya see it. Take your time with it; we're all hopin' y'all can help us make some heads or tails of this situation."

"Well, I think I'm done in here; let's head back downstairs to see if we can learn who was workin' this weekend and go from there."

Travis looked over and said, "Madison, why don't we take your things down with us now. You won't be stayin' here any longer, it's too dangerous." Travis wasn't much of an investigator, but he did care about Madison's safety.

"Hold up, Travis!" Wyatt exclaimed. "If someone took the trouble to actually break into the room while the women were gone, that means they were lookin' for somethin. Right?"

"Right."

"Well, it would seem that they obviously didn't find what they were lookin' for, and the only thing missin' is a personal item of Madison's—the saddlebag she'd received last week. Madison, did y'all have anything in the bag?"

"No, it was empty. I was going to pack it with my things to bring home."

"The only item missing, as far as we can tell, is a personal effect. And the writing on Madison's car was also a personal message to her, assuming the person who was in the room also left the message on her car."

Travis turned back to Wyatt and said, "What are ya gettin' at, then?"

"What I'm sayin' is that we should leave most of Madison's things here to see if this person decides to come back again. Now that the cameras are workin' again, we might be able to catch them in the act."

Madison shrugged her shoulders and said, "Fine, but let me just grab a few things to take with me, and if you gentlemen will all excuse me for a minute, I'd like to change out of these clothes." The outfit she'd thrown on looked quite ridiculous and she wanted to change.

"We'll wait for ya in the hall," said Wyatt.

Back downstairs, Deputy Malby had gotten a list of all the names of the people that had been on duty over the weekend and would come back in the morning to interview them. The hotel manager said he would call each one in to be there by 10 a.m. Wyatt took the investigation folder from Bud, and they all left the hotel with a plan to reconnect the next day.

He sat on his chair with a cold beer, holding the saddlebag. He knew Madison would find it missing, and it was exactly the message he wanted to send to her—I can get to you no matter where you are, bitch!

He rubbed his fingers over the initials that had been etched into the leather: JBW. Madison hadn't even noticed the lettering when she first held the bag; she was more interested in its contents at the time. Inside the bag was a worn tag that read: Walker Saddle and Bridle Shop.

He took a drink of his beer and looked out the window, wondering why his brother had come to town. He'd seen him walk out of the attorney's office shortly before Tessa and Edward. What was he doin' in town, and, more importantly, what did he find out at that meeting? Was it possible he too knew something about the bonds? In fact, maybe Lane knew more than he thought he did. And maybe, just maybe, Lane would lead him right to them.

He decided to keep an eye out for him and follow him for a while longer to see what he was actually up to. He was getting bored with Madison. She annoyed him more than anything. He knew she'd take refuge with others; if she didn't than she was a dumber bitch than he'd figured her for.

Madison was exhausted and tired from all the events that just occurred and wanted to be alone. She excused herself once back at

Travis's, and he showed her to her room. He had a four bedroom home, two of which were guestrooms, one an office and study, and then the master bedroom.

She sat in bed for a moment then reached for her purse, taking out the keys she'd stashed away from the saddlebag. Sitting there with the keys in her hand, she began wondering if this was what whoever had broken into her room wanted? She was glad she'd kept them separate from the bag, but she also knew that if whoever it was wanted the keys, they'd be back.

Travis was tired and decided that he, too, should get some rest. He gave Wyatt a hug and said, "I'm really glad y'all here. It's good to see ya."

"I'm happy to help. This is all a bit of a mystery to me right now especially with the events that have taken place this evening. I'm gonna stay up a while and try to familiarize myself as best I can. We need to move quickly here to cover a lot of ground. The murderer has a huge jump start on us all."

"I'll see ya in the morning. Good night."

Once in bed, Travis laid there and thought about how he'd seen Madison check out Wyatt earlier in the evening. He knew women found Wyatt attractive. They always did back in college. He had a way about him that women found irresistible.

Wyatt's last long-term relationship had been with a woman he'd met while they were at Harvard. They broke up shortly after graduation when Wyatt decided to work for the FBI. She had been looking toward their future: being together, raising a family, and buying the white house with the picket fence. They both realized quickly that he couldn't give her that nor was he ready to settle down.

Over the years, he knew Wyatt to date periodically but also knew the demands of his profession and his passion for it yielded his chances of having a long-term relationship. Lying there, he felt a sudden twinge of jealousy over catching Madison looking at Wyatt. Had she done the same with him? Had she looked at Travis with the same interest when he wasn't looking?

He didn't like the notion of being jealous at all. That was definitely not his style, and yet, he couldn't figure out why he felt it. He'd thought a lot about Madison since he first met her and was extremely fond of her. Why couldn't he bring himself to want more with her? More importantly, why the jealous thoughts now? Wyatt was one of his best friends, and he would never stand in his way of happiness. Besides, Madison was leaving in just a few days to head back home, and Wyatt would be on his way down to Charleston.

He decided to let things be for the moment and get some rest. He had to go into the office in the morning and get caught up since he'd been out the last couple days, and Madison would be safe with Wyatt.

Wyatt began going through the police report as well as the information Travis had given him on the events since Madison and Samantha Jo's arrival to town. He started a list based on the facts he decided were credible.

FACTS:

1) Doors were locked when crime unit found Hazel Walker
2) No sign of forced entry at the home (visit self to see if anything different than report, prints)
3) 2 wills from Hazel
4) 2nd will leaving property to Lane and Leroy to share – no money
5) Hazel's neck cut from ear to ear – body laid back on bed?
6) Nothing of monetary value missing from home?
7) Green car following Madison (talk to Bud about car)
8) Check out property listed in town (check for prints)
9) Break-in to Madison's room – Saddle Bag missing (Who and How)
10) Madison's car vandalized – BITCH (personal???)
11) Money left in estate – to whom??? (talk to Travis)

To Do:

1) Courier prints from hotel room in the morning to Mikey.
2) Meet up with Tate Malby at hotel in the morning for interviews

After four hours of reviewing and three beers later, he felt he had a place to begin in the morning. For now, both his body and mind were exhausted.

Chapter 13

Samantha Jo opened her eyes and heard the TV in the background. Lane saw her wake up and said, "I got y'all somethin' to eat and some coffee. I'll untie your hands so you can eat but only on the condition you don't try anything stupid!"

She nodded and tried to speak, but her mouth was dry and she started going into shock. She was frightened that she would never make it out alive and even more scared for her daughter's safety. She was starting to fade into the deepest and darkest places of her imagination. "I mean it. Y'all scream or try anything stupid and Shelby Lynn . . ."

"Please don't hurt her!" she cried. "I'll do whatever y'all ask just don't hurt her."

Lane untied her hands and retied the rope around her ankles. Better safe than sorry, he thought.

Samantha Jo rubbed at both of her wrists. Her arms were numb from being tied behind her back. The rope had dug into her skin and left indentations on both arms. She sat up and adjusted herself with her back to the headboard.

Lane placed a bagel with cream cheese and a cup of coffee in front of her. She nibbled at the bagel as if to please him but had lost all her appetite and will to fight. It was as if she had given up hope. Lane looked over and said, "Y'all better eat up. This here ain't no restaurant, and I don't intend on spendin' a dime on ya or day longer with ya than I have to!"

Samantha Jo's eyes began to tear up as she thought to herself, "He's really going to kill me, too. My own father." Her hands trembled terribly as she tried to hold the bagel up to her face, smearing the cream cheese across her cheeks and chin and getting it caught in her hair. She brushed the hair away from her face and felt a large bump on the side of her head where he'd hit her the day before.

Her bed smelt of human urine, and she soon realized that she had peed herself during the night. She felt a wave of hopelessness overtake her. She slumped over to her side and fell fast asleep.

Lane had panicked after he had brought Samantha Jo back to the hotel. What was he plannin' to do with her once he was done? There was the strong possibility that she didn't know a thing about the information he was lookin' for. Making her talk wouldn't be a problem if he used her daughter as the pawn. How did he plan to keep her quiet, though, while he searched for the money?

He was angry with himself that he hadn't a better plan in place, but he was desperate to find what he felt was his entitlement. "That fucking attorney Mr. Jackson sat there in his chair tellin' me I don't get shit because of how the old bat died. And to top it off, I gotta split it with Leroy. Who the hell did she leave all that money to?" he thought. His head hurt as it often did from the massive migraines he'd suffered from his whole life.

He needed to rest and the only way to keep an eye Samantha Jo was to knock her out as well. At least, until he could figure out when and where to get rid of her. He'd crushed up a couple sleeping pills and laced her coffee and bagels with them. She'd be out for hours. He lied down on his bed and put the TV on mute.

Madison rolled over onto her side and squinted to read the clock; it was almost 9 a.m. She'd been so stressed out and tired from everything that happened the day before that she'd slept in some. She sat on the edge of the bed, dangling her feet, when she smelled bacon and coffee. She threw on a pair of shorts and walked down the hall to the kitchen. Wyatt had his back to her, scrambling eggs, and turned when he heard her feet come padding into the dining area.

"Good Mornin'," he said.

"Morning."

"I figured you were pretty tired, so I was gonna let ya sleep just a bit longer."

"Thanks."

"Would you like fresh-squeezed orange juice or coffee with your breakfast? I made both."

"Um, coffee would be great."

She pulled out a bar stool from the center island and sat down, staring out the window to the backyard and thinking that, yes, coffee would be great. Madison had a hard time moving in the morning, much less having a conversation, until she had her coffee.

She glanced back over at Wyatt and noticed, "My God, he's even attractive in the morning, and he cooks!" She admired his muscular legs and then his butt again. He had on a pair of khaki cargo shorts and a white t-shirt. He was handsome, and she found herself lost in lustful thought, wondering what his body would feel like next to hers.

Wyatt turned around to finish the eggs and smiled to himself. He'd noticed her small, perky breasts bouncing slightly as she walked into the room. There was something about Madison that was beginning to drive him crazy. He was happy that he would have the day to spend with her even if it was work related.

He pulled two plates down, filled both with eggs, bacon, and toast, and finished each with a fresh strawberry. He placed Madison's plate in front of her with a hot cup of coffee and said, "Y'all might want to eat up. It's supposed to be another hot one today, and we have a lot to get done."

"Oh. What did you have in mind? And where's Travis?"

"He left already for the office this morning, but we'll stop by later to see him. I need to get to the post office so I can FedEx the prints from the hotel to my buddy Mikey at the Bureau, and we have to be back at the hotel by 10 a.m. for the interviews. That really shouldn't take too long, and I believe Officer Malby will be joining us."

"Should I be there while you're interviewing these people? Won't that seem a bit awkward with me in the room?"

"It will, and that's why I want you to stay by the pool if ya can and try to remember anything else that y'all haven't already told me. We can discuss it later at lunch."

"Anywhere else we need to be today, then?" Madison knew he'd want to see Hazel's house and the crime scene, and she wanted to be there when he did.

"Well, I reckon we should all head back over to your grandmother's house so I can take a look around. I understand if that is too hard for ya; I could drop you off at Travis's then?"

"No, I want to go with you. Really, I've seen it once; a second time won't make much difference."

"Well then, y'all better eat up because we need to get on the move here in about twenty minutes."

Madison finished her breakfast and took her coffee back to her room to get ready. She could shower and be ready in minutes. Besides with the heat that'd set in, it was easy to throw her hair into a ponytail and put on a baseball cap.

They drove straight to the post office, and she waited in the car while Wyatt ran in to send off his package. She looked around to see if the green car was in sight.

Thinking back, when was the last time she saw it? She counted back the days and events and remembered, "Thursday! It had to be then, that's the day I went to the stables, got the saddlebag, and drove into town to see Travis." Where was that damn car hiding? She hadn't seen it in almost five days (granted she was gone for two of them), but she was sure the car had seen her. Not seeing the car made her more nervous and left her always wondering when and where it was going to appear.

It bothered her that things were moving so slowly with the investigation. Why was that? She had a hard time understanding what it was that Bud and his crew were missing that they couldn't find the killer on their own and why they were taking advice from an FBI agent. Former, that is.

Wyatt opened the door and hopped in, startling Madison. "Y'all all right?"

"Yeah, I'm fine. I guess sometimes I get a little too wrapped up in my thoughts is all."

"I know the feeling!"

While at the hotel, Madison sat outside in a shady spot near the pool. She pulled over a lounge chair and drew her dark shades down to her face. She wondered who was inside and what they were saying. Madison had seen Officer Malby as she walked through the lobby towards the pool in a small room with the sign **Personnel Only**. Inside, she had noticed at least ten people standing there. She'd figured they were the staff being interviewed.

She hadn't recognized any of them, but then again, why would she? She and Samantha Jo had not spent much time at the hotel, and when they were there they stayed in their room. She hadn't talked to any of them, except for the nice man that gave her the directions to the stables last Thursday. She thought she could remember him again if she had to.

Thinking about someone being in their room gave her an eerie feeling. That person could have come in anytime. They could've come in the middle of the night then too, if they wanted, and killed them. Her mind began racing with the many ways a person could do that and do it without anyone knowing.

He could've slit their necks, too, and there wouldn't have been a sound. He could have smothered them with a pillow or . . . "Jesus Christ, Madison, get a grip on yourself. You're gonna make yourself crazier than you already are." Obsessing about it wasn't going to help.

She thought back to the saddlebag—why would they want it? And why was it the only thing missing? She began tracing back and thinking about the facts without trying to scare herself more. Thank God for Travis and Wyatt. At least she felt safer with the two of them in her company.

Madison grabbed a piece of paper from her purse and began her own list of facts:

1) 4th Key on ring
2) Green car following them
3) Lane at the Monday meeting
4) Hazel's death itself – how and why?
5) Encased flag and medal missing
6) Break in to hotel room
7) Saddle bag missing

She paused for a moment and remembered the meeting on Monday. Travis had said that the money portion of the estate was intended for someone else and only to be discussed with that someone else. That meant the person had not been in the room. Who had been missing?

There had been an empty chair . . . Leroy? No, it couldn't be. There was no way in hell she would've left all the money to him. But he was the only one that could've been missing. After all, Lane was there. Was Travis expecting Leroy? Had Leroy contacted him, too?

Who was the money for? She hadn't given it any thought since the meeting but now she couldn't stop herself from wondering who the hell was getting the money. She made one more entry to her list:

8) $$$ from estate – who?

It was noon, and there was still no sign of the green car as Madison and Wyatt drove back towards town.

"Are you hungry?"

"Not really, I'm still full from the breakfast you made. Thanks by the way. I can't remember the last time someone made me a homemade breakfast like that."

"You're kidding me, right?"

Madison shook her head.

"Well then, it was my pleasure."

They stopped at Travis's office for a short visit to check-in and say hello. "So what's next on your list today, you two? Where are y'all headin' off to next?" Travis asked.

"Madison and I are going to stop back at Hazel's house and take a look around. I need to compare the notes from the original report to see if I can find anything they may have missed."

"Madison, are you up for that? It looked like it was pretty hard on you the last time we went out there?"

"I'm fine. Right now I have more questions myself, and I just want to put this whole damn thing behind me."

"Be careful, y'all, and I'll see ya back at the house tonight. We can throw those steaks on that we didn't cook last night and relax."

"Sounds great, Travis. We'll see y'all then. Oh, and if Bud calls, give him my cell number would ya?"

"Sure thing."

Back in the jeep, Madison asked Wyatt if he'd found out anything from the hotel staff. "Not really. All the employees were accounted for and their duties performed. I wish those damned cameras had been working. I'm really hopin' Mikey can help us out with the prints. He'll be able to run the prints pretty quickly and get back to me by morning."

"So what you're sayin' is that it was a waste of time then, this morning?"

"No, not exactly. There was one employee that was working the front desk over the weekend not present this morning."

"Well, where was he? I thought everyone had been rounded up?"

"No. Evidently they couldn't reach him. One of the other employees said that he'd left town on Sunday evening after his shift. The manager looked, and he's not on duty again until Thursday. He's the only one we've yet to account for."

Madison didn't say much after that. She thought about the nice gentleman that'd given her directions and wondered if it was the same person. He seemed so nice. Was it possible he was involved somehow? She didn't know him any more than he knew her. There were so many loose ends and questions mounting by the minute; it was making her head spin.

They reached Hazel's house, and Travis paused before getting out. "I forgot to stop by the station and ask Bud for the key. We'll have to turn around."

"No we won't. I know where she kept the spare."

Wyatt looked at her and smiled, "I knew there was a reason why I brought you with me today."

They walked up the steps and around to the back. Madison found the bird house and pulled the top off. The key was there. Wyatt asked for the key and said, "Why don't you let me go in first just to be on the safe side." Madison was an independent woman and while any other day she would have said, "Bullshit", this time she handed the key to him without argument. She was beginning to like the southern hospitality and charm from these men.

Wyatt put the key in and opened the door. The cool air inside felt good considering the sweltering heat outside. He turned around, expecting Madison to be right behind him, and saw her still standing motionless at the door. He noticed her face had turned white as if she'd seen a ghost. He slowly walked back up to her, studying her. "Madison, what's wrong? What is it?"

"The . . . The . . . The . . ."

"It's okay; take your time. I know this must be hard for you."

"No, it's not that. Someone has been here. Someone's been in the house since I was here last."

"Fill me in here, Madison; how do you know that?"

"The air conditioning is on! It wasn't last week when Travis and I met the sheriff here. I know it wasn't it! Ask Travis. It was hotter than an oven in here."

Wyatt pulled his index finger up to his mouth, motioning for her to keep quiet. He pulled his gun from the back of his shorts and began creeping slowly through the house, ready to fire. He returned from the bedrooms and motioned that he'd be back in a minute. He needed to check the lower level.

Madison stood frozen in the doorway, holding her breath. The last time she was alone out back she'd heard something in the woods. This place was beginning to creep her out more and more.

Wyatt quickly returned, put his gun back to where he'd pulled it from, and said, "It's clear. If there was someone here they're gone now."

He held out his hand for Madison to grab and helped her into the house. She noticed the smell had gotten worse but at least was more tolerable with the air on. She wondered if that was the reason why whoever had been there had turned it on. She noticed the flies had been busy and multiplied since her last visit.

Wyatt called for her to come to Hazel's room. She stood in the doorway when he asked, "Was this how things looked the last time you were here? I'm referring to the room and its contents."

Madison scoured the room with her eyes. Something caught her attention and she looked at Wyatt, shaking her head.

"No, it's not. Someone has been in here moving things around again."

"Again?"

"Yeah, again. Last week when I was in the room there were items strung about the room and drawers with things hanging out of them like the killer had gone through looking for something. This time the drawers look different. A few of them were left opened last time, and now they're shut with clothes sticking out of them."

Wyatt didn't need to ask for reassurance. He believed her. From everything he'd gathered so far one thing was for sure: she was observant, a quality he admired. He went from room to room as if taking mental notes and didn't say a word. Madison wandered back out to the living room and stared at the spot on the wall where the enclosed flag had been.

When Wyatt was done, he came back out to the living room and stood next to her. He saw instantly what she was looking at. He, too, saw the dust particles clinging to the wall and the slight shadow they left behind. "Madison, what was on the wall?"

She turned to him and knew she needed to tell someone. She'd been holding back a lot of information, and maybe she was the one holding up the investigation. "It was a flag given to my grandmother when my grandfather had passed away. She had it enclosed along with his medal."

"Did you mention this to Bud? I didn't see it anywhere in his report last night when I went over it."

"I . . . I didn't. I guess I figured at the time why bother? He didn't exactly seem, at the time, that he much cared to pursue anything further with the investigation to look for her killer. So I just kept it to myself, figuring it didn't matter since we all suspect who the killer or killers might be anyway. What difference would it have made?"

"Madison, I get the feeling there's more going on here than you're telling me."

"What do you mean?"

"I mean, I think ya know more than you're telling anyone, and ya may be holding onto some crucial evidence that could help with this investigation."

"I don't know anything. In fact, I have so many questions myself that I feel as though my head is goin' to explode!"

Her eyes began to tear up out of all the anger and emotional stress. Wyatt pulled her close to him and just held her for a moment. He felt her heart pounding through her shirt against him. Her body was trembling, and he stood there with his arms around her until he felt her body give in to his and begin to relax.

He leaned back and placed his hand under her chin. "Let's get you outta here. I think we're done here."

They got back in the jeep, and Madison asked, "Wyatt, there is something else that I haven't told anyone. I wasn't sure it was anything."

"I know about the noise you heard from the woods that day if that's what you're referring to. Travis had told me about that out of concern for you and your cousin's safety."

"No, it's not that. In the saddlebag from the stables there was a set of keys that I kept and put into my purse. I couldn't figure out why they were there, and I can't seem to figure out what the fourth key belongs to." She reached into her purse and pulled the key chain out to show him. "See, each of these keys is marked but the fourth one. I've been trying to figure out what it belongs to."

"Madison, why didn't you tell anyone sooner? Do you understand this could be what the killer is looking for?"

"I hadn't thought about that. I was so concerned with trying to figure out the last key, and I was afraid if I told the sheriff he'd take the keys from me."

"Okay, Okay. I'm glad you told me. Now at least we have a motive of some sort if, in fact, this is what the killer is looking for. What does B.H. stand for?" he asked as he held the key up.

"It belongs to an old, blue house in town. There really isn't much there but things my grandparents stored over the years."

"Well, I think we should go have a look. What'da say we go there next, or would you rather go to the farm?"

"There's nothing left at the farm. Nothing, anyway, that is of any value or worth looking at. Hazel took all that she needed with her when she moved out of there. She hated going out to the farm, and I guarantee you she wouldn't of left anything there that she'd want to keep close to her."

"All right then, the blue house it is."

On the drive to the blue house, Madison and Wyatt mostly made small talk, but it was enough that both began to learn more about each other. Wyatt found himself more intrigued by the minute and yearning to spend more time in her presence, longer than he knew was possible. She would be leaving for good in forty-eight hours.

Wyatt parked the jeep in front of the house. The grass looked as though it hadn't been cut in some time, and the house was in rough shape. They walked up to the door, and Madison used the key to open it. It looked the same as it did over twenty years ago, only dustier and dirtier. The living room floor was still caved in, and she could see that the mice had taken shelter in the home as well.

Wyatt took one step in, exclaiming, "My God, what a mess!"

"I know. I told ya all they did was store things here." They walked into one of the bedrooms filled with boxes and junk piled everywhere and began searching through the boxes, not really even sure what they were looking for. Wyatt grabbed a photo and asked if it was of Madison when she was a little girl.

She turned to look at it, saw the blue dress with the white-crochet collar and said, "Nope, that's my uncle Lane, Samantha Jo's father."

Wyatt stood there, holding the picture and looking at Madison, waiting for her to laugh or say, "I'm just kidding." But she didn't. She turned around and went right back to searching. She thought to herself, "Someone has got to throw that photo away!"

After an hour of looking through boxes of old store merchandise, knick-knacks, and junk, Wyatt said, "There's nothing here; we're really just wasting our time. Besides I can't take it much longer in here with the heat. It's gotta be over 100 degrees in this house."

"I agree. She wouldn't of left anything here, either."

"What do you mean?"

"Well, whatever that key belongs to, I doubt she would of left it here amongst all this crap with the rats."

Wyatt smiled and said, "Then let's get outta here and head back to home base. Travis will be home soon, and I could use a cold beer. How 'bout yourself?"

"You're on!"

Travis got home and found Wyatt and Madison out on the deck drinking cold beers and talking. He watched them for a moment from inside and noticed Madison was actually smiling and laughing. He hadn't seen that side of her. Most of the time he spent with her seemed to revolve around Hazel's death or some other unpleasant event.

Standing there watching her, he noticed that he no longer felt jealousy but comfort in that she looked to be enjoying herself for the first time since her arrival to Blackberry Creek. He smiled to himself and headed for his bedroom to change before joining them on the deck.

He sat parked in his car quite a distance away from Lane's motel room and watched through his binoculars. Lane's old, blue Chevy Malibu hadn't moved all day. In fact, the only movement at all was when he walked to the gas station and back with what he guessed was a bag of food. What was he doin' in town? He couldn't have been looking for the bonds, too, or he'd have followed in footsteps similar to his own. No, Lane was up to something else.

It frustrated and angered him that Lane had gone to the meeting the day before. What was it that he learned at the meeting that they didn't already know? What the hell was he still doing here? At this point, he was only in the way just as Madison was. He decided that Lane should move up on the list of those to be taken care of. He'd come up with a plan for him, but for now, he'd give it one more day to see if Lane made a move.

Samantha Jo slowly opened her eyes. She was extremely groggy and quickly losing track of the days and of reality. Lane saw her out of the corner of his eye and got up. He grabbed a soda and poured some in a glass for her. In it, he mixed more crushed sleeping pills. He'd also made her a laced jelly sandwich. He wanted to make sure she stayed quiet until he could figure out what to do with her.

Samantha Jo didn't even try to speak. She ate a few bites of the sandwich which he had to feed her and took a couple sips of the soda. Her eyes slowly drooped shut again, and she fell back asleep. Lane stood over her for a moment, watching her sleep. He remembered back to when she was a baby, and he'd sometimes get up and watch her in the night to make sure she was breathing. Today he stood over her making sure she kept her mouth shut.

After dinner, the three continued sitting on the deck talking into the night. Travis and Wyatt were both recalling college stories of one another while Madison listened and almost peed in her pants from laughing so hard.

Around 10 p.m., Madison began yawning. "You two have quite the stories I must say. It has been the most enjoyable evening I've had since back in Blackberry Creek, but if you'll both excuse me, it's been a long day and I need to go lie down. I think the beers have caught up with me."

Both men stood up as she did and said good night. "Thanks again Travis for everything. The dinner was delicious, and I appreciate you letting me stay here."

He smiled and said, "Madison, believe me; it's been my pleasure."

Madison went to her room and was asleep before her head hit the pillow.

Back in the kitchen, Travis loaded the dishwasher and said good night to Wyatt before heading to bed himself. Wyatt stayed out in the kitchen, finishing his beer and looking back through the police report and interviews taken earlier in the day. He pulled out his laptop and quickly sent Mikey an email:

Pull Comfort Inn inbound and outbound calls from Thursday – Sunday.

Fax to 843-799-3586
WP

He shut down his computer, finished his beer, and headed to bed. He went back over the day in his head, over Hazel's house and the keys Madison had found. He had no intentions at this time to tell Bud what she'd found. It wouldn't help to shed any new light on things. He did, however, feel obligated to tell him about the air conditioning being on as well as about the missing flag that Madison had not yet mentioned. Bud needed to know that the original report's claim that nothing was taken from the house was incorrect.

Somehow, though, he needed to find the connection between the smaller key and the murder. Something was missing in this puzzle, and somehow Madison had everything to do with it. Madison—her name ran through his head and he couldn't stop thinking about her.

He was drawn in by her smile and her eyes. They were hazel green and extremely seductive. He was convinced she had more than 100 smiles and that he'd only yet seen a few. He wished he had more time to spend with her before they both left to go their separate ways.

"Madison, Madison." He felt himself hardening at the very thought of her. "Calm down, think of something else. Baseball. Baseball's good. Did the Cubs even play tonight? Think, think, think . . ."

It was of no use; his mind returned right back to Madison. He imagined the softness of her skin touching his and longed to explore every inch of her body. She was smart, sexy, and independent with a take-no-prisoners attitude. Yet there was a soft and secret side to her he found most intriguing.

He replayed the morning in his head in the kitchen, seeing her breast bounce just enough for him to witness and her nipples hard from the cool air in the house poking into her tank top. "Madison." His body began to ache for her, and he found himself gently stroking himself and saying her name over and over in his head. With his eyes closed, he couldn't get the picture of her out of his head. He suddenly realized that she had taken a hold of him, and he was helpless.

Feeling the blood rush with more hardening, he rolled to his side pushing his head into the pillow and thrust his lower body back and forth as quietly as he could. He was physically powerless by the very thought of her and found himself ejaculating into the sheets whispering, "Madison."

Chapter 14

Madison awoke early and went out to the kitchen to make coffee. Travis was sitting there reading the paper with a cup in his hand. "Good morning. Did you sleep well?"

"I did, thank you."

She poured a cup for herself just as Travis stood up and said, "I've got to get into the office this morning for a meeting. I'm sure I'll talk with you and Wyatt later on today."

"Hey, Travis, I need to ask you something."

"Shoot."

"At the meeting on Monday there was an extra chair that no one sat in and . . ."

"And you were wondering if it was for Leroy?"

"Yes, actually I was."

"You'd be correct, then. I hadn't heard a word from him, but since Lane had stopped by my office the week before, I half-expected him to walk in too."

"I guess that's logical. But you hadn't heard from him at all?"

"No. I've never met him or spoken to him since I've known Hazel."

"You mentioned at the meeting something about the money when Lane got angry, saying that it was a private matter with the party involved."

"Yes, that's correct."

"Well, then, since Samantha Jo and I were the last ones to leave, am I to assume that person was not in the room with us?"

"Madison, I wish I could tell you who and more, but, at this time, I feel I can not divulge that person to you. Bud and I have discussed it and based on the investigation right now and all the incidents that have occurred, we feel it would be best to keep it quiet just a for awhile longer. I'm sorry, but y'all have to trust me on this one."

"I do trust you, Travis, and I trust that your decision is based on protecting everyone involved. I'm sorry, and I hope you're not upset with me?"

"Not at all. In fact, if I were in your shoes, I'd probably do the same. I gotta run." He gave her a smile and reached for his briefcase on the way to the door.

Wyatt woke up an hour later, showered, and walked out to the kitchen. He found Madison there drinking her coffee and texting on her phone. Joe had sent her a text and she thought she'd better reply now while her head was clear and she had the time. She'd scrolled through her other messages and, again, decided to deal with them once back home. She told Joe that she was fine and that she and Samantha Jo were enjoying some poolside time. She hated to lie, but there was too much going on and she didn't want to worry him or go into any details. She'd fill him in later but for now it was best to keep him at arm's length.

She looked up and smiled good morning. Wyatt poured his coffee and sat down by her. "What's on our agenda for today?" she asked.

"Well, Mikey should be getting back to me this morning with the prints and other information that I've requested he fax to Travis's office. In the meantime, how about breakfast before we leave and go into town?"

"That sounds great. I am feeling kinda hungry."

"Good, then I'll whip up some pancakes for us."

Lane was pacing back and forth in his motel room. He'd screwed up and was just now realizing how bad. His reckless and irrational behavior had been getting him in trouble for years. There had been no reason for him to abduct his daughter other than that the moment had presented itself and he had acted on impulse.

Now he was stuck with the daunting process of figuring how to get rid of her. He couldn't let her go, that was a given. She'd run straight to the police and that'd be the end of it. He had to come up with a plan and fast. Time was running out and, sooner or later, someone would find her abandoned car at the gas station.

Eventually she'd also have to answer her phone and return home. He'd noticed all the texts and missed calls before it died. No, time was running out for him, and he knew that he needed a plan and would have to leave town tonight. Staying any longer was much too dangerous.

Madison sat on the deck after breakfast and snuck a quick cigarette while Wyatt cleaned up. She sometimes enjoyed sitting with her morning coffee and a cigarette to unwind and think. She found herself thinking of Wyatt and how something about him made her stomach flutter. The way he looked at her made her feel safe and wanted. She began comparing him to Travis in her mind.

Travis was attractive, handsome, and very charming, yet she didn't feel the same around him. Her heart didn't pound profusely, and she didn't find herself sneaking a peak at his ass either. Either way, she reminded herself that tomorrow she would be leaving town and a life with either of the men was out of the question.

Wyatt came outside, interrupting her deep thought, and said, "Travis called to let me know a fax came for me. Let's run into town quick, and then we'll stop off at the hotel to check on your room and the surveillance videos."

"Let me get changed quickly, and I'll be ready."

They walked into Travis's office, and Doris was there to greet them both. "Good morning, y'all. Go right on in."

Travis handed the fax over to Wyatt, and Madison watched him while he studied it with intent. "Hmmmm," was all he muttered before saying, "We need to head over to the hotel and check on a few things there. Could you do me a favor and call Bud? Ask him if he's found out anything yet on the background of the hotel employee that couldn't be found for interviewing."

"Sure thing. I'll call ya on your cell if I hear anything back."

"Thanks."

Madison and Wyatt drove to the Comfort Inn. Wyatt was in deep thought and didn't say much at all.

"Was there anything in the fax you'd care to share?" Madison asked. "Did you find any fingerprints that would help us?"

"No, there weren't any prints from the room that we didn't already expect to find. What I mean is, there were plenty from you and Samantha Jo and the hotel cleaning staff."

"You fingerprinted them, too?"

"We had to, it was the only way to confirm who the prints belonged to. Look, Madison, I know that your father and uncle both have a history of trouble with the law . . ."

"Please do not call him my father. He has been nothing even close to a father!"

"I'm sorry; I didn't mean to upset you. Lane and Leroy both have a record and their prints are on file. We didn't find either of their prints in your room. I didn't really expect to."

"Why? Because you don't believe they're responsible?"

"On the contrary. From what we know so far, this all points in their direction; that's for sure. We just need the evidence that will prove it. No, I was alluding to the fact that I suspected whoever was in your room wore gloves."

"That would make sense but it surprises me."

"Why?"

"I honestly didn't think either would be smart enough to do so."

"Huh. Well, they did. The only other thing in the fax was a record of three calls that were made to a prepaid cell phone. That will make it impossible to trace, but the times of each outgoing call was made when Henry Arnold worked."

"Who the hell is Henry Arnold?"

"He's the only hotel employee that we can't seem to find to question, and we're just waiting for him to return to work tomorrow."

"Tomorrow? Wyatt, I am leaving tomorrow."

"I know, and, to be honest, it is probably in your best interest that you do."

"I don't feel as though I can. I mean, this whole mess just seems to get bigger, and I feel as though I have more questions now than I did a week ago. I can't leave now, I need to know what really happened and why!"

"Madison, I can't imagine all that you have been through since this whole thing started, but listen to me. Staying here is dangerous for you. You need to head back to Minnesota, and let the rest of us here solve this."

"Why? Can't you solve it with me here?"

"I didn't say that. I could, but right now, I am more concerned about your safety and knowing you're okay will allow me to focus."

"You mean I'm in the way."

"You're not in the way. In fact, you've been the one to help shed some light on things we didn't know yet. I just would feel better knowing you're safely back home with your son."

She could see the sincerity and honesty in his eyes when he spoke. She knew he was right. It was crazy and dangerous for her to stay in Blackberry Creek any longer than she already had. Deep down part of her longed to catch the next flight out, while the other part whispered for her to stay.

Checking Madison's room took only a moment. Nothing had been moved, and the cleaning staff had been told to not enter the room under any circumstances. The surveillance cameras showed nothing. Wyatt was beginning to feel extremely frustrated by the lack of urgency in the small town. He was used to it since he grew up in the south, but on the job, he needed and wanted things to move at a much faster pace. He longed for his equipment and desk back at the Bureau. He hated having to wait for others to get back to him with information he could have accessed much quicker on his own.

As they were finishing up, Wyatt's cell phone rang and he answered. Madison listened and saw his eyes widen.

"We'll be right there!"

"What is it?"

"They found Henry."

Madison and Wyatt hopped into the jeep to head towards town. "Damn I'm outta gas!"

"There's a gas station just right up the road about a mile." They turned the opposite direction of town and found the gas station.

Madison sat in the jeep while Wyatt paid inside and bought a couple of Cokes. It was still steamy hot outside, to the point where it literally took your breath away. Madison sat staring out the window when something caught her attention.

She got out of the jeep and began walking towards a row of cars parked in the far lot of the station. As she walked closer to one particular car, she saw the rental car sticker and noticed the color was the same as Samantha Jo's car.

Wyatt came out and saw the door to the jeep ajar and called for Madison. He dropped the Cokes, ran to the jeep, and began looking around. Turning, he saw her standing next to a row of cars, not hearing his voice. He ran up to her and said, "What are you doin' over here? You scared the crap out of me!"

Madison stood there and pointed at the car. "That's her car!"

"Who's?"

"Samantha Jo's. It's her car."

"Are you sure? There are a lot of cars like that on the road."

"No, I'm sure. Look, there's the rental sticker."

Wyatt looked more closely at her and saw that Madison was not backing down. She was absolutely positive and not about to budge.

Wyatt had no reason not to believe her, crazier things had happened before.

He wrote down the car's plate numbers, make, and model. "Come on Madison, let's get back to the jeep, and I'll call Bud and have him look into it."

She kept looking over her shoulder as he walked her back. Her heart sank with fear. She knew it was Samantha Jo's car, but where was Samantha Jo? The last she'd heard from her was via text when she got to the airport. But, then again, anyone could have sent that text from her phone. Her mind went to her darkest fears—Samantha Jo, she never made it home.

"Bud, I'm on my way with Madison to the station, could you do me a favor and run these plates for me? We'll be there shortly. Thanks."

"Madison, I'm sure it's just a coincidence, and she is just fine. When was the last time you heard from her?"

"Right after the meeting on Monday, she packed and left. On my way to Travis's house that night, I panicked when I realized someone had been in our room while we were gone, and I called her to make sure she was okay."

"Did you actually speak to her on the phone?"

"No, she sent a text back that she'd made it to the airport. That's the last I've heard from her."

"Is there anyone you can call to confirm she did?"

Madison began to cry. "I don't know her mother's number or new last name. Oh my God, Wyatt. What if something terrible has happened to her? I should of drove with her back to the airport!"

"Madison, whatever has happened could have very well included you if you'd been with. You can't go blamin' yourself. We're not even sure it's her car yet." Wyatt put his hand on her shoulder and tried to comfort her, but by now he was beginning to worry himself. They drove in complete silence to the police station.

By the time they got there, Bud had run the plates and was waiting for them in the lobby, looking concerned. Madison saw his face and knew in that moment that she'd been right. Samantha Jo was missing. She sat down, put her face in her hands, and began crying. How could this happen? What the hell was going on in this town? Her emotions got the better of her, and she lost herself thinking about Samantha Jo.

Meanwhile, Bud informed Wyatt that it was indeed the car Samantha Jo had rented from the airport. The rental car company been trying to reach her for the last twenty-four hours and had called the Charlotte police to report it stolen. Bud took care of the details, and the car would be returned after it was done being inspected as evidence.

"Bud, this is beginning to get out of control. First, their grandmother and now Samantha Jo is missing?" Just then he paused and thought for a moment before speaking again. "Bud, with Samantha Jo missing, and Madison probably not far down on the list, that would mean the murderer is possibly still in town?"

"I suppose it could."

"Well then, get that car towed to the station for me to inspect, and meanwhile let's have a chat with Mr. Arnold to see what he knows."

"I don't think that's going to be possible."

"Oh?"

"I didn't want to tell y'all this on the phone, but Mr. Arnold won't be doing any talking,"

"Why's that? Did he already call for an attorney and lawyer up?"

"No sir, he's dead."

Wyatt stood there for a moment then pulled Bud aside and away from Madison. She was under the distress of Samantha Jo's disappearance; the last thing she needed was to hear details of Henry's death.

"After y'all were done at the hotel yesterday, I took the liberty of running a background report on him," Bud said.

"I did the same; we found nothing at the Bureau. He has no priors."

"That's what we found as well. Still, I wanted to know where he'd run off to without his cell or no one able to find him, so I got a search warrant."

"Bud, I don't think we had enough probable cause yet otherwise I would have asked you to do the same."

"Well, by the time I was done talking with the county judge, he felt there was enough evidence to do so." He gave Wyatt a quick wink. Wyatt knew exactly what he was getting at. Small towns have their own laws and ways of doing things.

"Well, the damned thing is, once we got to his place and knocked down the door, we smelt his decomposing corpse just the same as we did at Hazel Walker's. Coroner says he's been dead since about 10 p.m. on Sunday."

Wyatt turned around when he heard, "Who's been dead since Sunday?"

Both men stood there looking at Madison without saying a word, waiting for the other. Wyatt broke in and said, "They found the hotel employee, Henry, dead. We're not sure yet why or how he's involved, but I'm willing to bet he's the one that placed the calls to the cell number I found on the call log."

Bud turned to Wyatt, and, before he could say a word, Wyatt informed him he'd requested them earlier and found a number that was called three times. Each time the number had been called, Henry Arnold had been working. Every one of the other employees all had alibis and could be accounted for during their shifts. He'd determined that with Henry working the front desk those evenings, he would've had the most freedom to make calls and allow access to rooms. It made perfect sense. He was somehow an accomplice only now that he was dead, they were back to square one trying to find out with whom.

Wyatt turned to Bud and asked him how they'd found him. Bud cleared his throat and said, "Found him slumped over his kitchen table with his neck slit from ear to ear."

Madison looked as though she were going to pass out. Bud offered to let her lay down on the cot in the break room for a bit. Wyatt waited until she was settled and handed her a glass of water before returning to Bud to go over their facts and devise a plan.

Madison lay there with her head spinning. Samantha Jo was missing, and she had no way to reach her mama. The hotel guy was found murdered just like her grandmother. Green cars following her, Lane showing up in town, people breaking into her room, and spray painting "bitch" on the side of her car. She realized the only one missing in this entire debacle was Leroy. Where was that piece of shit hiding? Things were starting to look as though Lane was the guilty party.

Her head began to pound. She dug through her purse and found a couple Excedrin to ease the pain. Her mind raced with thoughts of Samantha Jo being tortured and in pain. She couldn't stop herself from going there, and her imagination was getting the best of her. She felt completely helpless and scared. Tears fell to her pillow, and soon she fell asleep.

Wyatt wanted to see the body and inspect Henry's apartment. He went to check on Madison and let her know he'd be back soon, but she had fallen asleep and he thought it best to let her rest. After all, he didn't really want her to come with him and Bud. Seeing another crime scene was only going to upset her more especially after the news that Samantha Jo missing.

Henry's place was clean. Nothing was out of place, and there appeared to be no struggle whatsoever. The door had been unlocked when they'd come to knock it down therefore leaving the only reasonable explanation that Henry knew his assailant. They spent some time going through Henry's apartment looking for clues before returning back to the station.

When they returned, Wyatt looked in on Madison who was still sleeping and hadn't moved since he'd last checked. Together, reviewing the evidence, Bud and Wyatt fell short in finding anything new. The dead corpse was not much help either other than the fact that the M.O. appeared to be of the same nature—throat cut from ear to ear.

"Bud, we have got to get some answers here and quick. That's two people murdered in the same fashion and one missing that we know of. Look, it's after dinner, and I'm going to run Madison home to stay with Travis. I'll come right back and go through Samantha Jo's car you had towed in earlier."

Bud was tired and frustrated, too, and, he knew they'd be working into the night as well. "I'll see y'all back here then."

Madison awoke to Wyatt gently saying her name and rubbing her arm. She had slept most of the afternoon. The stress had finally gotten to her, and she felt numb. "Come on. I'm gonna take you home. Travis is there waiting for you."

"Where are you going?"

"We've got a lot more to do here tonight, and I think y'all be more comfortable at Travis's."

"Did you find Samantha Jo yet? Have you heard anything?"

"We're still looking at all the possibilities, and Bud has notified all the surrounding counties. Everyone is looking for her, Madison. Don't worry, we'll find her." She followed him out to the jeep, and again they said nothing the entire way back to Travis's.

She wished she could stay with Wyatt and help him, but she knew at this point she was of no help. She could barely think straight for herself. Wyatt had already called Travis to notify him of the events that had taken place since he saw him that morning. Travis had been working all afternoon to locate Samantha Jo's mother so he could find out if she had made it home. He, too, had come up empty trying to locate her mother.

At home, Travis was waiting and had made up some dinner for Madison. She hadn't eaten since breakfast, but with everything that had happened she'd lost her appetite. Wyatt didn't stay long and said that he'd be back later. He pulled Travis aside and said, "Keep an eye out for her and make sure every thing's locked up. I don't want to take any chances with either of you." Travis agreed with him and said good bye.

He'd been watching most of the day again, just sitting in his car looking through his binoculars, but still no movement. The sun had gone down and dusk was setting in when he saw the door to the room open. Lane's car was backed into its place, and he noticed him come out to throw a duffle bag and a suitcase into the back seat. Next, he popped the trunk and went back inside. A few minutes later he came out with a sheet wrapped around something he'd thrown over his shoulder.

As he leaned towards the trunk, a woman's arm fell out from the sheet. He sat there watching and thinking to himself, "What the hell has he gone and done this time? Always the stupid one and always getting caught." Lane never did have any patience nor did he think things through. Whatever he'd done, he'd gotten himself into deep water this time.

He decided to follow from a far distance to see what he was up to and where he was going with a woman's body stuffed in his trunk.

Madison managed to eat some soup, enough to get something into her stomach. Travis sat with her while she ate and didn't say much. He didn't want to push her to talk about it if she didn't want to. He stood up and put on some music to ease the tension in the room.

He grabbed a beer and asked if she'd like one as well; she nodded. They went back to the deck to sit and drink their beer. Madison asked, "Do you mind if I have a cigarette?"

"Not at all. In fact, in light of the day you've had, smoke all ya want."

Then he looked at her and said, "Mind if I bum one from ya?"

Madison laughed and handed him one. She didn't question why he wanted it. She realized that since she'd come to Blackberry Creek, all she did was ask questions. Always with the questions and never any answers. Maybe she felt it wasn't her business, and maybe she just enjoyed the company; either way, she didn't say a word and just handed him the lighter.

They sat on the deck drinking their beers and watching the sun fade slowly into the horizon. It was getting dark, and the bugs were coming out in full force. The heat and humidity certainly didn't seem to bother them any. Madison and Travis went inside, and he said. "I'm gonna clean up out here and grab a shower to cool down. Can I get you anything?"

"No, you go ahead. I'm fine."

She grabbed her purse and walked down the hall to her room. She threw her purse at the bed, missing it by a few inches as it slid to the floor. She picked it up and the keys from Hazel's bag fell to floor.

She picked them up and sat on the edge of the bed, holding them in her hand. She began to study the small key again and tried to imagine what it unlocked. Rubbing her hand over the arrowhead, it suddenly hit her and she froze. "She said it'd be right under my nose . . . Of course! I know where it is!"

She'd been so consumed with analyzing the key itself that she'd forgotten what Hazel had told her. Something inside Madison kicked in, and she felt herself want to fight. Fight back for Hazel and fight back for Samantha Jo. She needed to do this alone.

Travis was in the next room, and she waited until she heard the shower turn on before she quietly opened her door. Leaving him to panic when he came looking for her was not her style, so she grabbed a piece of paper and wrote:

Went to house to get something. Be back in a snap.
-Madison

She paused for a moment before opening the front door, remembering someone crazy was out there and once she opened the door she was on her own. She thrust her shoulders back, saying, "Fuck it!" and walked out the door.

In the shower, Travis couldn't help but feel so helpless and sad for Madison. He wished he could help and comfort her. He remembered how he caught her staring at Wyatt and how comfortable they both seemed to be in each other's presence. What confused Travis the most was that he truly cared for Madison and wanted only the best for her. Since he'd first met her, he admired her beauty and enjoyed her sometimes sarcastic humor. She was intelligent, funny, and compassionate—all qualities he looked for in a soul mate.

In that moment, he realized that his jealousy for Madison was similar to that of a protective brother. It wasn't that he was jealous of his friend, not at all. He loved Wyatt and knew he was a good man. "That was it," he thought. "I've been trying to protect her and keep her safe since the moment I met her and now Wyatt is here and he's doing the same thing." The only difference was that they seem to be attracted to one another. He could see the chemistry between the two when he was in the room with them. It was electric and obvious. He decided that when the time was right, he'd let Wyatt know that there was nothing between him and Madison and that he should do what he could to get her.

Wyatt and Travis had been friends way too long to break their code of friendship. Travis felt obligated to give him the go ahead if he chose to move forward with Madison.

Madison arrived at the house just as it had turned completely dark. She'd not paid any attention to the time of day it was when she left. All she could think about was getting to the house and finding it.

She pulled into the driveway and shut the ignition off. Madison dug the key chain out from her shorts and decided to leave her purse in the car. Her phone was on vibrate-mode in her purse, causing her to miss Travis's frantic calls.

She started walking up the steps to the back and realized she didn't have a flashlight with her, but she knew if she gave herself just a few moments, her eyes would adjust. She remembered seeing a small gardening spade by the back door and fumbled around until she found it.

The moon was almost full and gave her just enough light to walk out into the garden, right up to the sun catcher. She kneeled down and began digging, listening to the sounds of the night surrounding her.

The humidity was still so thick she could cut through it with a knife. Around her she could hear loud bullfrogs croaking away in unison.

She'd dug nearly a foot when she felt his eyes upon her. She could feel him staring right through her body. She stopped digging and rested her hand on the ground.

He laughed and said, "Y'all gonna have dig 'bout another three feet deep and five wide for when I'm done with y'all." Madison slowly turned her head and looked into the eyes of the devil.

There, standing over her with a shotgun pointing at her head, was Lane. She didn't move or say a word.

He turned on the flashlight he held in his other hand and shined it right into her eyes. Blinded by it, she turned her head towards the ground. "Stand up!" he ordered. She slowly turned her head back towards him and noticed tiny eyes staring at her from behind him. She froze. Again, he yelled for her to stand up, and again she kneeled there, frozen. Behind him was a large Cotton Mouth snake, nearly three feet in length.

Lane began to take a step towards her, and the tiny eyes moved in a quick flash, making its strike. Lane arched backwards with a shrilling scream and pulled the trigger of the gun. The shots missed Madison's head and grazed her right shoulder. Immediately, she scrambled to her feet and ran toward the opposite side of the house.

It was dark and she began stumbling. Trying to get her footing, she tripped and fell down the side of the hill toward the front of the house. She pulled herself up and breathlessly stumbled her way to her car. She felt as if she was in one of those dreams where she was trying to run, but her feet wouldn't move. In the fall she had twisted her ankle which made the car seem like it was so far away as she limped towards it.

Her heart sank as she got closer and realized the bastard had blocked her in. She could hear his screams of pain coming from the backyard. She knew the damage one bite from a Cotton Mouth could do with its venom and that he would be paralyzed with extreme pain.

She went to see if he'd left his keys in the ignition. Her body was in a complete state of panic when she realized they were with him. There was no way out of here, except for on foot; walking was her only chance to escape. She slowly limped towards the street. However, she stopped dead in her tracks as she reached the end of the driveway.

There, leaning up against the hood of his car, was the Monster himself. Leroy. "Come to Daddy," he said.

Madison's mind screamed for her to run but she couldn't. He was holding a gun as well. He walked towards her, grabbed her by her arm, and threw her in the front seat where he could keep an eye on her. Her shoulder was bleeding, and her entire body ached with pain. She had no idea where he was taking her, and she wondered if it was even worth screaming. Who would hear her?

As he drove, he ranted on about what a pain-in-the-ass daughter she was and how he should have done away with her years ago. Madison's mouth began to speak before her brain could stop her, "You mean the time you tried to kill us all you Crazy Fuck!"

Leroy had lost all his patience with women years ago, and he was done listening to their lip. With one swift move of the hand holding the gun, Madison's head hit the window, leaving her unconscious.

After his shower, Travis knocked on Madison's door to see if she needed anything. He reminded himself to not be the annoying, doting father figure. Madison was an independent woman, but she'd had a pretty traumatic day. He waited and heard nothing. He knocked again and still no word. Figuring she'd fallen asleep, he went to the kitchen to get another beer and relax.

At first, he didn't see the note on the counter and walked right past it. It wasn't until he walked back towards the patio door that he noticed it. Running for his phone, he began to panic and tried to remember how long she'd been gone. He dialed her number repeatedly; each time it just rang and rang then went to voicemail. Travis's hands were shaking so badly he could hardly scroll through his phone to call Wyatt. He'd tried to reach Madison without any luck, and by his count she'd been gone for almost thirty minutes.

Wyatt answered, "Is everything okay?"

"Madison is gone!"

"What do y'all mean gone. I told ya to keep an eye on her."

"I was, I did, I . . . I . . ."

"Slow down man, take a deep breath. Tell me what happened."

"I went to take a quick shower, and several minutes later, I came back out to the kitchen and found her note saying she'd gone to the house."

"Shit. She went there this time of night alone?"

"I'm sorry, Wyatt."

"Hang up now and call 911 to send an ambulance out to the house. Bud and I are on our way."

Wyatt had been inspecting the car when Travis had called him. He ran back inside to find Bud, but he was gone. An officer he hadn't met yet was sitting at his desk and said, "He went for a bite to eat, and he'll be back shortly."

"Radio him and tell him to meet me out at Hazel Walker's house. Now!"

Wyatt ran to his jeep and began speeding through town to get to the house. He kept repeating to himself, "Please be okay, Madison, please." He arrived before the ambulance or Bud and noticed two cars parked in the driveway: Madison's and one he didn't recognize. The driver's side door of the unfamiliar car was open, but there was no one in it. He looked up toward the house and saw that it was dark. Not knowing who or how many people could be inside, he quietly reached around and pulled his gun from behind. He slowly tiptoed up the steps towards the back.

As Wyatt got close to the top, he heard a dull moan come from the backyard. He stood with his back to the house and gun in hand while trying to peer around the corner. It was too for him to see much, but he thought he saw a body lying on the ground. "Oh dear God, Madison," he thought. He slowly crept up closer and saw that it was a man on the ground.

When he was close enough, he turned on his little flashlight and saw Lane lying on the ground with his shotgun beside him. Wyatt reached down to pick it up and asked, "Where is she?" Lane lay there, still moaning and paralyzed by the venom that now had spread into his bloodstream. Wyatt screamed it louder, "Where the hell is she?"

Lane tried to speak, but it was more of a mumble, "I donnano . . ."

Wyatt took the gun with him and went back down to where the cars were parked in the driveway. He walked out into the street and began shining his flashlight back and forth, looking for signs of another car. In the distance, he heard the sirens coming and knew they'd be there shortly to take care of Lane.

His light flashed over something on the ground, and Wyatt moved in closer for a look. Another car had been here; the condensation from the AC had dripped onto the street. He started to walk backwards to get a better visual and felt something crunch under his boot. He shined the light in front of him and found tiny clusters of dirt. They looked like clumps of mud that had fallen off the bottom of a work boot.

He knew it was a long shot, but the farm was the only place they had not yet been to search. Wyatt jumped back into his jeep, passing Bud and the crusade heading towards Hazel's house. He didn't have time to wait for them or to inform them. After all, he wasn't even sure where Madison was, it was just a strong hunch that he needed to act on.

Madison started coming to, and her body ached with pain. She opened her eyes, still covered with dirt from when she was trying to avoid Lane's gunfire. Her clothes were sticking to her, and the blood from her arm was slowly dripping onto the floor. Remembering the gun shot, she looked at her arm and saw all the blood. Her mind registered the injury, and instantly it began to throb.

She attempted to wipe the hair and dirt from her eyes when she realized she couldn't move her arms. He had tied her hands with a rope hanging from the rafters above her.

There wasn't much light in the room, and all she could do was squint because of all the crud in her eyes. Nothing around her looked familiar, and she kept mumbling, "Where am I?" After several minutes, she noticed the ceramic jugs around her lined up on a shelf and along the floor. They were old and dusty, and she knew exactly where he'd taken her.

She was at the farm in the old shed by the spring. Panic and fear immediately set in, and her heart began racing. In that moment she knew that he was going to finally kill her, too. She knew no one would hear her scream at the top of her lungs from the farm—it was hopeless. It was like a nightmare, and the Monster in it was real this time.

She tried to listen for him but couldn't hear a thing. She began sweating more profusely as her fear worsened. Madison knew right then that this was where she was going to die. Just then, she heard footsteps coming towards the shed. She heard him mumbling to himself and wondered what was taking him so long. He'd finally get his way, and she'd be gone for good.

Tears ran down her cheek as she thought about Mason and how she'd never see him again. She tried to wiggle herself around to loosen the ropes, but it was no use. She didn't have the strength to hold her own body weight anymore than she already was, and all the moving around placed more pressure on her arms tied above her head. She felt her knees weakening and the salt from her tears burning her mouth where he'd hit her.

It was hopeless. She was never going to see her son or family ever again.

Wyatt turned off the lights to the jeep and parked it near the entrance to the dirt road. He walked quietly along the road for several hundred yards when he spotted tail lights off in the distance near the woods. He reached for his gun and sat a minute, taking in his surroundings and the situation. It was dark enough that the person in the car might not even see him coming. Or, he could wait where he was and then make his move.

"Ah, hell," he said and began quickly and quietly walking towards the woods. He knew he'd have a better chance if he went towards the car than if he stayed, and time was of the essence. Madison's life depended on it.

He crept in from the far right, as if closing in on a prey, and there, through the trees, he saw him. He recognized him instantly from the photo he'd studied earlier. Leroy was pacing back and forth, mumbling to himself as if he were talking to someone else. Wyatt looked to the left of Leroy and saw the gas can sitting near the shed. It was possible Madison was still in the car, but Wyatt's hunch told him otherwise. She was in the shed, and Leroy planned to set it on fire.

Wyatt crept in closer for a better shot then slowly cocked his gun and rested it on his other arm for aim. He was a distance away, and Leroy was a moving target, pacing back and forth. Wyatt leaned in, and as he did, the weight of his body snapped the twig he'd stepped on.

Leroy stopped walking and looked in the direction where Wyatt knelt, frozen. Leroy slowly moved towards him and Wyatt fired. Leroy stumbled backwards as the first shot hit him in the left shoulder. He was still standing and began staggering in Wyatt's direction when Wyatt fired again, this time into his right leg. Leroy fell to the ground and laid there motionless. Wyatt quickly ran up, took the gun that was sitting on the hood of the car, and opened the doors to the shed.

There, Madison hung from the rafter with her hands tied above her head, covered in dirt and blood. She began screaming the minute the door opened, knowing that Leroy was coming in to finish her.

Wyatt ran up to her. "Madison, it's okay; I'm here. It's Wyatt. You're okay." He cut the rope with his pocket knife and caught her in his arms as she fell into him. She opened her eyes and saw the familiar blue eyes she'd been longing to fall into.

Wyatt carried her back to his jeep and said, "We need to get you to the hospital."

"No, really, I'll be fine."

"Madison, this is one of those times where we're gonna do it my way."

"Okay, Okay." She rested her head on his arm when his phone rang. It was Bud.

"Y'all right? I passed y'all on the road earlier, drivin' like a maniac."

"I'm fine, Bud. We're fine. I've got Madison here with me safe and sound, but y'all need to send a car over to the farm. I left y'all something back in the woods by the pasture."

"I'll send Tate over there now. Did y'all say ya got Madison?"

"Yeah, she's fine. A little banged up, but she'll be fine."

"Well if ya can, I think ya should come back to the house; I've got something for ya too."

"We're on our way."

They pulled in near Hazel's house and saw there were two ambulances parked. Wyatt went to Madison and helped her down from the jeep. Bud walked over to them and motioned towards the second ambulance.

As he opened the door, Madison's eyes widened when she saw Samantha Jo lying there, hooked up to an IV. She turned to Bud and asked if she was okay. Bud explained how they found her in the trunk of the car when they began searching it after getting Lane into the ambulance. She was extremely dehydrated and drugged but would be okay.

Madison reached over and gave Bud a hug and winced at pain in her arm. Bud stood back for a moment, and he, along with Wyatt, realized she had been bleeding. "Madison, we really do need to get you to the hospital and have you checked."

She agreed and asked if it would be okay if she rode in the ambulance with Samantha Jo. Wyatt said he'd meet her there; he needed to tie up few loose ends at the house. Bud handed Madison her purse as he close the ambulance doors; he'd found it on the front seat of her car. Wyatt called Travis and told him the good news and asked him to meet them at the hospital. He was a complete wreck and relieved to hear that Madison was okay and that they'd found Samantha Jo.

Back at the hospital, Wyatt sat with Samantha Jo while she slept, waiting for Madison to return. The doctor told Madison she was lucky that the pellets had only grazed her arm. She didn't need stitches, but she would need to keep it clean and bandaged. Her ankle was a bit swollen, and he told her to keep it iced for the next few days. Overall, she was very lucky that she was still alive in spite of the events that evening.

Madison walked to Samantha Jo's room and looked in through the glass window. There, she saw Wyatt sitting next to her bed holding his head in his hands.

He had saved her life tonight and she was forever grateful. She watched until he noticed her and looked up. Neither moved while staring back at one another, until Samantha Jo's doctor interrupted them. He went over with Madison the trauma that Samantha Jo had suffered both physically and emotionally and said that they would keep her there for the night and monitor her. For now, she needed rest, and everyone would need to leave her room for the evening.

Out in the hall, Bud stood waiting with Travis. Wyatt and Madison walked over to update them on Samantha Jo and let them know that she was going to be fine. Both were relieved to hear this, and Bud mentioned that he'd make sure an officer was stationed outside her door. Madison thanked him and said, "Why would she need an officer outside her room? It's over, right? You have everyone."

"Madison, we didn't find Leroy back at the farm. When Tate got there, he was gone and so was his car. We've searched the entire farm, and he's not there. Now, I don't want y'all to panic. We've put out an APB on him as well as his car."

"You mean he's gone? How is that possible?"

"I'm not sure, but I doubt he'll get too far. Wyatt got a couple shots in em, and I bet he'll be looking to stop somewhere for medical attention very quickly."

"You said his car was gone. Was that him in the green car this whole time? Why didn't you pull his DMV information before when I first mentioned the car?"

"As a matter of fact, we had pulled his info. Honey, he drives a silver Impala."

"He what?" Come to think of it, everything had happened so fast and it was so dark out that she hadn't noticed what color his car was when he shoved her in it.

"We did find the green car though. It was hidden at the farm under a tarp. I suspect that's the car you've seen followin' ya 'round town."

"What about Lane? What's going to happen with him?"

"Lane didn't make it to the hospital in time. The poison from the venom was such that by the time we got to him, he was barely alive. Listen, Madison, I don't want for you to worry. We're gonna find Leroy and when we do, he won't ever bother you, or anyone for that matter, again. The best for thing y'all to do is to go on home and get some rest tonight. We've got everything taking care of here and will keep a watch on your cousin all night. You have my word."

Travis turned and gave Madison a hug, then scolded her for leaving like she did and scarin' the hell out of him.

"I'm sorry, Travis. I really thought I'd be back before you knew it."

"What the hell y'all go out there for anyway?"

In all the commotion of the night's events, Madison had forgotten why she'd gone out there in the first place. She looked at Travis and said, "There was just something there I wanted to get before I had to leave in the morning; it was nothing."

Travis looked to Wyatt who shrugged his shoulders. He was just as clueless as to why she was there in the first place. "Well, I brought your things to the hospital. I didn't know if you'd be stayin' here or not tonight."

"Thank you, Travis, for everything, I mean it. I think tonight, if it's all right with you, I'll just stay at the hotel. I've got to check on Samantha Jo in the morning and hopefully take her back with me to the airport."

"Speaking of which, I hope you don't mind, but I took the liberty of changing both your flights to an early afternoon. You'll both be flyin' out within a half hour of each other, and it'd be my pleasure to drive you both there."

"Travis, you're too much. Really."

"Madison, it's the least I can do. So, I'll meet you back here in the morning then. Wyatt, I'm going to assume y'all will stay with her tonight?"

Madison looked back at Wyatt who just nodded his head in agreement.

"All right then, I'll see you in the morning." Travis gave both her and Wyatt a hug before leaving.

Wyatt carried her things down to the jeep and helped her in. They had pulled out of the hospital parking lot when Madison turned to Wyatt and said, "I need to go back to the house . . ."

Before she could finish her sentence he said, "I know." Reaching over, he held her hand as they drove back to the house.

They drove in silence, and Wyatt kept thinking to himself how scared he'd been thinking that something awful had happened to her. At the time, he was acting like the investigator that he was, never stopping to realize the emotional attachment that he'd developed to her. Tonight he'd almost lost her, and the thought of it terrified him.

They parked the jeep, and Wyatt grabbed his flashlight. He followed Madison to the garden without saying a word. She knew what she'd come for, and he followed.

She found the spade still lying where she'd left it and began digging again. It was a matter of minutes before she hit something hard in the dirt. Madison dug an inch around in a square shape until she could reach down and pull the metal case up. She wiped as much of the dirt off as she could and carried the silver case back to the jeep.

Neither spoke. Wyatt understood that whatever was in the case sitting on her lap, it was important enough to her to risk her own life. What it held were answers that would set her free. Madison sat looking straight ahead with her arms cradling the box the entire drive back to the hotel. She would wait until later to view the contents.

Back at the hotel, Wyatt sat watching TV while Madison took a shower. She still looked awful, like something out of a horror movie. Her hair was plastered to her head from all the sweat and her clothes were filthy with dirt and bloodstains. When she finished, Wyatt took his turn using the shower.

Madison put the case on the table, dug the keys out, and placed the small key into the lock. It fit perfectly, and the case popped open the minute she turned the key. She sat there for a moment, bracing herself for what she was about to find—answers. She really had no idea what to expect, but felt relieved and anxious at the same time.

She waited until she heard the shower turn on, then flipped the top up and took the first item out. There she found several bonds which she figured were worth nearly 250,000 dollars.

Immediately she knew this was the reason Hazel had been killed. Her death was over money, just as she had suspected all along. Lane and Leroy had been fighting her for the money since her grandfather's death, and they'd finally given up waiting. It was sad that her life meant nothing more to those two bastards than what Madison held in her hand.

Setting them down, she reached back into the box and pulled out a torn piece of red satin and an old, deteriorated picture clipped to a worn newspaper article. She picked up the picture and her heart sank immediately. It was a picture of the Klan, and in it, the swearing-in of a new Grand Dragon. She turned the picture over and written on the back was the year—1963.

Madison realized instantly what the article was without even reading it. She unfolded the newspaper clipping and saw a black and white picture of each of the young boys that had been murdered after walking home from their church. Her eyes filled with tears as she struggled to hold them back. Those poor boys and their families. She was repulsed by the fact that her family was responsible for this horrible act. It seemed that all her family did was bring violence onto others.

How was it that she and Samantha Jo were so different from the rest? They were nothing like their fathers and certainly nothing like their grandfather. Madison felt no love towards Leroy and hoped that he had driven off a cliff somewhere tonight. Lane got what he had comin' to him and was no loss to society. It was difficult for her to explain to anyone, including herself, her feelings towards her grandfather, Jethro. She once thought he walked on water, and now she knew he was the spawn of the evil Monsters that had taken over the Walker family.

Madison reached back into the case and felt around with her hand, grabbing the last item: an envelope. She carefully opened it and removed the letter inside. She unfolded the letter and began to read:

I don't want no trouble from y'all whatsoever, but I thought ya should know I had a baby. I know it's yours and I promise I ain't said nothin to no one about it nor will I ever. I don't want no money and I don't want no help raisin this baby, we just wanna be left alone. I wanted ya to know that ya have a son. His name is Travis.

M. Jackson

Madison set the letter down and sat back in her chair, absolutely speechless. There were no words to explain what was running through her mind. She couldn't believe it.

Travis was actually her uncle.

It all made sense to her. She, too, had been feeling confused about Travis since she'd first met him. He was handsome and charming, and she enjoyed his company but felt nothing more than a close kinship to him.

This was not going to be easy for him to hear, and there was no easy way to break it to him gently either. He already had a story about his father and one that he'd grown to accept. By his count, his father was a good man that had died in a bad accident. But Madison held the proof in her hand that claimed otherwise. He, too, came from the same crazy family as she did.

This was going to be extremely difficult to explain to him. "Sorry, Travis, your mother was raped by my grandfather who is really your father." There are no words to describe a situation like that with a positive spin.

Wyatt came out from the bathroom and saw Madison sitting there, looking deflated. "I know it's none of my business, and I don't know quite what to say or do at this moment, but I'm here to just listen if you need or want to talk."

She turned around, facing him, and he could see it in her eyes that she had something to say but couldn't speak the words. "I . . . I need to talk to Travis."

"Look Madison, I understand, and, believe me, the last thing I want to do is come between you and Travis. He's my best friend, and I have the greatest respect for him as well as you."

Madison tilted her head to the side and smiled, "You think there's something going on between Travis and me?"

"Yes . . . No . . . Hell, I don't know. Is there?"

"Yes, there is, actually, but not like you're thinking."

Wyatt looked utterly confused and puzzled. "I don't . . ."

Madison interrupted him by saying, "He's my uncle."

Wyatt sat there, staring at her in complete shock "But I . . ."

"I know, right? But it's the truth. Please don't say anything to him about this. I'm pretty sure he doesn't know, and I need to speak with him in the morning."

Wyatt just sat there, nodding his head with a confused look on his face.

Madison stood up and put the items into her work bag. She had no intentions of lugging that case back home with her. She was tired and needed some rest. She crawled into her bed, facing opposite of Wyatt.

Her turned off the light, took off his shorts, and laid there wide awake. "He's her uncle," he kept repeating in his head. It still hadn't sunk in. But the more he thought about it, the more it made sense. He'd been trying to hold himself back and restrain his urges toward Madison so he wouldn't upset Travis.

Through the silence of the room, he heard Madison say, "I don't want to sleep alone tonight. Will you lay with me?"

Without any hesitation he crawled into her bed and lay next to her, spooning her from behind. Not sure where to rest his arm, he laid it upon hers and tried to keep his mind in check. He had always been respectful of women and just because she invited him to her bed did not mean she wanted anything more than to be held.

His thoughts were interrupted when he felt her hand reach around and pull his over to rest on her thigh. His heart raced as he slowly moved his hand, feeling the curve of her body following her panty line. In an instant, he felt himself harden as she pushed her body back just enough so their bodies were touching. Her skin was soft and silky just as he'd imagined. He rested his head into the small of her back and took in a deep breath, smelling her skin.

She rocked back just enough for him to know she, too, wanted him. His hand found its way under her panties, and as he began to softly touch her, he felt the warmth and wetness between his fingers. She rolled over and kissed him passionately, locking her long legs in with his. His desire to know and feel every inch of her body became more and more a reality as each minute passed.

She straddled him on top and arched her back as he gently caressed her breasts cupped in his hands, reaching every erotic nerve in her body. Slowly, she raised her body up and guided him into hers. Their passion for one another was one they could no longer avoid as they continued into the night, making love.

Chapter 15

Wyatt awoke early and lay there watching Madison sleep so peacefully in his arms. He couldn't understand how he'd managed to fall in love with her in a matter of forty-eight hours, but he had.

He knew that if he lay there any longer he'd never want to leave her side, but it was time for him to continue his journey to Charleston. He gently moved so he could slip out of the bed without waking her and sat at the desk. Noticing the hotel tablet and pen, he began writing her a letter.

Madison,

You are the most beautiful woman I have ever met and I'm glad to have gotten to know you. Please don't be mad that I left before you awoke, but if I hadn't I would have never been able to leave.

I wish you all the best and a safe trip home.

Sincerely,

Wyatt Parker

Madison rolled over and began feeling around with her hand for Wyatt. She opened her eyes, saw the note on the pillow, and smiled. She, too, felt the same and knew that waking up next to him would have made it harder for her to leave. She needed get back home to her son, her career, and her life. She ordered up room service for coffee and got ready to go to the hospital.

When she arrived, she found Samantha Jo sitting up in her bed with color back in her face. Madison ran to her bed and gave her a big hug. "I was scared to death you were dead. I'm so glad you're all right!"

"I thought for a time that I was dead. Did they tell ya he didn't make it?"

"Yeah, I heard. How are you doin' with all that?"

"I'm not sure right now, I guess. I'm just relieved that this is all behind us, and we can go home, for real this time. The doctor said I was okay to travel back home today, but that I still need a lot of rest and will need to take it easy for a few more days."

Just then, Travis tapped his hand on the window. Madison gave him the signal to wait a minute.

"We need to talk," she said as she grabbed his hand, leading him down the corridor. He followed her into a room and she shut the door behind them.

"Madison, you're making me nervous; what's goin' on?"

"Travis, I need to tell you something very important, and I've been trying to find a way to do it and there is really no other way than to just say it."

"Well? What is it?"

"Travis, I know who your daddy is. I have the proof that I can show you, and he is not the man you thought he was."

He stood there thinking, "I've spent my life looking for information on him, and now she's here less than two weeks and claims to know more than I do?"

"Travis your daddy didn't die in a car crash before you born."

"Oh come on, this is a joke, right?"

"No, Travis, I'm serious." She pulled out the note from her purse and handed it over for him to read.

Travis read the letter and looked up at Madison, with a white face and eyes bulging from his head. He shook his head back and forth, and said, "No, this can't be true. I'm sure it's some coincidence."

"I don't think so, Travis. What was your mother's name?"

He looked at her as tears began to fill his eyes, and he could hardly find his voice while trying to speak her name: "Mary Anne."

"Travis, you and I both know this is not some coincidence. Believe me, I wish I wasn't the one having to tell you this.

She sat down next to him, put her arm around him, and told him the story Hazel had shared with her five years ago. Anger and pain overtook him, and he cried in her arms until he could gather himself. When he calmed down, he looked at Madison and said, "Well this explains a lot of unanswered questions I've had with regards to you."

Madison smiled back and said, "Ditto!"

"Madison, there's something I need to tell you, too."

"What is it?"

"I couldn't say anything before and to be honest I wasn't quite sure what to do, but your grandmother, Hazel, left all the money in her estate to me. I didn't understand it and was trying to find a way to sort it out while y'all were at the meeting. Now I think I understand."

"It was the right thing for her to do, Travis. You deserve it after what my grandfather did to your mother. He should have been hung from his balls for what he did to her. I'm just sorry that you had to find out this way. And I'm also sorry that you're cursed with the truth of knowing that you, too, are a Walker."

"Madison, you have to remember that it is just a name. You and Samantha Jo are nothing like your fathers or grandfather, for that matter. What they've done and who they are as people are not who you are."

"I know what you're saying is true, Travis, but it's still hard to separate myself from the fact that they are related and I come from the same DNA, just as you do"

"Well then, Madison, I say this. From this moment on is a new beginning for the Walkers. And it starts here today with me and you and Samantha Jo. Deal?"

She reached out to shake his hand. "Deal!"

"I just want to say one more thing, and that is I won't ever say a word to anyone, Travis. You have my word. This is your secret to do with as you wish. I wouldn't blame you one bit if you chose not to acknowledge this publicly. Believe me, it's not easy being a Walker."

"I appreciate that, and for now I agree that we should keep this just between family."

They hugged and talked for a while longer before returning to Samantha Jo's room and getting her ready for discharge.

An hour later, Samantha Jo was discharged from the hospital and they began the drive to the airport. As they drove out of town, Madison saw the sign with the boys' pictures in front of the Baptist Church and asked Travis to pull over for a minute. Samantha Jo and Travis remained in the car and gave each other a look, not knowing what she was up to.

She pulled an envelope out from her bag and slid it under the door to the church.

Inside it were the bonds she'd found in the case. The money meant nothing to her, and it gave her great pleasure to donate it. It would never bring back the lives of those boys that were taken from their families nor would it heal their pain, but it was the right thing to do.

Along the way, Madison and Travis explained their news to Samantha Jo, and she was ecstatic to learn of her new uncle. Jokingly she said, "I hope you're better than the other one." They all laughed.

At the airport they said their goodbyes and hugged at the curb, promising to stay in touch and talk often. They decided to start their own Walker traditions and would pick a time to have their own reunion soon.

Madison helped Samantha Jo get situated on her flight first. Hers didn't leave for another thirty minutes or so. She found an open chair in her gate and sat down.

She felt her phone vibrating, and she took it out and answered. It was Tamara on the other line. "Where the hell have you been? Joe said he's been trying to reach you for the last two days."

"I'm fine. What's with the all the excitement?"

"We got it!"

"Got what?"

"We landed the Landis McNeil project! When are you coming back into the office?"

"I'm flying out now and will be back this evening. Tell John I'll stop by the office tomorrow for the highlights."

"Is everything okay, Madison? You sound different."

"No, everything's fine. I'll see y'all tomorrow." She cut Tamara short and ended the call.

Finally after all that she'd been through over the last two weeks, she had some quiet time to herself and could relax. She'd gotten some answers to some of the questions that had accumulated over the years. She felt relieved, relieved that she wasn't crazy and that some things had finally been laid to rest. Restitution had been made and dues had been paid.

She wondered for a moment about Leroy and where he was. It was highly unlikely that he made it out of the county in the condition he was in. She knew it'd be a matter of time before he'd be found somewhere, dead in his car. For now, she and her family were out of danger, and Hazel could rest in peace.

She heard the announcement that her flight was boarding, and she stood to get in line. Once situated on the plane, she dug into her work bag and found the novel she'd brought with to read on the flight down. Her trip had been quite a nightmare, and she needed a change of pace. Maybe a little romance novel would do her good. She opened the book to the first page and a note fell out into her lap.

Madison,

Hopefully you are reading this after I've left and you're on your way home. I miss you already as I sit here writing this letter while watching you sleep. I long for more time with you and to wake up with you in my arms every morning. Timing is everything though and for now I know we must go our separate ways. You've taken a hold of my heart and I want you to know I will wait for you. When you're ready, I'll be waiting for you in Charleston.

Love,

Wyatt

Madison rested her head back and closed her eyes for her flight home, smiling from ear to ear.

The End

Here's a sneak preview to the introduction of

Wild Dunes

By Rachel McCoy

A sequel to Blackberry Creek

Introduction

Before he could say another word, Madison whispered "I don't think I'm alone in the house." He kept calling her name into the phone, but it was of no use. They had lost connection or so he thought. Wyatt hadn't picked up on the fact Madison's voice had turned into a low whisper of someone who was in shock. He assumed it was the horrible reception he was receiving on his cell phone.

Little did he know. . .

CPSIA information can be obtained
at www.ICGtesting.com
Printed in the USA
LVHW110853251020
669749LV00005B/352